2

First Edition 2022
Yorkie-Montague Books
Devon

ISBN 978-1-7398275-0-2

Historical terminology

Addle-pated	Foolish or stupid.
Approver	A criminal at trial might name others as complicit in their crime, or even of another unconnected crime. Turning approver wouldn't usually confer a lesser sentence, but through corrupt agreements might confer some benefit or serve as a means to wreak revenge on one's enemies.
Arming Jack	A padded jacket worn under a Knight's armour. For poor soldiers it might be worn as the sole torso protection. Also known as a gambeson or padded jack.
Bardiche	A type of polearm weapon.
Bailiff	Subordinate to the sheriff. Largely an administrator, the bailiff was responsible for helping to collect taxes and appointing the jury of the hundred courts.
Beshrew	Curse.
Brais	Medieval undergarment worn under hose. Similar to long johns
Bullock	The bullock dagger was so-called because the in place of the normal cross guard were round ball shapes resembling testicles. It was a type of 'Rondel' dagger with a long, thin blade. It could be used for general purposes, but one of the primary benefits for it as a weapon was that it could easily slide through the eye slits of a fallen Knight's helmet.
Chaperon	A man's hat. Available in many different styles, tend so to be a large puffed out hat with one or two 'tails' hanging down from it
Coroner	Not a medical practitioner like the modern version, but an essential part of the judicial system. The coroner would determine cause of death, if there was any doubt over how someone had died, and was required to be present at any

execution. Even if a criminal was caught red-handed in the act of a capitol crime, they could only be legally executed on the spot if the coroner was present to confirm the legality of the matter. A coroner could also sit in place of a sheriff if there was a conflict of interest on a particular case.

Crispinette — A lady's headpiece, usually a band around the head and the hair tied up into mesh buns above the ears, somewhat reminiscent of a 'Princess Leia' hairstyle. The Crispinette is usually adorned with gold and/or jewels and usually accompanied with a veil.

Distraint — Seizure of property in lieu of money owed.

Doublet — A medieval tunic usually made from wool. In 1402 the common style was waist-length and buttoned up at the front. They sometimes had detachable sleeves and may have been more than one colour.

Fare — 1. Food/meal, or 2. A commotion.

Farming — Unlike modern square fields, medieval farming was organised in strip farms. These were long strips of land with no boundary wall or hedge. There were often many side-by-side. Labourers worked on their lord's land for several days per week and then on their own land the remainder.

Forest — In the medieval period the term forest didn't denote an area of woodland, but rather hunting land owned the crown and subject to 'Forest Law'. Sherwood Forest is the most famous example. The Dartmoor Royal Forest boundary covered a vast area; although Sampford Spiney and the surrounding area are within Dartmoor, they fall just outside the Royal Forest.

Fuller — The poor folk who cleaned freshly sheared wool and treated woven threads by stamping on it in to remove grease/impurities. Modern sources often refer to the fuller working in vats of urine to treat the wool, but this method wasn't in common usage in the Middle Ages and was outlawed at certain points - although that may have made little difference in many rural areas. Sometimes the wool may have also been dyed during the fulling stage.

Hamsoken
A common legal term used to describe an assault on an individual in the victim's own home. Such attacks were considered a more grievous classification of assault.

Hose
Medieval trousers made up of two separate leggings, usually woollen, worn over an undergarment (brais) and supported by leather thonging tied from a belt or other garment.

Hundred
A medieval administration subdivision. There were thirty-five Hundreds (also known as wapantakes) in Devon. A hundred organised the collecting of local taxes and held its own judicial courts held every three-four weeks. A jury of twelve could preside over minor and serious cases (not crown offences such as treason), but execution sentences had to be confirmed by the county court. In reality, sentences were often carried out immediately and then confirmed by the court later on – Lydford was notorious for this practice.

Kettle Helm
A steel soldiers' helmet, often resembling a World War One era British infantry helmet.

Lauds
One of the canonical hours, signalling the start of the day and morning prayer. Depending on time of year, between 5 and 8am.

Lych Bell
The ringing of a bell to announce a corpse being taken to a place of burial.

Lynchet
Ridges along the sides of farm strips formed by ploughing.

Minuta
A time measurement equating to 6 modern minutes.

Money	In coinage the penny was most common. The groat which is worth 4d (pence). The quarter-noble is worth 20d; the noble 80d. There were no coins for shillings or pounds. A shilling is 12d; a mark is 13 shillings and 4d; a pound is worth 3 marks. It would seem from the evidence of surviving documents that the privileged preferred to work in marks rather than pounds.
Nones	One of the canonical hours, equating to around 3pm in modern time.
Priests	Catholicism the predominant religion in England, although Protestantism was in its embryo stage in the form of the Lollard movement, which was not tolerated by the church or state. Rural priests often had to work the land like the villeins and would often have small gardens or strip farms on church land. A priest was correctly referred to as 'sir' rather than father in the early 15th century.
Quillion	The cross guard of a sword.
Rakefire	Medieval slang: a guest who has overstayed their welcome or taken advantage of hospitality.
Retainer	Could be anyone working for a landowner, but usually refers to one of the military retinue.
Sheriff	There was one sheriff per county, although later in Devon, Exeter also had its own sheriff. The sheriff was responsible for taxes, raising local militias for the king, and administering county justice. Many sheriffs were notoriously corrupt, which is probably why the Sheriff of Nottingham is such a villainous character.
Sherman	A sheep shearer.
Simpkin	Simple-minded; a fool.
Solar	The medieval living room. In common housing this would often double as the bedroom. In a longhouse, like those on Dartmoor, the solar would occupy the upper end of the longhouse.

Villeins

The entrance hall was in the centre, and the lower half was the shippon, where animals slept. These were the bottom of the social order, the feudal tenants working their Lord's land. The term peasant wasn't used in medieval England; the term peasant is derived from the Old French word 'Pais' to mean 'of the countryside' and was only used by English and Welsh soldiers on campaign in France to describe the French villeins in a derogatory way.

Wandought

A weak man or the offspring of a prostitute.

The Sampford Slaying

I

Robert Wood dismounted at the pillared gateway to the estate of the Sheriff of Devon. He removed his plumed riding cap and wiped his perspiring brow with a sleeve. A gap formed between his black beard and bushy moustache to reveal large gleaming teeth that grinned up at his mounted companion.

'This be it, Guy. Our fortunes change this day - forever.' Robert said. He handed the horse bridle to his friend. 'Stable the palfreys and get yourself fed.'

'Yes, Master Robert.' Guy said, inclining his head and touching the brim of his brown pointed cap. His thin lips twitched in a hint of a smile; the long pink scar running down his pale face from brow to lip prevented the smile spreading further.

Robert inhaled, filling his lungs full of summer air. He removed his riding gloves and sucked in his gut as he tucked the gloves into his belt. He placed his fists on his hips as he surveyed the estate.

The manor's dull, grey, granite walls and slate roof contrasted with the verdant foliage surrounding it. Pastureland, bushes, and trees with leaves all shades of green flourished in the June sunlight. Insects hummed around the array of coloured flowers in the garden. The manor's largest windows glistened with reflected sunlight while smaller, unglazed windows conflicted with their grander cousins by fading into squares of varying darkness. A thin trail of smoke escaped one of the chimneys, dissipating into azure sky. Stone slabs lined the path to a large oak doorway, while a dirt trail diverted east toward the stables and lesser servants' lodgings.

A man in a sweat-soaked coif and shirt advanced from the stable, summoning Guy with a jovial wave.

Robert walked toward the house, enjoying the metallic click the hobnails on the bottom of his boots made on the pathing stones; it felt like strolling in a grand city rather than the moorland.

The manor door opened revealing a grey-haired servant dressed in the red and yellow colours of his lord. He hurried toward Robert despite an obvious limp and bowed his head in a sharp pecking motion.

'This is most unexpected, Master Wood,' the servant wheezed. 'I do not believe Sir John is expecting you.'

Robert flashed a wide smile. His broad chest heaved under the tight-fitting green tunic as he released a few barks of a baritone laugh.

'I am indeed expected by your lord and have brought the… gift expected by him.' Robert patted the red leather purse on his right hip and idly rested a palm on the hilt of the sheathed arming sword dangling from his left hip.

The manservant hummed, scowling at the purse. His lined and sagging face creased as he wrinkled his nose, scrutinizing Robert for a few moments before finally grunting.

'Well… I suppose. Come inside and I shall announce thee.' The servant made a flourishing gesture, indicating for Robert to walk on in.

Robert strode to the entrance, pausing to check that the soles of his knee-high boots were clean. He fanned himself with his hat as he walked with a confident swagger.

The anteroom was well illuminated by two large windows. The stone floor was worn smooth over time by the scuffs of shoes. Large sun-faded tapestries covered the walls. The only items of furniture were three wooden chairs and a small table with an unlit tallow candle in a bowl.

Robert waited beside the table - only mildly irked that he wasn't invited to sit, he supposed the Sheriff wouldn't keep him waiting long.

The stooped and withered servant pushed through the groaning, iron-studded oak door to the hall and closed it again behind him.

Robert scratched his beard as he glanced over the tapestries. The weaves displayed images of hawking, winemaking, and stag hunting. He ran his fingertips over the surface of the nearest tapestry, feeling the rough thread of the heavy fabric. He harrumphed and shrugged his acceptance of the quality of the weaving. He leaned against the nearest tapestry and unsheathed the bullock dagger he kept next to his purse and used it to clean his nails while whistling some half-remembered tune, then recalling some of the words he sang:

'Merry 'tis while Sumer-y last. With birds in song...' his memory snagged on the next lyrics, so he returned to humming the tune. He inspected his nails, finding them satisfactory. He slid the thin-bladed dagger back into its sheath and frowned at the doorway to the Sheriff's hall. The manservant could have at least offered some refreshment. He'd been better received on his previous visit. Robert wondered if he should relate his lacklustre treatment to the sheriff, then shrugging, he dismissed the idea: it wouldn't do to sour a perfect day - the most fortuitous day of his life.

The door to the hall squeaked and the circular handle clacked as the door was jerked open. The servant inclined his head and gestured for Robert to walk on in.

'Robert Wood of Woodtown, m'Lord,' the servant declared.

The room was awash in a hazy, dust strewn light. Large windows with latticed glass panes lined the length of the stone wall opposite Robert. Above the windows were smaller, yellow glass panes in the shape of the cross. The flanking walls were covered with patterned dark wood panels, the centre of each panel bore a painted carving of Sir John's coat of arms.

Each of Robert's footfalls upon the thick wooden floorboards echoed up into the vast ceiling where gargoyles and the painted heraldries of the sheriff and his ancestors were interlinked by cobwebs. A dozen lit candles lined the corners and recesses of the room, contemptuous of the wasteful expense of keeping them burning during daylight hours.

Sir John sat in a high-backed chair behind a long table. A clerk sat to his left, the seat to his right was empty. Parchments, inkpots, and books cluttered the tabletop.

'Ah, Master Robert,' Sir John croaked. He nudged his brightly coloured chaperon so that it tilted to one side of his head: the angle matching the slant of the wearer's frown. Although about the same age as Robert, Sir John's face was gaunt and pale. His cheeks and nose were red, and half the hairs on his chin were grey. His left eyebrow pressed down in permanent scrutiny, the right brow occasionally joining it.

'My Lord.' Robert's voice echoed around the chamber. He bowed at the waist, extending one leg so he could bow all the lower.

'What brings thee today, Master Robert?' Sir John beckoned Robert with two gold ringed fingers.

Robert walked to the table, stopping a few steps short. He fiddled with the buckle on his purse, causing the contents to jingle.

'Were you not expecting me so soon? I've come to pay my dues, m'Lord.'

'Your dues?' Sir John looked to the white robed clerk beside him.

The clerk shrugged as he continued to clean the tip of the quill he'd been using.

Robert unfastened his purse and produced a small linen bag which he deposited onto the table with the unmistakable clatter of coins. He undid the top two buttons on his tunic, reached inside, and took out a small but bulging pouch from about his neck and tossed it next to the linen bag where it landed with a short, tinny ring.

'My dues,' Robert grinned, 'in thanks for my appointment as bailiff of the hundred. As was agreed.'

'Oh.' The Sheriff clicked his tongue against the roof of his mouth as he frowned with both eyebrows at the two bags of coin.

Robert swallowed and cleared his throat. He looked around again at the splendour and expense of the hall, and then at the coin purses which contained perhaps enough to buy two or three horses. How many mounts had the sheriff in his stable? He hadn't paid much notice but was sure it would have housed half a dozen.

'We have something of a misunderstanding, Master Robert,' the Sheriff said in a rasping voice.

'A misunderstanding?' Robert echoed. He wiped his sweaty palms on the leggings of his hose.

'Yes, Master Robert. A misunderstanding.' Sir John forced a thin smile.

Robert took a deep breath and closed his eyes for a heartbeat before speaking.

'Forgive me, m'Lord... I don't fathom what the nature of that misunderstanding might be. I stood afore you here but ten and four days ago whereupon you offered unto me the position of bailiff of the hundred. We talked about my likely earnings in the capacity of bailiff and agreed a deposit to compensate you for your time and consideration, and a quarterly fee...'

'No, no, no.' The Sheriff waved his hand irritably, his voice breaking through the rasp. 'Offer, thou say? Offer thee? Nay. Negotiate we did, as thou say. Offer? Not so. A misunderstanding, Master Robert. That's all.' He rested his elbows on the table and entwined his gold and jewel-laden fingers over which his long, thin smile mocked.

Robert looked up at the glass crosses as he gathered his thoughts. The light through the glass illuminated a slow rain of dust.

The servant cleared his throat behind Robert.

The clerk turned his attention to a parchment. The scratching of his quill filled the chamber.

'No.' Robert strode forward and stabbed his finger onto the tabletop. 'There be no misunderstanding. I've brought you six marks as agreed! Your damnable clerk wrote the words. I put my mark to it and you - *you* put your seal to it!'

Sir John leaned back into his seat, moving his elbows onto the armrests. 'I say, Master Robert, I don't like your tone. In my own house too!' Sir John coughed into his fist and turned to his clerk. 'Where's the paper? It's among these here. Or those there.'

The clerk thumbed through papers, picking up some and glancing at them before discarding them until he finally put one before the sheriff.

'Ah, yes. That's it.' Sir John murmured to himself as he glanced over the paper before pushing it across the table toward Robert. 'Read it your own self.'

Robert tried to control his breathing. He balled his hands into fists to stop the digits trembling. A trickle of sweat rolled down his temple. He ignored the document, keeping his gaze on the sheriff.

'Ah!' Sir John clapped his hands and winced. 'My apologies, Robert. Apologies! I forget: thou cannot read, isn't it so?'

The shaking travelled up Robert's arms to his shoulders. He bit his jaw closed to compress his expulsion of outrage into a short, strangled sound.

'Read the document for him, will you?' The sheriff handed the paper to his clerk.

The young clerk sniffed and clicked his tongue against his teeth. His eyes scanned over the first words of the paper before he began.

'On this day...'

'Yes, yes. Miss all that! To the point!' Sir John flicked his hand irritably in the clerk's direction.

'...Master Robert offers six marks, followed by an annual fee of twelve marks, to be paid in instalments of two pounds each quarter day if he should be enrolled as bailiff of the hundred at Lydford for the term of one year. This amount is agreed to cover such costs as incurred by the sheri-'

'Yes, that's enough!' Sir John barked. 'There, you see, Robert? *If he be installed*, it says. *If* he be.'

Robert looked over at the parchment. The writing was unintelligible to him, but the words sounded like those agreed on his previous visit. He'd seen the clerk scratch the letters down as the sheriff dictated, and the sheriff applied his seal to it along with a second, shorter parchment summarizing the details. All that was required was the payment of the fee. Or so he'd thought.

'What I offer thee, are almost my entire life savings.' Robert said, his voice barely above a whisper. 'I sold me own best horse to make up the shortfall. If it be the amount which distresses you, or if you need more...'

Sir John waved his hand as if he were trying to swat an irksome bee. 'Not so. Not so! It's not money. Look about: do you think a few pounds per annum will make a difference to me? A more suitable candidate came to mind, that's all.'

'We can't have an illiterate as bailiff,' the clerk said, his young voice high-pitched. 'I don't believe such ill appointment could ever come to pass.'

'Indeed,' said the sheriff with a sigh. 'I suppose there is no need to keep the agreement any longer. It is null.' He gestured to the clerk and then to the document. 'Burn it, if you please.'

The clerk's chair grated on the floor as the young man pushed himself up from the chair. He padded over to one of the candles and held the corner of the parchment to the flame, then walking back to the table with the burning paper, he deposited it into an iron dish on the tabletop.

Robert closed his eyes and let out a long, slow breath. So that was it. The sheriff had written down the proposal to show it off to another candidate as a way of getting that fellow to increase a competing offer. Robert realised that he had never seriously been considered as bailiff. He'd been stupid to think he could come to the sheriff and try to bribe his way into respectability. Not when he was barely above a villein in the Knight's eyes.

'So,' Robert managed after a long pause, his voice quavering. 'Who shall become bailiff?'

The sheriff scratched his chin and looked up at the ceiling beams. 'Hmm, well… If you must know now... it's to be William of Sampford Spiney. He will take office after the St. John's day feast.'

'William Spiney?' Robert growled.

'Just so. William Spiney of the Sampford Spiney estate.'

Robert opened his mouth to protest but the words wouldn't form.

'Please, pick up your coin, Robert.' Sir John extended a bony finger toward the two small pouches. 'Perhaps, if you can learn to read and write, the next sheriff may consider you for bailiff next year.'

Robert clenched his teeth. He could feel his cheeks warming. In his mind's eye he lunged across the table, taking Sir John by the head, and dashing his skull against the table. He unclasped his stiff fingers and reached for the purses while his eyes continued to bore into the sheriff.

Sir John shifted in his chair. He glanced nervously at the young clerk to his side, releasing a relieved sigh when Robert withdrew the coin purses. He nodded at Robert and flapped the fingers of his right hand toward the door.

'Good day, Master Robert. I am sorry you travelled this way for naught. I shall look forward to seeing you and your good wife again on St. John's day.'

Robert stuffed both coin bags into his leather purse. His fingers fumbled the buckle, so he left it unfastened. He turned without bowing to the Knight, marching back toward the antechamber where the manservant stood holding the door open. Robert heard the sheriff tut. He didn't even glance at the crippled servant as he passed him - not trusting his temper should the servant be wearing an expression which might cause offence.

The manor door creaked closed behind Robert as he emerged from the shadow of the great house. The warmth on his skin now annoyed. He wanted to rip off his doublet, throw down his hat and scream at the sun, but to do so in the sight of the manor would be to ensure ridicule by the entire household. Instead, he unfastened the remaining buttons of his tunic. His shaking fingers failed on the last button, so he tore it off and threw it onto the grass.

Guy sat on an upturned bucket outside the stable, cutting slices from a whitened cheese as he chatted with a smiling young maid. He ate a slither of the cheese off the end of his knife and said something which made the girl giggle.

The maid slapped her hand to her chest to exaggerate the humour, then snatched the hat off Guy's head, revealing his short-cropped blonde hair.

'Oi!' Guy laughed and took a swipe for his hat which the girl held teasingly above his reach.

'Guy!' Robert roared, 'bring the damn horses. We are leaving!'

Guy stood, knocking the bucket over. He tossed the cheese to the young girl and ripped his hat from her grasp. Without excusing himself from her company he rushed to the stable where he conversed briefly with the stablemaster. They saddled the horses as the mounts drank from a trough. The horses resisted being pulled away from their water and feed, but Guy cursed them and tugged sharply on their bridles and led them to his master with a rein in each hand.

Robert snatched the offered rein, putting his foot into the stirrup, he pulled himself up onto the saddle while holding down the pommel of his sword so that the sheath wouldn't slap against the beast's backside as he mounted.

Guy remained silent, watching his master, and awaiting any comment or instruction.

Robert scowled and urged his horse on. He kept his horse at a trot through the estate grounds onto the open moorland, not letting it slow to a walk until they had passed over the next hill and into the valley toward the River Tavy; far from the sight of the manor of Sir John Herle, Sheriff of Devon.

II

Robert stopped his horse atop a valley hilltop. Below, the River Tavy twisted between steep hillsides flecked with chunks of granite. Descent into the valley would necessitate navigation through tufts of undergrowth, brown bracken, untamed yellow grass, and clusters of spiny gorse bushes dotted with yellow flowers over which swifts flitted from one shrub to the next. Near the river a spread of hare's-tail cottongrass swayed in a gentle breeze; from a distance the sprinkling of white cottongrass appeared like sheep's wool caught on reeds. The river was little more than a stream in the June heat, but come the autumn could swell and transform the dark peat into bog up to a hundred yards from the river.

Robert yelled into the valley. His long, deep, roar put small birds to flight from ground nests, their flight paths skimmed over bushes and stone. The bellow resounded through the valley for a moment or two after it had departed Robert's lungs.

Guy reined in his horse next to his employer. The horse snorted; Guy patted the beast's neck while quietly humming to calm it.

'He's done made fool of me, Guy,' said Robert. His chest heaved. His voice cracked.

Guy cocked his head but said nothing.

'Damn all those highborn.' Robert spat onto the grass and plucked the riding gloves from his belt to wipe his mouth with.

'I'll grant that readily enough, aye,' Guy said, his voice soft and songlike.

'Well, dammit man, aren't you going to ask me what happened?' Robert blurted, spittle flecking his beard.

Guy sniffed and sucked his teeth before replying. 'I gathered enough. Supposed they refused you the bailiff 'n sent you on yer way. I wasn't wanting to cause anger in the asking of it.'

'Aye, well you presumed rightly enough,' Robert said, his baritone returned to a conversational volume. 'Played me for a fool they did, Guy. Played me. And those Spineys' had a hand in it too.'

'The Spineys?' Guy arched a thin blonde eyebrow.

'Aye. That bastard, William Spiney. He's to become Bailiff. Out-bribed me he did, Guy. Out-bribed me!'

Guy nodded and began to hum. His attention turned to a kestrel hovering above a mound of granite as it searched for prey among the foliage.

'What can be done, Guy, eh?' Robert reached across and grabbed Guy's arm.

Guy flinched but remained in Robert's grip. He looked at Robert's arm - the muscle evident under the tight-fitting sleeves of the green doublet, and then turned his gaze up to meet his master's.

'I don't see as there's anything what can be done, Master Robert. Sheriff ain't gonna change his mind on account o' the displeasure of a wool merchant, if you'll forgive me for sayin' so.'

Robert released his grip. He puffed out air and adjusted his position in the saddle. 'Well, Guy, you're right about that. Right indeed.' Robert scratched his beard.

The two men sat in silence, studying the view. Robert's horse bowed its head to sniff at something on the ground. Clouds lurked on the horizon some ten miles distant.

'Maybe we should be on our way, Master. We've few hours of sunlight left and we're yet to 'ave supper.'

'Spiney,' Robert growled.

'Master?'

'You're right. There might be naught to be done, but I'll have words with that bastard Spiney. He's no more highborn than I. Tis a betrayal of neighbourly trust: he knew I was proposing to stand as bailiff and he didn't say a word of it. Not a word!'

Guy sighed. 'He were probably fearing you might take sourly to any intent of competition on his part… I dunno why he'd think such a thing.'

Robert's eye's widened. His nostrils flared as he sucked in breath like a dragon preparing to incinerate its foe.

Guy's mouth spread into a lopsided grin.

Both men erupted in laughter. Robert's bawling crescendo almost smothering Guy's high-pitched yap.

Robert slapped his companion's arm then spurred his horse onward.

Guy tugged the rein on his mount and made a clicking sound for the benefit of the horse as he followed his master.

They cantered down into the valley, heading for the ford where pebbles had built up so that in the hotter months the current merely trickled submissively between the stones. The river wasn't deep or wide enough to provide any real obstacle for the horses, but the banks were steep in places and partially screened by reeds and boulders, threatening a small element of risk of the mounts making a misstep.

Robert led the way, encouraging his bay onward with short grunts and nudges. Once across the riverbed they followed a trail through long, tangled moorland grass. The occasional farm, hut, and church steeple that were visible in the distance were the only signs of humanity's imprint on the moorland until finally, they reached the granite tor above Sampford Spiney.

The hill they occupied offered a perfect panorama of the moors and the western edge of the Royal Forest. To the North-West, Brentor Church was a far-off shadow atop its steep promontory: a dominating landmark which overlooked many farmers for every day of their lives. To the East were the hills, woodlands, and grasslands of Dartmoor Royal Forest. It was not indistinct from the rest of the landscape except in that everything falling within its significant, unmarked boundary belonged to the crown.

To the south, Sampford Spiney: an unremarkable village with a small church, a dozen or so thatched houses and thrice as many long, thin, strip farms. At the heart of the village stood the prominent farmhouse of the Spineys, which looked like a half-size version of the Sheriff's residence. A half-mile beyond the village was the small hamlet of Woodtown, sat on the edge of a large area of woodland.

'Is ye really gonna to confront Spiney?' Guy said, wincing at the Spineys' estate.

'Well... we have to go by way of his house to get to mine. It would be rude not to visit our neighbour and hail his great accomplishment at becoming bailiff.' Robert spurred his horse onward, ignoring Guy's impertinent sigh.

Bent-backed men ceased toiling among their strips of farmland, standing to watch the two riders come down from the tor. The land they worked was their master's - their own meagre strips could only be farmed during their free time or by their wives and children. One villein wiped sweat from his brow and waved at Robert, who ignored the gesture.

'Master...' Guy urged his horse forward so that he rode beside his employer as they neared the manor, 'I know you'd not asked, but I'd advise against inclinations to violence. Plenty hereabout to raise a hue and cry. There'd be nothing but trouble in striking a bailiff.'

'Guy, what do you take me for?' Robert scowled. He touched the brim of his hat, nodding to Randalf Hoccleave, the local pastor who was attending his own small lot of land adjacent to the graveyard around the small stone church.

The priest was on his knees, his face wet with sweat, he raised a trowel in salute to the riders before returning to his labours. His blonde hair was shaven on top, leaving a sunburnt circular cap of flesh on the crest of his head.

Then the riders were at the gates of the large farmhouse. The perimeter wall was drystone with a brick arch around it just high enough for a rider to duck under. An stone cross stood at a crooked angle just outside the estate, local legend held that it was built to ward off the devil after he had failed to destroy Brentor Church.

The manor, as the Spineys' fashioned it, was a large farmhouse with stone walls and a thatch roof. It was bigger than the other houses in the village and had two chimneys, its own well, a barn and a stable. Chickens, roosters, and ducks waddled about the courtyard while a pair of idle goats chewed acorn bread.

Robert jerked the reins of his horse to bring the beast to a stop. The horse snorted, shook his head, and stamped one of his forelegs in the dirt.

Guy began to dismount until Robert reached over and snatched the sleeve of his doublet.

'Remain mounted. We'll not grace this place longer than needed.'

Guy nodded and settled back into his saddle.

'Spiney!' Robert bellowed toward the house. 'Spiney! Come out here and face me, you thieving whoremonger!'

Some of the hens clucked and bobbed their heads. A goat regarded Robert while continuing to slowly chew. The priest stood up from his patch and covered his brow with one hand to shield against the sun as he peered at the riders.

'Spiney, you coward! Come out here!'

The farmhouse door opened with a protesting groan. William Spiney emerged, hatless and chewing a mouthful of food. He tossed a half-eaten chicken bone aside. His pointed goatee beard was finely combed. Although not yet thirty, his brown hair was receding. His tunic was undone, and his shirt laces loosened. He dabbed his mouth with a square of cloth.

'Robert. Good afternoon. I was at the table. What brings you here with such vacuous cries?'

'What brings me?' Robert's cheeks warmed. 'By God, Spiney, do you dare to feign ignorance of your betrayal?'

William's wife and eldest son came out of the house. The wife, Mathilde, as usual wore a fine dress with a long train, and she had her hair tied into a jewelled crispinette. The son wore mud-splattered hose and boots and came out clasping a wooden cudgel and snarling under a mop of tangled hair. He made to advance on Robert, but his father waved him back.

'I assume you are talking about the bailiff business?' William said.

'Of course I'm talking about the bloody bailiff! You know how I toiled to save enough coin for that bloody Knight's bribe. I agreed an amount with him on paper, just for him to use it to get a better price off you! How much did you pay him, bastard?' Robert sprayed spittle as he yelled.

'You apologise to my father, immediately!' The son took a step forward, halted by his father's hand on his chest.

'Stay your hand, Son. This is just a misunderstanding.'

'Misunderstanding?' Robert stabbed his finger in William's direction. 'You stole my fate from me, bastard.'

Mathilde gasped and ran back into the house as quickly as her chubby legs and dragging dress train would allow.

William held up his hand and frowned at Robert. 'I would remind you, Robert, that you are insulting me on my own land. I know you were intent on becoming bailiff - so was I, but I have no idea what paper you refer to.'

'I agreed a fee, in truth twas a bribe, with the Sheriff. I made my mark n' he placed his seal, promising me the job of bailiff.'

William stroked the tip of his beard and sniffed. 'You're telling me that the Sheriff signed and placed his seal to a document confirming acceptance of a bribe for you becoming bailiff of the hundred?'

Robert dug his nails into his saddle. 'Verily, and don't dare pretend ignorance of having seen it!'

'I've not seen it, Robert, because it doesn't exist.'

Robert turned to Guy. 'I'm going to run him through, Guy. Don't try to stop me.'

Guy shook his head and smirked. 'Don't do that, Master. Your sword'll become stuck in his guts.'

'No, really,' William said, walking toward Robert with his arms folded. 'There's no chance Sir John will have recorded a bribe. Think about it: anyone might use it against him. I don't know what he got you to sign, but it wasn't a bribe. I can assure you. If you wish I will inspect the-'

'How much did you pay? Bastard.'

'I don't really think that's any of your concern.'

'I swear in God's name: if you don't say it, I shall cut you in half. And if that boy of yours creeps any closer with that cudgel, I'll cave his skull with it.'

William looked sharply around at his son and then back to Robert. 'I agreed and paid ten marks with nine marks to be paid quarterly.'

Robert's breathing came heavily. He bit his teeth together and stared into William's face for several long moments, trying to detect any indication of dishonesty.

'Nine? Quarterly? You couldn't hope to earn that much in bribes and fees from the prisoners during the whole year long term - unless they imprison a noble or his favourite whore.'

William shrugged. 'It's not about money, Robert. It's about power. It's a first step to raising oneself up from being one who works to becoming one of those who lead. Surely you understand, or you wouldn't be investing so much of your little wool trade into it.'

'It's both betterment and livelihood for me,' Robert sneered, 'and you have taken it from me. Know that we are now enemies.'

William sighed, shaking his head, he put his hands on his hips. 'Be reasonable, Robert. I can make use of you - you can still profit from this. You must have known that Sir John wouldn't appoint you as bailiff: you don't read. I've taken nothing that wasn't already out of your reach.'

Mathilde came running back out of the house, puffing with the effort and her expression flustered. A household servant followed her, brandishing a mallet.

'Get away from here, Robert Wood!' Mathilde cried out, 'you scoundrel! I'll stand for no threats to my family and estate.'

The servant fell in alongside William's son. The two young men held their improvised weapons with both hands and adopted combative stances.

Guy released a snorting laugh. Robert frowned at him.

'I've said my piece,' Robert said, 'I'll be on my way. Any o' you come over the threshold of your estate afore we ride off and I'll cleave your skull in two.'

Mathilde cried out and made the sign of the cross.

'This whole area is my estate!' William shouted.

'I'll have no violence!' the pastor called out in a high-pitched voice.

Robert had forgotten the priest loitering at the corner of the drystone wall. Randalf scurried forward, holding up the copper cross he wore around his neck. His off-white robes were muddied at the knees and his sandaled feet the colour of the earth.

'Violence or not is up to them,' Robert growled, 'I've said my bit, Sir, and will leave in peace as you command. For now.' He turned back to William. 'But know this, Spiney. I will have my revenge upon you - it won't be a long time coming either. I'll see you ruined, imprisoned or dead. I swear it.'

'Peace!' Randalf called out. He hurried to stand between Robert and his quarry. The Priest held his cross aloft and waved the holy symbol at Robert as if he might direct divine retribution at him.

'My fight's not with God, Sir, just with one of his bastard creations.' Robert tugged on his horse rein, turning the creature about.

'Blasphemy!' Randalf screamed.

Robert ignored him. He led his horse along the earthen track which wound among the rows of strip farms toward Woodtown.

Guy spurred his horse so that he fell in alongside his master.

'Well…' Guy sniffed and shrugged. 'That went better than I feared it might.'

III

A dirt trail attached the hamlet, Woodtown, to its slightly larger neighbour like an umbilical cord. The little village of Sampford Spiney occupied the higher ground overlooking the tiny hamlet, guarding, or perhaps even dominating it with its tall church steeple and expansive field system. The road down to Woodtown was dusty in the summer, a mire in the winter, and downhill all the way. Robert and Guy followed the track into the hamlet of seven thatched homes and a half dozen outbuildings situated just above the River Walkham. Thick woodland guarded its back, blocking the view of the river, although after a heavy rainfall the rush of water could be heard through the whole community. During the warmer months the surrounding pastureland was home to grazing livestock from the lowlands.

The track cut through Woodtown, creating a central street; on the north side two small cottages with smoking chimneys housed women who worked as spinners. The spinners' families toiled two small fields behind their cottages where golden barley swayed with the breeze, ready for the coming harvest. A four-wheeled cart sat outside the second of the cottages alongside a threshing platform. Several chickens wandered at will, pecking between tufts of grass, looking for spilled morsels of grain.

On the West side lay Robert's longhouse: twice the length and half the height again of the other abodes in the hamlet and boasting two chimneys. A laundry line connected the longhouse to a ramshackle stone shrine, referred to locally as the chapel, its slate roof was moss-covered; a wooden cross and a crude statue of St. Mary inside the doorless structure were visible from the road. A large stable stood nearby, behind which a fenced-off enclosure housed two dozen sheep. To the north of the longhouse were twin cottages with doorways on the gable side, housing the fullers who worked the wool. South of the track were two smaller cottages: the first housing the sherman who sheared the sheep. The last home was missing its door and had been empty since the last occupant died heirless three winters previously, the run-down homestead now only served to contain the produce of the wool trade before it was shipped off for sale.

As Robert and Guy reached the outskirts of the hamlet, one of the labourers ran to the longhouse and hammered on the door. After a few moments, a young lady emerged wearing a long white and yellow dress with a moderate length train behind it. She wore her golden hair tied into the netted bunches of a crispinette with a large jewel in the centre of the headband. The labourer bowed to the lady and indicated Robert's arrival, then rushed back to his work.

Robert muttered under his breath.

Guy looked at him with a quizzical eyebrow.

'Alice is dressed in her finest,' Robert sighed, 'expecting me to be raised to bailiff.'

Guy nodded.

Robert swung his left leg over his horse's back and dropped down from the saddle. He handed the bridle to Guy. 'See to the mounts. After you're done, stay outside for a bit. I must console the wife.'

'Yes, Master Robert.'

'Ah, bugger.'

Guy titled his head, and then nodded when observing the source of Robert's exclamation: A man stood in the cottage doorway, dressed in a gaudy attire and shoes curled at the toes in finest court style. The chaperon on his head boasted excess tails of material which draped almost to his waist.

Alice rushed to Robert, the veil from her crispinette wafted in her wake.

'Robert! Oh, you were gone longer than I expected. I'd almost begun to fear you were waylaid by outlaws.'

'Alice, my dear.' Robert opened his arms and forced a smile.

His wife rushed into his embrace. She pecked him on the cheek then pulled back. Her face was unblemished and smooth, almost milky-white. She looked at least a decade younger than Robert's forty years. Many might mistake Alice Wood in her finery as a noblewoman: she spoke in a practiced accent reminiscent of French but betrayed by a Devonian tinge. She held Robert at arm's length as she examined his face.

'What is it, my love? Why do you look so pained?' Alice's large blue eyes begged. Her lower lip hung moist in mimicry of sorrow.

'Ah, wife! I can hide my mood from ye for but a second. I wouldn't deign to explain all to you here where all the spinners and muckers will strain their ears and wag their tongues. Let us go inside and I'll spill the tale of our fortune over some bread and wine.'

Alice bowed her head and curtseyed. She turned, almost colliding with the gaudily robed man behind her. She tutted and walked around him to the house.

'Eustace!' Robert barked. 'I thought you were in Plympton where you belong.'

The man smiled and nodded. The tails of his hat flopped around his chest.

'As much as it tires me to come to this dreary place, I couldn't miss the opportunity to congratulate my brother in his latest endeavour.'

'Bah! Come for alms have ye?'

'Oh Brother, you judge me harshly!' Eustace stepped back, folding his arms over his chest. He pursed his lips and frowned, slowly shaking his head. 'You wound me. I wish only to partake in your rejoicing.'

'I'll wound you alright.' Robert sniffed as he walked past his younger brother and pushed through the door of his longhouse.

The interior was partitioned into a central hall with doorless chambers on each wing. A small square firepit smouldered upon the compacted dirt floor, its black wisps trailed up to the rafters and through a round hole in the thatch topped by a slate chimney cover. Daylight spread through a single square un-paned window. One of the wooden shutters hung at limp angle from a broken hinge. The only items of furniture were a wooden chest, a shelf supporting a few pieces of pottery, and a low, rickety bench. Robert headed for the chamber on the right: the solar. The entrance was shielded on the far side by a painted wooden privacy screen which he walked around.

Alice was pouring wine into clay cups. She turned to Robert as he entered, offering him a libation.

Robert raised the drink in salute and gulped it down. A trickle from the corner of his mouth seeped into his beard. He gasped and passed the beaker back to his wife which she dutifully refilled.

The solar was well lit by a large, un-paned window. The floor was masked by a thick layer of rushes which crunched underfoot. A polearm with a blade browned from rust rested against a large unlit fireplace. Four knee-high stools surrounded the wooden table upon which the wine was served.

Eustace followed his brother into the chamber. He accepted wine from Alice and sat on the stool nearest the fireplace.

'So, what's the story, Brother?' Eustace yawned.

Robert muttered a curse, drained his second filling of wine, and scowled at his smooth-faced brother before returning his attention to his wife.

'Bastard Spiney.'

Alice and Eustace exchanged confused glances.

Robert paced the room. He unfastened his belt, sword and purse still attached, and dropped them onto the table. 'Bloody William Spiney has gone n' bribed the sheriff so as to become bailiff.'

'What?' Eustace sprang up. He swept the hat off his head and kneaded it with his hands. 'By god… how could he? I thought it was all arranged?'

Alice took Robert's hands in hers. Her eyes moistened. 'Oh, Robert. How could this befall us? Did you offer the sheriff the agreed sum?'

'Of course I did!' Robert snapped. Immediately regretting his outburst, he sighed and softened his tone. 'It was never going to be. I could never be bailiff because I don't… ah, it doesn't matter.'

Alice lifted Robert's knuckles to her lips and kissed his hairy fingers. 'Oh, husband. Let's not dwell on it. We shall have a better summer season this year. I know it. Then we'll show those Spineys!'

'He said you don't what?' Eustace said, running a hand through his straight, black, jaw length hair.

Robert fixed him with a stare.

'Ah… it's because you're not one of them,' Eustace smiled. 'They don't want a raised commoner. An illiter-'

'Enough!' Robert ripped his hands from his wife's hold. 'Maybe the wrong son went up there, eh? Maybe the son who apprenticed as a scribe afore falling into cups of wine should've tried out for bailiff instead of the one who went to Brittany and through his own toil raised his family out of the ditches!'

'Peace, please!' Alice hooked her arm around Robert's elbow and patted his chest. 'Gentle Eustace isn't criticising you, please don't be angry with him.'

'Yes, apologies, Brother.' Eustace bowed his head. 'I don't criticise, of course. We are all grateful for all you've done for us.'

'Aye.' Robert eyed his brother. 'You do a good enough job managing the books and numbers. Not every son can grow into a proper man.'

Eustace nodded, smiling. 'Yes, of course, Brother. I'm sure one day you will produce a son, proving beyond all doubt that thou art a proper man.'

Robert tensed. He felt Alice squeeze his arm. He released his breath and gave her a peck on the forehead. His brother could play his clever word games: it was all the bookish waif was capable of. He held his wife's shoulder and looked down into her blue eyes.

'Soon, wife, we shall have a son.'

Alice smiled and rested her head on Robert's chest. 'Yes, Robert, dear. A boy. Big and strong like his father. Beautiful like his mother.'

'Intelligent, like his uncle.' Eustace raised his cup, accompanied by a lopsided grin, then tossing his head back he gulped down the wine. He wiped his mouth with the back of his wrist and sighed. He picked up the wine jug and poured the last few ounces into his cup.

Robert stepped away from his wife. He lifted the drink out of his brother's grasp as Eustace was raising it to his lips, and drank from it himself, swilling the wine from cheek to cheek as he stared at his younger brother. He swallowed. The beverage left a dry sensation on his tongue. He passed the cup back to Eustace. 'What will you do when I have a son and heir, Eustace?'

Eustace shrugged. He put the empty vessel down on the table and stroked his chin, avoiding eye contact with Robert. 'Well, I suppose that's up to you, Brother. Perhaps, as the only male literate, I will educate your son.'

'Ha!' Robert grunted. 'You could do as father intended for you all those years ago and join the priesthood.'

Eustace shrugged and looked over at the empty wine vessel. 'Well… at least there is a plentiful supply of wine in the church.'

'There is a plentiful supply of wine in my larder, except after your visits.' Robert growled.

Alice tugged on Robert's sleeve. 'Oh, come. You are always so hard on your younger brother. He does a good job as you say with the ledgers. We couldn't do without him.'

Robert cupped his wife's cheek with a tender hand. 'I tell thee, that bastard Spiney could have all the wealth in the kingdom, but his wife in all her finery is like a smouldering tallow candle next to your flame.'

'Oh, Robert.' Alice put a palm over her mouth and averted her gaze in a show of embarrassment.

'I saw her today. Stopped by the Spiney place to give the bastard a piece o' my mind. She appears as a beggar compared to you.'

'Oh really? What was she wearing?' Alice squeezed Robert's arms, her bashfulness vanished as she looked earnestly into his eyes.

'Nothing, really.'

'Nothing?'

'I mean, rags compared to you, wife. Rags. Red, I think.'

'Velvet?'

'Could've been. But her crispinette wasn't half as nice and the train was short.'

'Oh, marvellous! What about her hair, was it unkempt? What else did you notice?'

'Ah, I regret saying about her now. I can't answer your questions, dear. My thoughts were only for you. I noticed only that she was inferior in every way.'

'What did you say to Master Spiney?' Eustace wore a deep frown. His arms folded across his chest with his ample sleeves covering his hands.

'I won't speak it all over again like a mummer's act. Needless to say, he was sufficiently scolded.'

Eustace closed his eyes and let out a long breath.

Alice bit her lower lip.

'What?' Robert barked, looking from his brother to wife and back.

'I say this without criticising, Brother…' Eustace flashed his teeth, licked his lips, his eyes searching the rafters. 'If Spiney is to be the new bailiff, he could make life very difficult for us. If he chooses to do so.'

Alice shrugged and allowed a weak smile.

Robert walked to the fireplace. He reached out to the polearm, taking it by the five-foot ash shaft. He examined the long, curved, rust-flecked iron head. The sharp edge of the glaive was burred in places and the pole was worn with small chips.

'The Spineys are not warriors. They will dare not provoke me further. They would be foolish if they did.'

'For God's sake, Robert!' Eustace said with an exasperated sigh.

'Eustace, blasphemy!' Alice hissed.

Robert turned to his brother. He rested the weapon back against the fireplace.

'Robert…' Eustace cleared his throat. 'Even you are not stupid enough to hamsoken a fellow landowner on his own estate. Or even threaten to. Unless you plan to ruin us all.'

'Stupid is it?' Robert said in an even tone. 'Was I stupid when I carried that very glaive on chevauchee in Brittany and won fortune for our family? We'd all be tilling Spiney's fields now if I hadn't used it to unhorse that Breton lord and win a share of his ransom.'

Eustace ran a palm over his face. He shook his head and took a deep breath. 'Brother, perhaps I misspeak when I say stupid, but this isn't Breton land: nobody is going to award you for slaying a bailiff. They'll hang you, and you know it. So please, stop this posturing. Anyway, you've not wielded that glaive at anything more than a branch in twenty years.'

Robert puffed out his chest and raised his shoulders. He regarded his brother for a few moments, then nodded. 'I do let my temper best me, but even in a fury I know when to stay my hand. We can endure Spiney as bailiff for a year. You will teach me to read words and I'll see about making a go of it next year under the new sheriff.'

'I don't know, Brother...' Eustace frowned at the floor while pinching his chin.

'What?'

'I could teach an ox to read in a year. I'm just not sure I could teach you within a year.' Eustace smirked.

Robert quickly closed the few steps between them and wrapped his arms around his brother's waist, lifting him off his feet, snarling.

'Not on the dirt!' Eustace cried out, laughing.

Robert dropped his brother onto his back and put a foot onto Eustace's chest. He bared his teeth in a wide grin, still growling like a beast. 'Yield, you little snot!'

'I yield, I yield!' Eustace laughed.

Robert removed his foot and offered his open palm, pulling Eustace to his feet.

Eustace dusted himself down, picking rushes off his tunic and muttering about dirt stains on his coat.

Alice had retreated behind the table, with her back against the wall. She smiled at the brothers and forced a little laugh, covering her mouth with her fingertips.

Robert gathered up the cups and headed toward the door. 'I'll bring some beer. Then we'll call in Guy and we'll cook the rabbit from the larder.'

'There's one thing I don't understand,' Eustace said.

Robert stopped beside the privacy screen and waited for his brother to continue.

'When you met the sheriff the last time, you'd signed an agreement. Why would he go through that charade just to betray you?'

'He used it to get a better price out of Spiney.' Robert shrugged.

'Who read the agreement for you?'

'One of his damn clerks. Why?'

Alice crossed herself on hearing Robert's cursing.

'Well, Brother. It just seems a lot of bother to fool you over the bailiff matter. Did it not enter your mind that the documents you signed could have said absolutely anything?'

IV

'I'll take that 'un too.' Robert pointed at the sheep he was examining. He released the struggling creature which bounded away, nudging a couple of its fellow ovine out of the way.

The lowland shepherd who owned the small flock signalled to a young lad, likely his son, to separate the chosen sheep. The boy waded among the flock and wrestled with the ewe, looping a length of worn rope around its neck, he pulled the protesting animal to where Guy watched over a half-dozen sheep corralled together inside a circular wicker sheepfold.

Robert stood among a small herd of forty or so sheep. Their wiry coats were thick and matted with grass, poop, and other matter. Robert scratched his beard and moved among the flock, occasionally grabbing a tuft of fleece and examining it before moving onto the next animal. If he was happy with the appearance of the wool he would take the creature's jaw in his hands, prising open the mouth to inspect the teeth before running his hands through the whole coat, feeling the body of the sheep to ensure it was suitably fed and without any obvious tumours.

'How many we got now?' Robert said.

'Seven.' Guy answered over his shoulder as he opened the corral wide enough for the shepherd boy to push the sheep inside.

'That's about all I'll part with,' the shepherd said. His linen shirt hung almost to his knees and was as stained with sheep-related matter as the creatures themselves. 'I brought 'em up to the moorland for grazin', not sellin'. I coulda herded 'em into Tavistock if I wanted to sell off the 'ole flock.'

Robert sniffed. He cast a look over the flock, feeling assured that he'd picked about the best among them. Sweat beaded on his forehead, and his linen shirt was stained yellow under the arms. It was too hot for a hat, doublet, or cloak, and he'd left his heavy sword at home.

'A shilling apiece,' Robert shouted to the shepherd, 'and I'll give tuppence for each shearing off the rest yer flock.'

'Nay.' The shepherd shook his head. 'I already told ya we always ask a shillin' and ten for each.'

Robert put his hands on his hips, threw back his head and released a bellowing laugh.

A nearby sheep jumped and bounded away a distance, frightening a few more. The boy moved to head them off, waving a stick as long as he was tall, trying to herd the sheep back together.

'You may ask a shilling n' ten, but you won't get it,' Robert said, pretending to wipe a mirthful tear from the corner of his eye.

The shepherd's mouth curled up on one side. He pointed at the corralled sheep. 'We shoulda agreed the price afore you gone fenced 'em. Yer wastin' me time, Sir. A shillin'? I'll be losin' money at such a price.'

'The fleeces are fair, but they're skinny and small. You won't get a shilling n' ten for them - even in Tavistock.'

'I'll get more'n a shillin'. They ain't skinny either. Anyhow, all you wants 'em for is the fleece. Even if they were under size, which they ain't, it be the wool you want off 'em not the mutton.'

'Are you stupid, man?' Robert said, crossing his arms over his chest. 'The smaller the sheep, the smaller the fleece, the lesser the wool. Isn't that right, Guy?'

'Yep,' Guy said as he fanned himself with his riding cap.

'And what say you, John?' Robert called out to a young man sitting on a boulder with shears and a long knife cradled in his lap, his hose covered in strands of white wool.

'Uhhhh, yes, Master?'

Robert glared at him. 'The sheep are worth a shilling apiece, wouldn't you say?'

'Oh, yessir. At least!' John beamed.

Robert rolled his eyes up to the clear blue sky, lifting his palms up, silently imploring the heavens. He turned back to the shepherd. 'A shilling apiece. I've been trading in wool for near on twenty years, and John he's been a Sherman for... well, his whole useless life most like. We know a good, fair price.'

'He said at *least* a shillin'.' The shepherd narrowed his eyes. 'They's worth a shillin'n ten any day.'

'Not so.'

'They is!'

'Not on a Sunday. Ye won't get anythin' for them on a Sunday.'

'You can't trade on a Sunday! Tis the sabbath!'

'That's my meaning! Ye said any day…' Robert sighed and shook his head. 'Very well… I'll give ye eight shillings for all seven.'

The shepherd smacked his lips and squinted at the sheep. 'Another quarter noble and we has a bargain.'

'I'll not be robbed upon mine own land, Shepherd. I'll pay nine shillings and that's the lot.'

'And tuppence fer each shearing,' the shepherd reminded him.

'Aye.'

Robert pointed at John the Sherman and then at the livestock. The youth slid off his rock and advanced on the nearest sheep with his cutters at the ready.

'I should take some off your pay for your blasted stupidity,' Robert sneered as the Sherman walked by.

John stopped and looked dumfounded at Robert for a moment until Robert waved him on.

'You can't get intelligent help,' Robert muttered.

'Lad's of your own loins, is he?' the shepherd said with a grin that displayed a mouthful of blackened and missing teeth.

'What say ye? Of course not!' Robert fixed the man with a stare, unable to ascertain if he was being made fun of. 'When my sherman has done his work, go up to the house. My brother manages the accounts n' purse. My man Guy will notch the tally stick for you.'

The shepherd sucked on his gums. 'Your bruvver ain't gonna count them coins out wrong, is he?'

'Forsooth, absolutely not! He apprenticed as scribe four years and manages my… mind your own blasted business.'

'Well, it's just you said you can't gets clever help. So, I is worried your accountin' bruvver ain't good help neither.'

Robert studied the shepherd's face, noting the twitch of a smile then the quiver of the lower lip and chin as the shepherd switched between mild mockery and worry that he'd stirred this barrel-chested and wide-armed brute to anger.

'Just get the bloody wool off the bloody sheep then go onto wherever you're grazing 'em for the summer.' Robert turned from the shepherd and beckoned Guy with a wave.

Guy walked over with the tally stick already in-hand. Robert could smell the man's sweat - likely caused by the black doublet and leather riding hose he wore despite the heat. At least he'd had the sense to remove the sleeves from the doublet, Robert thought, then realising he'd never seen Guy wearing any other clothes, he considered that they were probably the only ones he owned.

Guy finished with the stick; carving the required number of notches for each shilling the shepherd was to be paid and pricking points into the stick for each penny. He handed the stick to the shepherd who scrutinised it.

'Have you attended the horses?' Robert said.

'Aye. Fed, watered, brushed down and put out to pasture. I mended the stirrup on yer saddle n' all. Twas frayed and might've snapped when mountin'.'

'Good.' Robert clapped his hand on Guy's shoulder. 'Stroll with me.'

They walked to the stable, stopping at the entrance. Hay and bags of grain were stacked against one wall. The pen in which the three riding horses and one carthorse overnighted was clear of manure. The troughs were full of chalky water. A rickety ladder led up to a living area in the rafters where Guy slept - except when it was cold, on which occasions he was permitted to sleep in the longhouse by the fireplace. The loft area wasn't visible from the ground, Robert reflected that he'd never been up there: it was Guy's space, and he could do with it as he pleased. Robert made a mental note to have a suitable pair of woollen hose made for Guy.

'We inspectin' the whole estate?' Guy said.

'Aye. Must be a week since I last did, so it's due. Why? Do you have something to attend?'

Guy shook his head and shrugged. 'No. I thought mayhap you'd other plans after what occurred yesterday n' all.'

Robert glowered. 'Take care not to speak of it in front of the workers. Forsooth, let's never mention it again.'

'Aye, Master.' Guy nodded.

Robert scrutinized him with a slight frown. 'What did ye think I'd be up to anyway? Revenge? Pay some old wife for a potion or curse? There's naught to be done.'

'I don't rightly know, Master.' Guy shrugged.

'Tell me something, Guy. I never asked you to tell me the tale of your service with the Courtenay household, but that scar down your cheek - did you get that in battle?'

'Nah, I took it fightin', but you wouldn't call it battle.'

'In the service of your lord?'

'Well, I were in his service at the time, but I didn't get it fightin' *in* his service. It were… a personal matter, Master.'

'Alright.' Robert carried on walking. He'd taken on Guy the previous summer on trust: it felt like a failure of that trust to pry too much into his past – especially since Guy was tight lipped regarding the rumours over his dismissal from the Courtenay household. 'I was just desiring to know if you're any use in a fight.'

'I do alright, Master.'

'Hah! Did I ever tell you how I cleaved the skull of a Breton during the siege of Nantes?'

'Yes, Master. Many times, as I recall.'

'Always on the front rank, I. Not a posturing garderobe sentry like Courtenay's men.'

'I don't recall ever watching the garderobe, Master.'

They crossed the earth track that divided the hamlet. A small square patch of garden lay outside the first residence. The soil had been turned over where root vegetables had been recently harvested. The cottage door was propped open by a stool and the sound of wood rubbing against wood emanated through the doorway. The two men stopped at the door; Guy had to duck under the rim of thatch which protruded two feet from the wall.

'I forget her name,' Robert said.

'This one's Muriel. The next one is Isolda.'

'Muriel!' Robert poked his head through the open doorway, but kept his feet beyond the threshold. 'Ah, there you are. Hard at work. No don't stop. I just wanted a few moments.'

Muriel stood working a large spinning wheel which reached to her shoulder. She span the wheel with one hand while pulling and twisting the thread as it wound around a small spool. Muriel's smile was wide but seemed full of effort under her sagging facial features. Her dark watery eyes shimmered all the more when she smiled, giving her the appearance of a constant state of mourning. She looked almost like a nun in her long grey woollen dress, white apron, and hood.

'What can I be doing for ye, Master Robert?'

'May I step inside?'

'Verily, you may. It be your land, Master Robert.'

Robert moved the stool which propped the door open and walked in, followed by Guy. Like most cottages and longhouses, there were no rooms. A curtain screen divided working space from the area beyond where she slept and ate. The area she worked in was bare of anything other than spools of thread, buckets of wool, an iron crucifix on the wall, and a chicken that strutted about looking for morsels among the rushes that covered the floor.

'Your husband, at the fields, is he?'

'Aye, Master Robert. He's working Master William's land today and tomorrow. If the weather holds, he'll be free to work our patch day after. We got a good little harvest of carrot. Perchance you'd like some for Missus's pot, Master?'

'Your husband was working Spiney's land yesterday, was he?'

'He were, aye.' Muriel's smile dropped. Her lower lip hung limp like she been scolded.

Robert picked up a spool of spun thread, turning it over in his hands. 'Did he return with any news? Forgive my trespass on private conversation between man and wife.'

The wheel stopped clacking. Muriel pursed her lips.

'It's alright, Muriel. I'll not be mad. I'm just curious what those soddomites on the Spiney estate are saying about what happened.'

Muriel winced and made the sign of the cross. 'They's saying you had a dispute with Master William.'

'And?' Robert put the spool back among the others. He smiled, displaying his big white teeth, then remembering that Eustace always told him his grin looked maniacal, he put his lips together.

'Well... I don't know, Master Robert. I don't really listen to gossip-talk, you know.' Muriel looked down at the ground. She fidgeted with a strand of thread.

'It's alright, Muriel. An imbalance of humours caused me to lose my temper yesterday. Today I'm calmness and peace.'

She regarded him with sad, unbelieving eyes. 'Well, Master Robert... they's saying you were gripped with the Devil's madness. That you were going t' cut Master William and his whole family to pieces with yer sword what you usually carries on yer person.'

Robert grunted and allowed a hint of a smirk. 'Forsooth, it wasn't that bad. But I did rise to anger, as I confess. I just wanted to be assured they weren't speaking untruths. Half-truths I can live with. I suppose the whole hamlet knows about it?'

Muriel seemed to shrink inside her robes. 'I don't knows about that, Master Robert. Maybe they does. I don't listen to or repeat gossip-talks. If I can help it.'

Robert glanced at Guy.

Guy shrugged.

'Well, don't let me keep you. If you'll drop a few carrots around to my wife later - your dozen best, I'll give you tuppence for them.'

'Oh, thank you, Master Robert.' Muriel smiled and bowed her head. She began spinning the wheel again as Robert turned to leave.

Robert crossed back over the track, heading toward the fuller's homes at the end of the hamlet not far from Robert's home.

'You're not visiting the other spinner?' Guy asked, his long legs easily keeping up with Roberts strides.

'Nah. I only wanted to find out what Muriel knew, being as her husband works on the Spiney estate. It'd be a good wager that all of Woodtown knows the same by now.'

Guy nodded his agreement. 'So, you're going to check on the fullers?'

'No. It's your job to check on the workers. I'm sure they're doing their bit.'

'You just don't like the smell o' the fullers' work.'

Robert arched an eyebrow. 'I've been doing this work for one score years; such scents long ceased to offend me. You've been in my employ for not yet one whole year. The solitary smells which stir me are those of profit and my wife's good cooking. Now, I will leave you to your work and I shall attend to my wife and brother. Come by later and we'll see what Alice has cooked.'

Robert slapped Guy's shoulder and strode on past the cottages belonging to the two fullers, both of whom were outside their homes, barefoot, with their shirts clinging to their sweating torsos. They beat wet wool laid out on a large sheet, their clubs raising and falling repeatedly, creating a muffled pounding on the ground. They were engrossed in their work and muttering between themselves, not noticing Robert as he passed by.

***

Robert sat on a three-legged stool at his table. Alice sat to his right with her arm hooked through his. Guy and Eustace sat on the opposite side of the table. They ate a pottage of peas and carrot accompanied with chunks of bread torn off a dark brown loaf and drank ale from leather cups. Fading daylight filtered through the gaps around the window shutters. A few long, thin tallow candles provided enough light to eat by.

'A tasty if simple dish.' Eustace smiled at his sister-in-law.

Robert kicked him under the table. 'Simple? And you're eating the King's venison every day when at my house in Plympton, are you?'

'No offence, Alice.' Eustace held up a defensive hand as he took a swig from his cup.

'Think nothing of it, dear Eustace.' Alice smiled and patted his hand. She wore her simple clothes: a commoner's rough woollen dress and linen coif, suitable for a day's work around the household, yet she retained a golden crucifix necklace and her fine emerald ring, which made her simple wedding band look stingy.

'I have a job for you two.' Robert bit into a husk of bread. He sprayed crumbs as he spoke and waved his stubby finger at the other two men. 'I want you to go into Plympton in the morn. The spinners have produced enough thread that along with what's in storage at Plympton should be sufficient to send up to Exeter.'

'But I only just got here,' Eustace whined, dropping his spoon into his pottage bowl.

'So? Thou did not come at my behest. You're supposed to be managing the shipping of the goods. Anyway, we need more wine and salted meat. That's why I'm sending Guy. He can come back with it.'

'You're just trying to be rid of me aren't you, Brother?' Eustace adopted a sulky expression.

'Yes, I bloody am. And if he tries to follow you back, Guy: break his bloody leg.'

The men chuckled. Robert and Guy knocked their cups together, creating a small spillage on the table.

'I thought you might want me to stay to look into the document the sheriff had you sign,' Eustace said.

'Nah.' Robert waved his hand like he was swatting a fly. 'I'll not dwell on that foul business any longer. To hell with them.'

'I thought you wanted me to teach you reading.'

'I just said to hell with them, didn't I?'

'Peace, husband.' Alice kissed Robert's shoulder and rubbed his forearm.

'I'll hear no more about it,' Robert said, dabbing the last of his bread into the remnants of his pottage and stuffing it into his mouth.

'We'll leave at dawn. After the church bell rings lauds,' Guy said. 'I'll return afore nightfall the next eve.'

'Depart at dawn?' Eustace's voice raised in pitch. 'I should like to eat first.'

'You'll leave at lauds,' Robert growled. 'It will take all day to get there with the cart. Anyhow, who eats at dawn? Before day's work has yet begun?' He pushed aside his empty bowl and stood. 'Guy, you can sleep upon straw at the far gable end or in the solar once you've collected up the wool and readied the cart. Eustace, if you wish to sleep here, you may, otherwise back to your own lodging at Plympton. You may finish your cups and whatever's left in the jug first.'

'As your guest, am I not sharing your bed?' Eustace said, his tone incredulous.

'Not tonight. The wife and I have business.'

'Oh, Robert,' Alice squeezed his arm. 'I've a sore mind from all this talk and I'm exhausted from all the excitement of late. Let Eustace share the bed. I'm sure he is tired. He's a soft man, not strong like you.'

'If he wanted a comfortable bed of feathers, he should've stayed in Plympton!'

'It's alright. I'll struggle with the earthworms on the straw,' Eustace said, sighing into his cup.

'Robert, please. He's your brother, and it's ill manners not to share our bed with a guest.'

Robert shook his head in surrender, knowing that his wife's begging eyes always defeated him and that the more he resisted the worse he would feel. He wondered fleetingly if she practiced the expression in a looking glass.

'I'm going abed,' Robert muttered.

'I'll come after I've drained these last drops,' Eustace beamed, holding aloft his cup.

'A pox on you, Brother,' Robert muttered.

V

Robert washed his face and hands in a bowl of cloudy water that Alice had left at the bedside. He'd slept fitfully, with three crammed in the bed, yet somehow slumbered on later than his wife and brother. It irked him that he'd risen last and made him feel lazy, more so because he often chastised Eustace for sleeping beyond dawn.

The bedroom was situated in the loft space above the larder on the East-gable end. The rafters met just above head height at the centre of the room - the only place in the bedchamber where it was possible to stand fully upright. Floorboards creaked as Robert moved to the small interior window which overlooked the firepit. He opened the shutter and found that nobody was below.

'Alice!'

Iron clanked against iron at the opposite end of the house. Alice emerged from the solar. She looked up at her husband while wiping her hands in a square of cloth.

'Alice. Has that rakefire brother of mine departed?'

'Eustace?'

'How many brothers have I, woman?'

Alice tutted. 'He departed with Guy, not long after sunrise.'

'Good riddance. We'll finish a jug of good wine tonight in celebration.'

Alice put her hands on her hips, frowning up at her husband. 'Robert Wood! Did you send those two men into Plympton just to be rid of your brother?'

'I wish for the day when we have our own son, so you can stop mothering my feckless brother! I know his hands and face bare the likeness of a baby's - surely the effect of never having done a hard day's toil in his life.'

Alice opened her mouth to speak but Robert pulled the shutter closed. He pulled on his hose, shirt and shoes and fastened his belt with the pouch and knife attached. He jogged down the stairs, through the larder and into the central chamber. He was about to walk into the solar when Alice's alarmed cry stunned him into pausing. He ran, pushing the privacy screen aside which clattered to the floor.

'Alice? Whatever is it?'

Alice startled and spun around. She was holding separate halves of a loaf in each hand. She held them out for his inspection. The bread was light enough that the grain appeared of good quality, but the centre of each half was pure white.

Robert dug his fingers into one half of the bread, pulling out a palm-sized lump of chalk. He looked his wife in the eye. 'From whom did we buy this?'

'Muriel sold it to us. Her husband bought several loaves from a baker in Meavy.' Alice sighed and threw both halves of bread into the fireplace. 'Oh, Muriel will be aghast that they have spent such coin on despoiled fare.'

'Bah.' Robert sniffed. 'Never buy bread from afar. The baker knows it's too far to return to make him acquit. I'll appeal him at the next hundred court.'

Alice looked about to say something but instead chewed her lip. Robert felt his face redden when he realised the implication of what he'd said: if he reported anything at the hundred court he'd have to deal with William Spiney and Sir John. By alienating them he'd made it difficult for his family and business to resolve any legal dispute.

'Forget it,' Robert sniffed, waving a dismissive hand toward the discarded loaf. 'It's just a penny loaf. If he's weighted it for us, he's done it to others. He'll get dealt his due one way or another. I'll have Guy pick up a couple good loaves for Muriel when he returns so she doesn't feel bad about her bread.'

Alice gave a weak smile and kissed the tip of Robert's round nose. 'Husband, you can be sweet of heart. Sometimes. Oh, you knocked over the screen. Do right it, please.'

Robert went to hold his wife's waist, expecting another kiss, but she was already turning away. He shrugged and walked to the screen and uprighted it, shuffling it back into the correct position.

'You know, Wife, I recall back in Britany when someone called me a sweetheart...' he chuckled to himself, lost in the memory for some moments, before remembering that he was recounting a tale. 'Ah, yes. Well… we had caught this lad stealing from the baggage and I…'

'I've heard this many a time, Husband. I dislike violent tales.' She swept the floor with a broom that had twigs for bristles.

'But it's humorous!' Robert laughed.

'Not for the boy, I think.'

'Well… At least he only lost a wager and a few fingers instead of getting get hanged. That's a happy ending, isn't it?' He slapped Alice's rump, ignored her tut and glare, and walked outside still chuckling to himself.

The sun hung low and bright in the morning sky. Robert closed his eyes and stretched his arms. There was no breeze. Birds chirped among the trees. The sun's blossoming glow was warm on his skin. He proceeded to perform his morning exercises, stretching his muscles and bending each joint. Untying the knots of an uncomfortable slumber.

Robert cocked his head, hearing a strange sound. At first, he dismissed it as a distant pipe or flute, then realised it was vocal. He looked North to Sampford Spiney, shielding his eyes from the sun. He could see the church; the conical columns on each corner of the tower pointed up toward the heavens, perhaps to better direct prayers to the Almighty. Most of the estate was hidden from view by clusters of foliage and the gradient of the land, leaving only thatched rooftops visible. Then he heard the sound again: It was almost like a long whistle, or a ringing bell, frozen and elongated at the moment of chime.

Eeeeeuuuuuw!

The noise continued, ceasing only long enough for the maker to catch their breath. Robert turned at the sound of footfalls behind him: it was John the shearer. He approached Robert with a confused expression.

'Do you hear that?' John said.

'Aye.'

'Is someone raising the hue and cry?'

'Aye. Sounds like it.' Robert turned back to the source of the noise. The sound was clearer now. The dirge had been joined by other voices.

'That's the cry for murder, isn't it?' John said.

VI

'We are beholden to see what it be about,' John the Sherman said. His jaw jutted forward in determination and shears held poised.

'Nah,' Robert snorted. 'It's up at the Spiney estate. No affair of ours.'

John's face twisted in confusion. 'But... master, isn't we obliged under law to go to the sound of the hue and cry as witnesses?'

'You desire to rush off seeking excitement? Chase down some bloody pickpocket and murder him instead of doing what you should be doing.'

John pursed his lips and frowned hard in thought. 'What should I be doing?'

'Bloody working, beshrew ye! It's shears your holding, not a bloody bardiche.'

John looked at the tool in his hand and then in the direction of the sound of the alarm. 'But we're bound by law, Master. And it ain't any pickpocket, Sir, it's the cry for murder, not for thievery.'

The door behind Robert creaked open. Alice stood in the doorway; she startled upon seeing the two men standing there.

'I thought I heard an awful sound,' Alice said, touching the small crucifix necklace that rested on her chest.

Robert opened his mouth to speak but John beat him to it.

'It be the hue 'n cry - for murder!'

'Oh!' Alice's eyes widened in alarm. She put her fingertips over her lips as if to stifle further panicked sounds.

'Master Robert says we shouldn't go to the cry. It's the cry for murder, it is!'

Robert glared at John, who shrank back a step.

'Maybe you should go, Husband. There might be trouble if you don't.'

Robert sighed, flicking another dark look at John, he nodded his assent. 'Alright. Stay here, Alice. And put the bolt across the door.'

Robert brushed past his wife and walked through the house to the larder. He put his foot on the first step to the bedchamber when he remembered that his sword was beside the fireplace. He spun around and strode to the solar. His shoulder clipped the wooden privacy screen making it wobble. Robert found his sheathed sword leaning against the wall beside the glaive. He snatched up the sword and slid it through the frog loop on his belt and put a hand on the glaive. His fingers tightened around the ash shaft momentarily before releasing it: such a weapon was overkill for a manhunt and would prove cumbersome if there was a chase.

Alice waited by the door in the solar. Robert kissed her quickly on the lips and went outside. Alice closed the door after him.

Robert waited until he heard the latch pushed into place, then turned to John. 'Rush on if ye wish. I shall ready a horse to ride. You'll be left choking in my dust if ye wait on me.'

John nodded, and without hesitation he launched into a sprint up the trail toward Sampford Spiney; arms pumping fast as he went and the points of the iron shears brushing just past his cheek with each movement of his right arm.

Robert shook his head and decided against calling a warning about running in such a way with a sharp implement - attracting the fool's attention was as like to cause an accident as to let him continue as he was.

There were two horses remaining in the stable following the departure of Eustace and Guy. Robert's favourite, a black and white mottled palfrey, turned her long head toward her owner and stamped a foot in anticipation of being let out. Robert found an old blanket hanging over the stable fence and threw it over the palfrey's back and tied a saddle over it. The horse bucked her head and snorted in eagerness of the coming exercise. Robert patted her neck as he slipped a bridle over her nose and made calming, hushing noises.

'Wait til ye get outside afore you start getting excited.' Robert led the horse out of the stable and shut the fence gate, then put his foot in the stirrup and hoisted himself into the saddle, with an involuntary groan at the effort of throwing his leg over the horse's back.

Robert kicked his heels into the palfrey's flanks and urged the beast on. The horse needed no such encouragement and erupted into a gallop, kicking up dry clouds of summer dirt along the track. Despite John's head start of a few minutes, Robert soon reached him, bouncing in the saddle as he overtook the footman. Robert grinned and cried out encouragement to his horse to go faster.

The outlaying fields of Sampford Spiney were empty. The hue and cry had ceased. Robert slowed the palfrey to a trot as he neared the manor. A group of labourers clustered around the manor gate and along the wall. A couple of villeins at the back of the group turned to see who approached, then returned to peeking over the shoulders of those in front.

'Stand back ye all. Keep well back now!' someone called out from inside the Spiney grounds.

Robert halted his horse near the stone cross opposite the manor. He pondered whether to head back: he had no wish to become entangled in Spiney's affairs. Robert was about to turn his mount about, then paused, considering that a murder on the Spiney estate might bode ill for William becoming bailiff. The musing jolted him: if Spiney or his son had committed a murder, Robert might get the bailiff position after all. How much gold would Spiney have to lay across the sheriff's palm to escape royal justice for such a crime? Robert couldn't turn back without finding what had happened.

Robert nudged his mount into a walk toward the gate. He could see that the doorway to the manor was open, but the villeins weren't paying attention to the manor. There was a gathering of servants around the stable. Mathilde was among them, although her face was hidden by the gilded bonnet she wore. Robert recognised the pastor talking with Spiney's grey-haired steward. Robert sat back in his saddle, deciding to observe quietly.

Mathilde ran back toward the manor house, sobbing loudly, with her hands clutching her cheeks. Her youngest son, a boy of twelve years, chased after her. Mathilde tripped on her dress, tumbling onto the grass.

Robert involuntarily barked two notes of a guttural laugh before he could stifle the sound. He rubbed his mouth to try to hide his mirth.

'Mother!' the young Spiney boy cried as he skidded to his knees at his mother's side.

Mathilde knelt with her forehead pressed to the grass and her arms covering her head as if from an assailant. The discarded bonnet lay forgotten beside her. The boy cradled Mathilde as she wailed. The eldest son rushed to join them, wrapping his arms around both sibling and mother.

Robert was looking forward to telling his wife about the spectacle Mathilde had made of herself. Alice would enjoy it, he thought.

The priest hurried toward the prone mother, he glanced in Robert's direction, then after another step his head snapped back toward Robert. His eyes widened and jaw dropped. He clasped his crucifix and pointed a trembling finger at Robert. 'There he is! Murderer! Murderer!'

Robert turned in the saddle to see if they might be pointing at someone beyond him. John was huffing his way nearer, with shears not quite so enthusiastically pumped as before; the priest clearly wasn't pointing at the sherman. Robert turned back to the priest. The accusing finger was still quivering in his direction. The heads of all the villeins were turned his way with expressions ranging from confusion to anger.

The small crowd fanned out from the estate entrance and formed a wide semi-circle around Robert. The villeins mumbled among themselves. A half dozen men among them hefted farming implements as makeshift weapons. The men looked at each other, unsure how to proceed. The law required them to apprehend the accused, but none were willing to make the first move against a mounted and armed opponent who so often boasted about his killings in France.

'What?' Robert spat, looking from one face to another. 'What madness is this? What are you talking about, Pastor?'

The elder Spiney boy left his mother's side, ran through the gateway, pushing past his field workers to stand at the head of them. The stablehand and one of the house servants raced from the stable to join their young master.

'Dare you feign ignorance?' The young man shouted, raising his fist. 'Get down from your horse and face justice! You damnable swine!' The boy's eyes were puffed red and his cheeks flushed.

Robert looked around for William Spiney: he had no intention of answering to his snotling son. 'Pastor, what is the cause of this raucous fare? Where is the elder Spiney?'

'You've slain him!' the eldest son screeched.

Robert's horse startled. Robert jerked the rein to keep the beast steady. 'Murdered? Nay, he's not dead. There be a mistake. Let me see!'

Robert swung down from his saddle and handed the horse bridle to John, glaring at the shearer when he was too slow to accept the rein. Robert walked toward the manor gate, intending to push past the eldest Spiney son, when the boy shoved Robert's shoulder.

'You shan't go near him! You're to be held as a cowardly murderer until the coroner can be called. And then I'll have your head!'

Some of his fieldworkers murmured their agreement and closed ranks behind their young master. Robert faced a wall of a dozen villeins and servants - half of them armed.

Robert held his sword sheath with his left hand. The forefinger and thumb of his right hand toyed with his brass belt buckle a few inches away from his sword grip. He looked each of the men before him in the eye, one after the other. All but a stablehand looked away as his gaze met on theirs. Robert locked eyes with the stablehand until the lad blinked and then turned his attention to the Spiney youth.

The younger Spiney blinked right away. He gulped and licked his lips, shifting his weight from one foot to the other. 'Bring me a sword!' he cried out in a hoarse voice.

Robert slowly shook his head and let his fingers dance on the sword hilt. 'I'd cut through ye like a scythe through wheat and take two more of your men in the same stroke by which I draw my blade.'

Young William Spiney's gaze dropped to the weapon. He clenched and unclenched his fists and glanced around at the nervous faces behind him. 'You heard him: he intends to do us all to death! He's lost his mind!'

A few of the men backed up a step or two, whispering to each other, one made the sign of the cross. The pastor pushed through the crowd and held aloft his crucifix, while his other hand rubbed the beads of his rosary, as if for luck or protection.

'The devil has taken his mind! God shall protect us against him! Have faith and bring the foul murder before God's good justice.' The priest snarled, stabbed his accusing finger at Robert, his chin raised indignantly.

Robert's fingers closed around the sword hilt. He drew the blade an inch or two.

The villeins tensed. A pair of the braver ones gripped their farming implements in defensive postures. A couple of the lesser brave manoeuvred behind their more valiant comrades.

Robert glanced behind and startled to find the sherman pointing his shears toward Robert with one hand while holding the reins with another.

'What in hells are you doing, you simple bastard?' Robert hissed.

'Best you let drop your sword, Master, n' face justice.'

Robert looked back at his would-be opponents: a pompous youth barely old enough to grow whiskers, a skinny servant, a filthy stable hand, and a handful of muck covered labourers. If he was to fight them it would be akin to murder.

'I didn't do it. I've been abed all night until just after dawn. I arrived here just now upon hearing the cry. I didn't kill William Spiney.'

'Yes, you did!' Cried Mathilde.

Villeins stepped aside to let her pass between them. Her tear-streaked face was blotchy and her nose ran freely.

'You slew my poor husband because he was to become bailiff. You swore your revenge and now you have it! I saw you flee right before they found my poor husband's body.'

There were tuts and mutterings among the assembled folk. All eyes regarded Robert with suspicion and disgust.

'Nay, wasn't I,' Robert said, his voice trailing off to a whisper. He knew they would never believe he didn't kill William Spiney - in their place he wouldn't believe it either. He closed his eyes. He would either have to surrender or slay one or two to enable his escape: he'd be outlawed, it would be legal for any man to kill him, and every man who lived within half a day's ride knew Robert by sight.

He unbuckled his belt and tossed the sword to the ground along with the attached dagger, belt, and knife.

The assembled villeins rushed him as the Spiney youth swept up the sword. Robert's arms were grabbed, and a dull hoe blade held against his throat.

The Spiney boy flung the sheath off the sword. He levelled the point an inch from Robert's neck. The weapon trembled in the youth's grip until he rested the flat of the blade on Robert's shoulder

'I would slay you here at the site of your foul crime... but it is more proper that I have you taken to Lydford to face justice.'

'The Lord's good justice!' chanted the priest.

The Spiney boy sneered. His breathing came hard and ragged. 'I'll see you hang, Wood.'

VII

Rope bound Robert's hands. Rough twine rubbed hot against his wrists. The binding was tight enough that it was too difficult to manipulate sufficiently to relive the growing friction burn on his skin. Attempts at wriggling the rope off raw areas only succeeded in spreading the pain.

Robert trudged behind Spiney's son's grey mare. The youth held the end of the rope to Robert's bindings and spent more time sneering around at his prisoner than he did paying attention to his horse, or the route. He had Robert's sword belt fastened about his own waist. He kept the sword drawn, and occasionally swept it as if to strike imaginary opponents.

Five others rode mounts: the stablehand; the steward rode Robert's palfrey; a tall, grim-faced, and wild-bearded farmer named Rowan the Large rode a fat draft horse; and two labourers rode donkeys. Two more farmhands and John the Sherman accompanied them on foot. John kept his mouth set in a determined pout and his eyebrows firmly knotted together. He shook the shears at Robert whenever the two locked eyes.

Robert's arms were violently yanked forward, unable to put his hands out to stop himself, he stumbled and fell, and was dragged over the long grass and over the lumpy terrain with the rope pulling urgently on his arms - stretching them from their sockets and sending a searing pain from the ligaments under his armpits down to his ribs. He was pulled for a dozen yards, his legs scrambling to regain purchase, before he managed to get to his feet and stumble after the horse.

The Spiney youth laughed at the cloudless sky, his shoulders shaking with his cruel mirth. One or two of his companions chuckled along with him. The steward shook his head in apparent displeasure at the treatment of the prisoner. The Sherman continued to scowl at his former master.

Robert tried to recall the Spiney brat's name. He remembered well enough the firstborn son, William, who died in infancy. There had been four children in all, of which only two survived.

Robert had been present at the christening for each, but had little to do with any of them since. What age was the eldest now, he wondered: twenty years, perhaps? It was only when he heard the steward mutter: 'Yes, Master Henry' in response to a command that the name was realised.

Henry fed the rope back through his fingers, giving Robert a couple more feet of slack; not out of concern for the comfort of his prisoner, Robert knew, but so he could for a fifth time that morning, eventually yank the rope again and drag Robert again.

Lydford was ten miles from Sampford Spiney. Robert considered that they'd already travelled halfway. It was not a strenuous distance, even by foot, under normal circumstances but the inability to control the pace, route, or have use of his arms led to a hastening of exhaustion. He'd not been offered either water or ale; he regretted not taking a drink when he awoke in the morning but was damned if he'd ask his captors to spare him any mercy. Robert reflected that when this was all over, and his innocence proven, he'd have little enough mercy on those responsible for humiliating him.

John caught Robert's narrowed eyes glaring at him and stabbed the shears toward Robert. The motion failed to produce any reaction, so he shoved Robert's shoulder, making Robert stumble a step. The glare continued. John stared back with his face twisted between fear and indignation.

Robert kept his silence. Content to bide his time. He'd hold no grudge against the servants of the Spiney household - they were doing what their master commanded and no more. Henry, John the Sherman, and the bearded bully on the draft horse were a different matter. He couldn't understand John's motivations: did he expect that the Spiney family would reward him for turning on his own master? Perhaps he was deluded that he might receive some elevated position on the Spiney estate or be rewarded for his duty to the law. He'd be back to shearing sheep on the morrow, and if Robert was back in his estate by that time, John would find himself quickly evicted and with little prospect of finding work, he'd likely come known as John the beggar.

Rowan the Large had a local reputation as a born bully. Robert had no prior dealings with him, but the big oaf's bullish behaviour had often been a source of complaint among the residents of Sampford Spiney and Woodtown. The large farmhand enjoyed shoving Robert and boasting of how he'd whistle a tune as Robert's legs danced when dangling from the rope.

Robert turned his thoughts to young Henry. He reflected that he couldn't slay the little snot: he'd be dragged back to Lydford to be justifiably strung up. Other options such as arson or sabotage of crops seemed somehow beneath him, but he checked them off in his mind anyway. He might have forgiven the upstart for the ignominious treatment if it wasn't that he'd seemed to enjoy it so thoroughly.

The company had been drinking plentifully from their flasks and waterskins. Some even showered water over their face and neck to relieve the heat. Some taunted Robert after taking a long draught, with water or ale trickling down the sides of their mouth they would pour some of their drink onto the ground in front of him. Rowan the Large even spat a mouthful of water at him. By the time they reached the River Tavy, most had exhausted their supply and began to complain about parched throats and the baking afternoon sun.

'Who has water?' Rowan demanded. 'Or ale?'

The men shrugged and waved their own empty water containers or shook their heads. The couple with remaining beverages were conspicuous in their silence. A labourer on foot put his waterskin inside his shirt, cradling it with both hands.

'Give it over!' Rowan shouted, leaning down from the draft horse and holding out an expectant hand.

'I shan't! 'Tis mine. You shouldn't have wasted yours teasing him.'

The big farmer pulled sharply on his reins, turning his horse abruptly and knocking into the footman. The labourer sprawled back on the ground, holding up a defensive hand toward his assailant while still gripping the valuable waterskin under his shirt.

'Stop this madness!' the Spiney whelp shrieked. He held aloft the sword, tip skyward, as if it were some talisman of command.

Rowan muttered and brought his horse back into formation. He kept his eyes down under the gaze of his master.

'We'll be at Lydford in a few hours. Then you'll all take food and drink. Well... maybe not all of you.' Spiney smiled at his prisoner.

Robert locked eyes with Henry but kept his face expressionless. The two looked at each other for a few moments before Henry turned his horse away and yanked on the rope, moving the company off again.

The group proceeded in sullen quiet. Each man suffered silently or with muttered complaints as they sweated, ached, and thirsted. Even those mounted, mostly unused to riding, were fidgeting uncomfortable in their saddles.

Robert endured in silence, reflecting that the short journey was nothing compared to the exhaustive journeying he'd endured day after day under the Duke of Gloucester. Robert had been a boy of eighteen years when he marched in the Duke's grand chevauchee of France, and when his boots wore out had to walk barefoot for a week.

There was no man-made trail directly linking Sampford Spiney to Lydford. Those who made the trip knew the route well enough, navigating by local landmarks such as the ever-present sight of Brentor Church atop its steep peak, the woodlands, river crossings, and the stone crosses which dotted the landscape to mark traveller routes and monk paths. Those who didn't know the route to Lydford well might have preferred to travel west to Tavistock and then follow the road which led directly to Lydford. Henry Spiney had attempted the former, but clearly did not know the way.

Henry seemed to have used Brentor to navigate by, but in doing so had fixated on it and was in danger of circumnavigating it. Robert knew that if they had followed the landmarks properly, he would be able to see the farms surrounding a hamlet a mile to the East, but they remained hidden behind the desolate sun-bleached hills of the moors.

Henry held up his hand for the group to halt. He turned this way and that in the saddle, then stood up in his stirrups and cupped his hands over his eyes as he peered at Brentor. 'It can't be much further!'

The moorland wind whistled over the hills, ruffling clothing, and gently waving through hair. Even during summer the high points were frequented by chill winds. From the vantage point of the heights it was possible to see south as far as Plymouth and St. Michael's island. The distant sea blended into the sky making it difficult to discern the horizon. Hills of gradually fading shades of green and brown dominated the other compass points along with scattered areas of woodland and rock-strewn peaks. Birdsong was a constant companion, even above the wind. A kestrel hovered over a deep gorge between two steep hills, flapping occasionally to steady itself against gusts as it searched below for food.

The group started off again. Travelling north-west on a heading which would take them just north of Brentor. Robert knew if they kept on in that direction, they would pass south-west of Lydford. They'd be certain to stumble along the road at some point, but they only had to continue directly north to go straight into Lydford. Robert said nothing: it wasn't for him to direct his captors, and he preferred to let them see how inept their leader was. Robert was curious how their morale would hold out if they became lost less than ten miles from their homes.

Henry Spiney forgot about tormenting his prisoner as it became increasingly clear to the motley companions that they were not travelling in a predetermined direction. Henry headed for every vantage point, leading them up bracken covered hills where the group would then stop for a time while Henry surveyed the landscape before setting off again. Robert wasn't sure if the boy was too proud to ask his underlings for the way, or if none of them knew the route to Lydford. Robert supposed it was likely that most of the group had spent most of their adult lives on or near to Sampford Spiney with the occasional trip into Tavistock or the surrounding villages for market days and celebrations such as May Day.

The sun began to sink low in the sky; they'd been out skirting the edges of Dartmoor Royal Forrest almost the whole day for what should've been a six-hour journey at a gentle pace. With no food, and the labourer guarding his last mouthfuls of water, the group glared, cursed, and complained among themselves - not daring to cast any blame at their young leader. For his part, the steward kept his silence except to offer whispered counsel to his master for which he received irritated, snapped responses.

'There's nothing for it!' Henry said, addressing the entourage, his face flushed. 'We shall have to stop. You men on foot are too slow and have delayed our journey too much. Perhaps on the morrow we shall split up. We'll have to rest on the moor and continue at first light.'

Robert looked down so that Henry wouldn't see his smirk. The men muttered complaints among themselves.

'You and you,' Henry pointed at two of the villeins. 'Go and collect wood for a fire. We'll take our rest sheltering among the granite atop the hill yonder. Tie the murder to the dead tree at the crest of the hill where we can keep a watch on him.'

The men set about their tasks. Henry dropped the rope into the hands of one of the farmers who led Robert toward the appointed tree. The stablehand followed on his mount, a hoe nooked under his arm like a lance pointed at Robert's back.

The tree was not much taller than a man. Its dark, dry surface was crumbling. Robert sat as directed with his back to the tree. The ground was hard, earthy, and bare save a few flakes of bark. The farmer looped the rope around Robert a couple times before tying it off. The binding was tight enough that Robert could only just exhale fully. He reasoned that the tree was decrepit and decayed enough that, if he was so inclined, he might be able to break free, although not without creating enough noise through the creaking and snapping of dead wood to alert his captors. Regardless, he had little intention of escape; there was no proof of his guilt and his brother and wife would account of his presence in his bed chamber all night- just as soon as they could get to Lydford and testify for him. There would of course be a matter of payment to the gaoler and the sheriff.

The mounts were all tied off against the same tree which Robert was secured to. One of the donkeys nuzzled Roberts ear, which made the stablehand laugh. The group set two fires as the sun was hovering over the western horizon: one a few metres from Robert, and another a little distance away for Henry and his steward.

The air quickly grew colder, as it often would on the highlands of the moors when the sum no longer warmed the earth. Only Henry had a riding cloak with him. Those who had travelled mounted wrapped their saddle blankets around their shoulders. The footmen who wore only shirts and woollen trousers grumbled at their comrades and tried to bargain for a sharing of the blanket.

'Givee water.' Rowan held his hand out to the labourer who was skulking behind a granite boulder.

'I shan't.'

'Givee or it'll be a whipping for ye.'

The labourer let out a cry of alarm as the big farmer lurched over the boulder with surprising speed and tried to prise the waterskin from the labourer's cradling embrace.

Henry looked over from the fireside where he warmed his hands. He said nothing as the two men tussled over the near empty vessel.

One of the other men rushed to join in. They pulled on the skin, elbowing, hitting, and cursing each other until finally the big farmer pulled the prize free of the melee. He held one combatant by the neck at arm's length, while the skins' original owner sat on the grass nursing a bloodied nose. The big farmer watched the man in his grip flail and choke. He forced the man to his knees then released the panting villein.

Rowan wasted no time in unstopping the skin and emptying the last few gulps into his gullet. He gasped and wiped his mouth with the back of his hand and threw the empty vessel at the injured labourer.

'Now there's nothing to drink or eat,' the labourer sulked.

Heads turned to Henry. He pulled his cloak tighter over his shoulders and frowned at his followers. Unperturbed, their collective attention remained on their master. Henry looked at his steward who shook his head.

'I could try for a rabbit,' said the bloodied labourer.

'As you wish,' sniffed Rowan, 'we be on royal land, so you'll be the one to pay for it.'

'Is not part of the Royal Forrest. That be east of here,' the labourer said, 'even if it were royal land, who's gonna accuse me if we all eatin' it?'

'Stop!' Henry stood, dropping the cloak from his shoulders. 'There's not enough meat on a rabbit for all of us. You'd need to catch three at least, and we've not an hour left of sunlight.'

The men looked at their master in silence, waiting for his solution.

Henry looked to his prisoner, the hint of a smile playing on his lips. He carried Robert's sword in his left hand- sliding the weapon from the leather scabbard and inspecting the blade as if for first time, before looking back to Robert. 'I've an idea,' Henry said, smiling at the assembled men. He let the moment hang, watching the interest, confusion and wonderment playing on the faces of his minions.

John the Sherman cleared his throat. 'Pray, you... you mean to say... we gonna eat him?' He looked between Henry and Robert; eyes wide and his lips pulled back over his gums. He shivered at the notion of feasting on human flesh.

One of the farmers gasped. Another whispered to his neighbour.

'No, you simple...' Henry tutted, shook his head, and marched to the tree.

Robert kept looking ahead into the flames of the small fire. The Spiney brat hadn't brought him all this way just to slay him for the sake of a missed meal.

Henry fussed with something around the tree stump. The gathered equines stamped and snorted at the interruption to their peace. A donkey kicked Robert's leg as it attempted to manoeuvre out of Henry's way.

Eventually, Henry moved away from the tree, leading Robert's palfrey by its bridle. He walked the horse around the gathered men until it was between the two fireplaces. He passed the reins to a labourer and stood back from the horse.

Robert tensed. His hands twitched but the numb fingers failed to clench; the sudden motion only created a tingling in his digits and amplified the soreness of his wrists.

Henry held the sword in front of his face in mock salute at Robert. He then turned to face the palfrey and brought his sword arm back ready to strike.

'I give you, horsemeat!' Henry cried as his blade arced down.

VIII

The sword sliced clean through the palfrey's throat, flicking blood for several feet. The horse collapsed onto its side almost instantly and lay with legs twitching. The beast lifted its head, blood still gushing out of the deep wound, then flopped back down. Breath came wheezing through the crimson crevasse in its neck.

'Finish it.' Henry said.

Three men rushed in with knives. They did their work with wet ripping sounds accompanied by the sickly stench of blood.

Henry walked to Robert, stopping by his feet. He pointed the sword at his captive, placing the tip of the blade under Robert's chin and lifting it so that the prisoner had to look him in the eye.

Robert met the gaze without betraying any emotion. He kept his breathing even and suppressed the shudder which he tried to dismiss as an effect of the cold evening air.

Henry cocked his head to one side as he studied his captive. He shrugged, wiped one side of the wet blade on Robert's sleeve, then the other side on Robert's other arm.

'Don't you have anything to say about me slaying your horse, Wood?'

'You owe me a good palfrey.'

Henry titled his head back and laughed. He took a step back pointed the sword at Robert. 'And you owe me a father. I'll repay my debt when you repay yours, Wood.'

Robert shut his eyes and fidgeted as best he could to make himself comfortable. He made a show of preparing for sleep-hoping the malevolent troupe might lose interest in him if he were considered asleep.

Henry's footfalls retreated to the warmth of his campfire. The other men bickered over the butchering of the horse: which parts to cut, how to cut it, and accusations of it not being done correctly.

'Just take the rump and flank,' Henry snapped. 'We only need enough for tonight.'

Searing horseflesh soon intermingled with the scent of burning wood. The fires crackled. Then men still argued.

'Don't cook it too long! We're starvin' here!'

'Wanna eat raw meat? Make ya sick, ya fool.'

'I don't want it raw. I want it afore my belly crawls on back to Sampford without me.'

A couple of the men laughed.

'This meat smells good,' Rowan the Large called out in his unmistakable baritone. 'You should partake of it, Master Robert.'

'Ya never know…' sneered another man, 'might take to likin' it so much that ya butcher yer other horses.'

'Oh, I've laid eyes on the best piece of meat in his stable,' Rowan said, lowering his strident bass to a conspiratorial rumble still loud enough for Robert to hear. 'That wife of his, Alice. Oh… I'd sink my teeth into her rump alright.'

Men snickered.

'Mayhap I'll pay her a visit after we witness Master Robert's hanging. Could be I'll wear his boots n' shirt. Come during the night so she thinks I'm husband returneth. She'll be waiting there… waiting for he. She'll not know any different until I'm astride her n' she finds out why they call me Rowan the Large.'

Several of the men roared with laughter – some even stomping their feet in excitement.

Robert opened his eyes. Rowan the Large, stared back at him, grinning. Robert only now noticed the man was missing one of his front teeth. *He'll be missing more than that when I'm free of these bonds*, Robert mused.

'Oh, looky yonder! Master Robert be awoken!' Rowan sneered. He knelt by the fire, toasting a chunk of horsemeat on a stick, turning it just above the flame. 'Oh, forgive my rudeness. Do you wish some?' Rowan pointed the dripping horsemeat in Robert's direction.

Robert closed his eyes again. It served no purpose to impotently vent frustrations on these men - not while he was bound anyway.

'Ah, he's not hungry!' a labourer cackled.

'He awoke at the thought o' me ravishing his wife. Master Robert fancies the idea of being shown how to treat her proper.'

'Be the only way his wife'd beget a child,' said one of the labourers. 'One of 'em be barren. That be the talk I hear anyways.'

'Oh! Forsooth, he's not a full man!' Rowan boomed. 'He be a man who acts so high n' proud like he's a lord just cos he owns a couple of furlongs n' mud huts. All play and bluster for being half a man.'

'Oh, and have you heard him going on about when he was in Breton!' John the Sherman whooped. 'Ay, ay, ay! A hundred times I heard talk of how he unhorsed some Frenchie. Bet he never was even there.'

The men forgot their bickering and enjoyed the tormenting of their stoic prisoner. Even Robert's lack of response did little to dull their mirth. Robert kept up the pretence of not hearing their words. He had little consideration for those jealous villeins who clung to the lower rungs of society's ladder and who despised their brethren who, like Robert, had managed to raise themselves out of the muck and above the seasonal worries that survival or starvation might rest on a harvest. Robert often witnessed such envy in the countenance, glances, and muttered words of men. He always considered such types as the lowest among villeins; incapable of improvement, and hateful of those who dared to enjoy a small taste of the luxuries of landowning class. The downfall of such a person could be a sweet taste to those who could never hope to sniff even the leftovers of a lord's table.

Eventually, the joints of horsemeat were ready for eating and the men took to gorging themselves. They sucked on their meats, chewing, grunting, and spitting noisily.

Robert's dry mouth began to water at the smell of the cooked meat. He swallowed and closed his eyes again. The night air covered his skin in a layer of chilled perspiration. His captors had placed the fire just far enough away from him that he could only feel an occasional flicker of warmth when the wind fanned the flames his way.

'Shall we feed the prisoner?' someone asked through a mouthful of food.

'Hmmm? Oh, well we should, shouldn't we?' Henry said, sounding disinterested, 'since he's tied up like a dog you may as well throw him such scraps as are deserving of such a beast.'

The sound of lips smacking together as the men ate irritated Robert. The wet chewing seemed to continue with a determined consistency that Robert found it difficult to distract from until he felt a moist slap in his lap as a lump of gristle was thrown onto him. Further lumps of stringy remains were tossed in his direction as the others ate their fill. Robert ignored them all. He was certain that his captors didn't believe he was truly asleep, but to feign unconsciousness seemed the best method when tied to a tree by vagabonds.

A wolf howled; it's lonely cry echoing through the hills, carried by the wind.

'He's smelling the horseflesh,' someone said.

'We shoulda slain the horse further from camp,' another said, 'if they come sniffing it'll scare the horses.'

'Keep the fires burning,' Henry snapped, 'gather more wood if you have to. One of you watch over the mounts and the prisoner. When the moon reaches its zenith, the guard wakes another to carry on the watch. And for God's sake, don't let the fires go out.'

Robert allowed himself a little smile as he heard the men groaning and footsteps going off into the darkness in search of twigs and branches for the fire. The men were cold, thirsty, tired, lost, and probably a little afraid. Perhaps he would sleep easily after all.

***

Robert woke with a flinch. Something had struck his leg. He blinked and tried to remember where he was as his eyes adjusted to daylight.

Rowan glared down at him and kicked him again before walking away.

The sickly stink of raw flesh assaulted Robert as his senses awoke. Flies covered the horse carcass. Two of the palfrey's legs were reduced to reddened stumps. Two of the labourers carried a severed limb each - likely to take home for their wives to cook.

The fires had reduced to smouldering, blackened stains. A golden sun was just emerging over the horizon, its blinding tendrils made slow work of warming the ground. Birds whistled and grasshoppers chirped in hopeful promise of an auspicious day.

A couple of the villeins still sleeping were kicked awake in the same fashion Robert had been. Henry's steward, a quiet man of confident stance, was saddling his horse. One of the men shivered and complained that he hadn't slept a wink.

Robert's clothes were damp from the early morning dew that made his shirt cling to his skin. He wiggled about as best he could so that a disgusting lump of chewed meat that lay in his lap dropped onto the dirt. The movement sent his back into complaints - resting rigid against a tree all night hadn't agreed with any of his limbs. His legs ached and the pain in his wrists quickly returned as soon as he moved his arms. Hair and beard both felt matted and smelt of woodfire; the taste of burnt wood also clung to his tongue. Two of the tacks on his boots had come loose leaving a parting between sole and boot around his right toe. His clothes were stained with grass, dirt, and horse blood. The knees of his hose were fraying from where he'd been dragged behind the horse. He was, however, consoled that all of Henry's men looked more miserable than he felt.

Nobody asked Henry how far it was to Lydford. Muttered remarks and dark looks at their leader gave clear evidence that everyone knew they were lost. Only Henry kept up the pretence of orientation; scanning the horizon and pretending to measure some sort of alignment between the sun and the nearest peak with his hands. Henry finished his act of navigation, sighed, and trudged over to his waiting horse.

'We ride north to Lydford.' Henry pointed in a direction that was a little east of true north.

Robert snorted. The little wretch had guessed luckily enough: if they continued that way, within an hour they'd stumble upon the road to Lydford and arrive at their destination a couple hours later.

Robert was untied from the tree. The end of the rope was given to John the Sherman who accepted the offered tether gingerly and accompanied with a reproachful frown at his ward. The grim party started out toward their destination, albeit at a slovenlier pace than the previous day.

'I need to pee,' Robert said. Despite having drank nothing, his bladder felt full.

John flicked a glare at him and yanked on the rope, but with too much slack between the two men, the action provided no result.

'Pee as you walk, Wood,' Rowan sniffed from atop his horse.

As much as Robert needed to urinate, he wasn't going to allow his undesirable companions the relief of laughing at him as he peed himself. If it came down to it, he'd be sure to relieve himself on one of his captors: Rowan the Large, if he had the chance.

The group stopped at the next hilltop. Robert took the opportunity to relieve his bladder, but with his wrists bound he struggled to refasten the front flap on his hose. At the next hill, the road to Lydford became visible. The company were unanimously relieved. Henry beamed triumphantly, seemingly self-deluded that his company were ignorant of the fact that he'd led them wildly astray.

'Down to the road!' Henry cried out, urging his horse into a canter.

Robert shook his head as he was bustled down the hillside. Rowan kicked him in the shoulder as he rode past, chasing after his master.

'Unhorse a Knight did ye?' Rowan laughed as he galloped on.

'Hurry up!' John snapped, pulling on the rope.

'Are ye afraid the road will vanish?' Robert growled, 'or that your new master will get ye lost again afore we get there?'

John tugged on the rope again and increased his pace. The men on foot broke formation, running after their master. One fell as he ran down the hill, tumbling head over heel, just missing landing in a bristling gorse bush. John and Robert were last to reach the road. The group reformed into a rough marching order. Henry looked irritated when he realised that his captive had been left to follow behind with just one guard - one of the prisoner's own men at that.

The road was little more than an earth track; wide enough to allow two carts to pass each other, and well-marked by cartwheels and hoof prints. The route was wooded along much of the path. The green fingers of oaks hanging over the road provided travellers with welcome shade.

'Hurry up Wood. You're not that old,' Rowan sneered.

'Older than you'll live to see,' Robert muttered as he walked past the big farmer's stationary horse.

'What say you?' Rowan snapped, nudging his horse into motion so that he rode alongside Robert.

Robert walked in silence, looking ahead, feeling the big brute's gaze on him.

'I asked: what did you say?' Rowan brought his left arm across his body; flattening his fingers ready to deliver a backhand slap.

Robert grabbed the farmer's boot with both his hands and pushed upward with all his strength, shoving the big man's leg over the saddle.

Rowan grasped at air as he tumbled off the saddle, slamming onto the dirt. He barely managed to bring an arm up to shield his face from impact at the last moment. The bully's right foot remained tied in the stirrup. His horse whinnied.

Robert yelled and slapped the horse's rump as best he could with his bound hands. The horse jolted, then ran down the path, brushing between Henry's horse and that of his steward. Rowan's head bumped against the leg of the steward's horse as he was dragged along. The steward's horse became skittish, but with a struggle the rider managed to keep his mount under control.

Dumbfounded, Henry watched the flailing farmer being dragged by. He turned in the saddle looking at Robert with an incredulous expression.

The steward calmed his mount sufficiently to give chase to the slower draft horse, quickly catching up, he reached out to grabbed the reins, bringing both beasts to a stop.

John Sherman watched the spectacle then turned toward Robert, his faced contorted. He launched himself at Robert, knocking him to the dirt, and pinning him down. A drop of his drool landed on Robert's eyelid. Others rushed to help tussle with the prisoner. Rough hands gripped him and pulled on his clothing.

'Seize him!' Henry cried, belatedly.

Robert was pulled to his feet. He heard the stitching of his shirt sleeve tear as he was dragged in differing directions by two men. Finally, they held him. Firm hands gripped his arms while John looped the rope around his waist a few times to increase his control over the prisoner.

'Trying to escape now that you're near to justice?' Henry said, walking his horse up to the captive until the horse's nose was a few inches from Robert's. The horse sniffed Robert's ear, and finding nothing interesting, turned its head aside.

The Steward helped Rowan to his feet, having untangled the flailing and cursing man from his predicament. Rowan's face was grazed and bloody from brow to jaw on the left side. His shirt was torn in at least two places and red streaks shown where his body had been pulled over jagged stones.

Rowan winced and gasped, holding a hand up to his injured face but afraid to touch it. The steward tried to get a good look at the facial injuries while Rowan held him away with his other hand.

'Get off me! He's ruined my face! I want his head!' Rowan pushed the steward aside and lurched toward Robert, baring his teeth, his fists poised for violence.

'Shut up!' Henry snapped. 'Your ugly face was already ruined.'

Rowan stopped immediately. He panted, spraying foamy spittle like a horse that had been run to exhaustion. His raw cheek was already oozing pus. He spat blood from his swollen lip and glared at Robert, visibly shaking with anger.

'You wouldn't believe I unhorsed a Knight. I merely showed you one manner of doing it. I'll show you another way some other time, friend.' Robert smiled. He'd promised himself he wouldn't provoke them, but decided that with an hour or so walk left, what could they do to him?

'Take his boots,' Henry ordered.

Two men kept hold of his arms while two others pulled off Robert's worn leather ankle boots. He didn't resist. One of the farmers measured them against his own feet and seeming to find them comparable he kept hold of the shoes.

The group started off again. Robert was shoved into motion by one of his guards. He'd only taken a few dozen steps when he stepped on the first sharp stone. Wincing, he limped a couple of steps and was pushed again for slowing the pace. The pattern repeated: every minute or so he'd step on a concealed, upward stabbing stone and when he flinched, limped, or hopped he was thrust forward by a sharp push from behind. Gradually, the tiny stone granules that stuck to his soles wore away skin and buried into flesh. The bloody wounds on his raw feet soon became smothered with dirt.

Rowan settled for glaring at his enemy from atop his horse - either too angry or too sorry for himself to even allow himself to take pleasure in Robert's obvious discomfort.

Robert was limping and lurching with almost every step by the time the outlaying huts and cottages of Lydford came into view. The proximity of the destination only served to make the last few hundred yards more difficult. He began to think that if he were dragged by one of the horsemen it would at least relieve his feet for this last distance, but his tormentors were satisfied for him to walk.

Lydford wasn't so much larger than Sampford Spiney. A village of one street, surrounded by trees and hills; one might pass within a half mile without noticing it. A stone keep at the centre dominated the village. Situated on a small mound, it stood fifty feet high and just as wide. If the walls had once been whitened with lime the elements had long since worn the coating away. The keep was cold grey; not even a banner topped the tower. One large window marked out the main chamber, the other few windows mere vertical slits.

A church stood beyond the keep. It was not dissimilar to the church at Sampford Spiney, if a little larger. Behind the church grassy ramparts marked out the remains of an earlier palisade. No more than two dozen homes lined the street. A strong smell of cow dung indicated the main local trade. Through thickets and trees were glimpses of pasture. From the far end of the street the sound of hammer against iron clanged in a constant rhyme.

The few people who were not tending to their animals or trades came out of their homes to watch the strange procession. They focused their attention on the prisoner, curiosity blatant in their expressions and whispers. A young boy brazenly ran alongside the steward's horse.

'What he do then, Sir? Is he a French marauder or somefink?'

The steward grunted a short laugh. 'Nay, not that. He's a murder and eater of little boys!'

The boy glanced at the shuffling prisoner, sniffed, and wiped his running nose in his sleeve.

'I be not afraid of he!' The boy ran over to Robert and kicked him in the shin before veering away, his legs carrying him as quickly as they could toward his hovel.

The group passed an empty pillory at the foot of the keep. Robert swallowed as he studied it, thinking he'd be lucky to only end up there. He'd been optimistic about his chances of being quickly found innocent of all accusations, but nothing in the long shadow of the dark, blank-faced monstrosity that was Lydford Gaol emanated a sense of justice.

Somewhere above a crow cawed.

IX

I oft have heard of Lyford Law,
How in the morn they hang and draw,
And sit in judgement after.
~Lydford Law, William Browne, 1590-1645.

A guard slumped beside the doorway of the keep. Noticing the group advancing up the track from the street toward him, he stood upright, tugging down his padded arming jacket and straightening his steel kettle helmet.

Henry led the company which had attracted several interested villagers to follow behind, muttering between themselves, but not engaging any of the miserable companions. The procession halted at a narrow wooden bridge which spanned a three-metre-wide ditch around the keep. The guard looked at the mounted men, and then behind him at the keep's doorway as if unsure if he should retreat inside.

'I've come to inter a criminal,' Henry said. His raised voice sounded nasal and whiney.

The guard licked his lips. 'Uh, what?'

'Bring him fore.' Henry clicked his fingers.

Robert was walked to the front of the group. John Sherman and one of Henry's labourers each held one of his arms.

The guard walked to the edge of the bridge, looking Robert up and down, then frowned at Henry. 'What you bringing him for? Never seen the likes of any of you before.'

'Because, you stunted imbecile, the man is a murderer. He slew my father and justly need be incarcerated pending trial.'

'Well...' the guard sucked his lips as he took a moment to think. 'Mayhap you is right, but you can't just bring any folk and drop 'em off. You ain't got a sheriff, bailiff, or even coroner or yeoman in your company. None of you lot is even tinners, is you? Mostly this be a stannary court.'

Henry closed his eyes and rubbed his hand down over his face. 'Look... Is there... someone else I can speak with? We've travelled overnight from Sampford Spiney. Not a drop of water nor ale has touched my lips since yesterday afternoon. Neither have I tasted any victual but unsalted horseflesh, and we are tired to the merest man, so verily do I refrain from wasting time explaining myself to a minion.'

The guard shook his head. 'Sampford Spiney? That be a half day ride, not overnight. Eat horseflesh? It's forbidden by the church, you know?'

Robert smiled. 'Just go and request audience with the sheriff or whoever is in charge. With haste.'

The guard considered the request for a moment before returning to the door, turning the iron door ring, and pushing through the doorway.

Henry climbed down from his horse and handed the bridle to his steward. 'Have the mounts stabled. Find somewhere the men can get fed and watered.'

The steward walked the two horses away, accompanied by Rowan the Large on his plough horse, and the two donkey-mounted farmers. The stablehand, John, and the two remaining farmers remained with Henry.

The group waited in silence for a short time until the guard remerged, accompanied by a man in his forties with long, stringy hair ringing his head under a bald mound. His nose was hooked, and his brow furrowed, which made it seem like he scrutinized everything he observed. He wore a threadbare doublet adorned with several pilgrim's badges. Although tall, his back was arched slightly. He descended the steps sideways, wincing with each lurched pace. Once he reached flat ground he shuffled, dragging his right foot across bridge. The tacks on his boot scraped over the wooden planks until he finally stopped before Henry. 'What we got here?' the man said, his eyes darting from one member of the group to the next before settling on Robert.

'This man…' Henry stepped aside to allow a clearer view of the prisoner. 'Killed my father, William Spiney. He was captured at the location of the crime armed with this.' He held out Robert's sheathed sword.

The man nodded as Henry spoke and grunted when he finished. 'Witnesses?'

'All those of us here were present at the arrest.'

The man's frown deepened. 'Witnesses to the slaying?'

Henry flinched, blinked and glanced about at his henchmen. 'Well, no. We raised the hue and cry and found the accused armed at the place of his crime.'

The man snorted. 'Has he confessed his sin?'

'No... sorry, who are you? You're not the sheriff.'

'Gaoler. Peyter's my name. Been gaoler here for-'

'I care not for your history, Peyter.' Henry snapped. 'No, he hasn't confessed, but he made threats to my dear father's life mere hours before he was slain.'

Peyter grimaced, sniffed and cleared his throat. 'I've seen him before about the village. I haven't seen the rest of you. Hard to trust the word of men you ain't seen afore.'

Henry glared at his prisoner. Robert remained silent and motionless, staring directly ahead.

'Do you two have some manner of business arrangement that he's protecting?' Henry sneered; his mouth close to Robert's ear.

'I don't believe I've ever spoken with him,' Robert said conversationally. 'Seen him about, as he says.'

'If you be wanting me to hold a man without proof or confession, I'll be wanting more than a stranger's word. If the sheriff comes and doesn't think he's worth referring to the royal court... well, I coulda spent coin on feed for him for weeks, cleaned away his filth, paid to have him guarded, and be out of pocket for the costs. Not to mention having a big strong 'un such as himself there holding grudge.'

Henry sighed, finally realising the gaoler's game. He opened the purse at his waist and fished around in it before retrieving three coins which he tossed to the gaoler.

Peyter, let the coins fall to the ground around him without trying to catch them. He looked down his nose at the money and grunted.

Henry sighed and tossed two more coins at the gaoler's feet.

Peyter nodded and gestured to the guard to pick up the money.

The guard scurried forward; snapping up the coins which he dropped into the gaoler's waiting hand.

'That'll do fer one month. Not sure what I'll do with him after that.'

'A month?' Henry sneered, 'that's enough coin to buy a fortnight's food and lodging at any inn in Devonshire.'

'Fortnight's not a month is it?' Peyter sniffed.

One of the farmers murmured something to the stablehand about being paid for their time; he made sure to say it loud enough for Henry to overhear.

'You'll get paid when we return to Sampford Spiney. I didn't expect to get swindled by that swine gaoler. There'll be an extra penny for each of you. Now, let's go find something to eat. It's a long way back.'

'One more thing,' Peyter said as Henry turned away. 'The sword.'

'What?'

'Belongs to your murderer don't it? Well… if he's found to be innocent, I'll need to return it. If guilty… well, it don't belong to you anyway, does it?'

Henry held the sword out, grip first, toward the gaoler, accompanied with a slight bow and an emotionless face.

Peyter nodded to the guard who stepped forward and took the weapon.

John the Sherman passed the rope to Robert's bindings to the guard. Henry and his entourage walked off toward the street. Only John glanced back at Robert as they departed.

'Well, well.' Petyer tutted and shook his head as he examined his new ward's dishevelled and stained appearance. 'Not taken fond care of you, has they? I seem to recall you as rather finely dressed afore.'

'Where's the sheriff?' Robert said, his dry throat putting a distinct rasp into his voice.

'Not about here, but don't worry; we'll take care of you.' Petyer smiled. He took the end of the rope from the guard and put a hand on Robert's shoulder and guided him over the bridge and up the steps to the prison keep.

The guard pushed the door open. Robert had only been into the keep once; almost twenty years prior when he paid his dues for the land which became Woodtown and paid the associated fees for his woollen business. Further quarterly payments had been collected by the bailiff, so he'd not needed to return to the passionless grey construct, until now. He recalled turning right beside the entrance and ascending stairs to a hall on the second floor where the sheriff at that time had sat dining with the magistrate, the bailiff, and some other officials. Robert didn't turn right this time.

They walked down a stone walled corridor only faintly illuminated by two candles: each candle opposite a wooden door. Despite the warmth outside, inside was cool, almost refreshing if it weren't for the foreboding of the darkness and the feint stench of faeces.

The guard opened the first door and held it open. Petyer gestured for Robert to walk through, which he did, the floorboards creaking with each step.

The room was unwindowed and unlit except for such light as filtered through the open doorway from the candle. There was a small table and stool by the fireplace, a bed of straw and a slop bucket. Robert decided it wouldn't be a comfortable place, but he'd expected worse: indeed, he'd lived in worse during his younger years.

The guard knelt and struggled with something on the floor. He grunted and then pulled open a hatch. Immediately the sickening stink of faeces, sweat and other unidentified foulness assaulted the nostrils.

The guard walked over to Robert and drew a knife from his belt. He cut through Robert's wrist bindings and uncoiled the rope from around him, allowing the twine to drop to the floor.

Robert's first instinct was to rub his sore wrists but flinched as soon as he touched them. Freedom from the bindings did nothing to diminish the burning sores from skin which had been rubbed raw. Robert flexed his fingers, then put one hand across his mouth and nose, trying to breathe only through his mouth.

'You best get used to the stink,' Peyter grinned, 'you'll probably be down there for a month or more. Court only be held each quarter.'

Robert peered down the hatchway. A ladder disappeared into blackness after the first six or seven feet. He stepped back from the trap door.

How stupid I am, Robert thought. *The room was for the damn guard, not the prisoner.*

'Down you go now,' the guard said, gesturing with his dagger.

'May I first take some water?' Robert croaked.

'Cheeky bastard!' The guard sneered, stepping forward with a raised hand to deliver a backhander on the insolent prisoner.

Peyter put a staying hand on his minion's shoulder. 'Leave him be. There be water enough down there. Go on now: it's better to climb down than be thrown down.'

Robert doubted that both men together were capable of throwing him into the oubliette. He considered briefly that freedom was two pounded heads and two unlocked doorways away, but then there'd be a hue and cry and he'd be outlawed: he could be killed on sight, and would be pursued with vigour; even those in his own hamlet would be duty bound by the tithing laws to pursue him. He closed his eyes. He had to prove his innocence. Guy would be back in Woodtown before the end of the day. Alice was sure to send him riding to Lydford to secure Robert's release. If he was lucky, he might be free before nightfall. At the worst he might endure one night of gaol.

Robert opened his eyes and climbed down through the hatchway. He paused near the top of the ladder; there was a low groaning from somewhere below. He cocked his head to listen. He could hear dripping and what sounded like someone muttering or praying.

'Go on, or I'll boot you down myself,' the guard warned.

Robert continued. The wooden ladder trembled as he descended. As soon as his head cleared the hatchway the door slammed shut. The bolt clanked into place. He was surrounded by blackness.

X

Ten men less room within this cave,
Than five mice in a lantern have,
~ Lydford Law, Robert Browne

Robert waited for his eyes to adjust to the dark; after a time, he could still see nothing. He closed and opened his eyes but could discern no difference. Blackness was complete; even the ladder rung he clung to bore not a shade of difference from the surrounding void. There was not a glint of light around the edges of the trapdoor nor any visible hues, outlines, or shapes either around or below him. Only the constant drip and the mumbled jabbering from below gave indication of any existence beyond the ladder.

The ladder creaked as Robert continued down. He took care to feel out each rung and moved slowly, unsure of the depth of the chamber, it was unwise to risk a fall. The stench from below was almost overpowering. The muttering grew louder, echoing through the chamber, making the oubliette seem like it was narrower than the room above. Robert counted stepping on fourteen rungs before his downward searching foot touched on something different to wood: soft, damp earth; perhaps, by the stench of it, mixed with human filth.

Something snatched Robert's elbow. He flinched, flinging his arm up. The hold was released.

'Peace, friend, peace!' a voice said in a tone barely above a whisper.

The mumbling continued: there were at least two other men beside Robert in the chamber.

'Who are you?' Robert demanded, tilting his head as he strained to locate the position of the speaker. He held his breath and tried to focus on listening, hoping he might hear movement or feel any nearby motion through the air.

'I mean no harm. Humble apologies for startling you, friend. I'm a prisoner, alike your own self. Here... do you wish for something to eat?'

Robert reached out, his fingers searching; he found clammy, cold flesh: a forearm. Bony fingers gently clasped Robert's wrist and guided his hand into a waiting palm which held some morsel. Robert took it, feeling the hard, smooth surface between his finger and thumb.

'What is it?'

The prisoner emitted a tinny, high-pitched laugh. 'When you've been down here a few days you won't ask what manner of victual it be - you'll just eat it.'

Robert popped the offering into his mouth. The smooth surface was sour; he almost spat it out but considered the stranger's warning. He crunched the tiny snack which released an almost sweet juice. He swallowed it, licking the remnants off his teeth. 'Pray, what was it?'

'Some bug or beetle.'

Robert suppressed a grimace; it hadn't tasted that bad, and he'd eaten worse during the siege of Nantes.

'Been hiding food from poor Gil?'

The voice had come from behind, but it was close. Robert turned, impotently trying to strain his eyes to see.

'Who's there?' Robert barked.

'Don't mind him. That's Gilbert,' said the first voice.

'Ooh, yes. Don't mind poor old Gil. That's right. Stay over your side and keep outta me way when they be dropping the food down, then ye won't have to be minding me.'

'Yes, best stay on this side,' said the original voice.

Cold bony fingers found Robert's shoulders and tugged him back into to what Robert assumed was the correct half of the cell.

'How many are in here?'

'Three. Well, four now - you being the fourth. You met Gilbert: he's uh... *innocent* of robbery on the road. Then there's mad Nate: he was here first. He jabbers mostly and quotes from the bible; likely mad on account of how long he's been here... however long that is. Then there's me, Cedric. Miller. Guilty. Unashamed and unrepentant as you please of non-payment of taxes, fines, fees and failing to answer the summons of the court until the bailiff came to, uh… escort me here.'

'Sounds like you all belong here.' Robert coughed to clear his parched throat.

'Not poor old Gil! Ye be careful about defaming poor Gil now. I can sniff ye out through the darkness and get my hands 'round yer grubby 'lil neck.'

Robert started to speak but Cedric squeezed his arm.

'What's your name, stranger?' said Cedric.

'Robert Wood of Woodtown. Landowner and wool trader.'

Cedric whistled. Gilbert laughed. Mad Nate stopped jabbering for a few seconds.

'Landowner?' Gilbert scoffed. 'You don't own enough land to lay down in now.'

Gilbert's resounding laugh bouncing off the walls gave an indication of the chamber's measurements: Robert estimated it to be less than twelve feet in length and width. Judging by the gaps between the ladder rungs he guessed the depth at about fifteen feet.

Cedric guided Robert by the arm to one wall, urging him to sit. 'Here you go, Robert. It's best to sit with your back against the wall. For sleeping, lay on one side with legs tucked to chest. There's not much room to lay flat out, and you might stray into Gilbert's half. He don't much like that.'

'Oh yes, poor 'ol Gilbert don't like that one 'lil bit.' Gilbert cackled.

'Mad Nate stays in his corner on our left,' Cedric whispered into Robert's ear. 'Don't stray more than a pace to your right because beyond is where we release our bowels.'

'Ah, for God's sake!' Robert hissed. 'I'm not sleeping next to where you all make your soil.' He stood up, brushing down the seat of his hose. He sniffed his fingers but was unable to ascertain if the stench of dung and urine was on him due to how strongly the stink permeated the entire cell.

'There's no avoiding it, I regret,' Cedric said, tugging on Robert's legging. 'It seeps into the soil and over the rock, and, well… as you can sense, spreads throughout. Nate tends to soil himself where he sits. Gilbert has the relatively drier half. He's not always… precise in placing his defecations, although he *is* sure to place them in our half.'

'That's it. I'm taking that fool's half.' Robert moved forward. His outstretched arm searched for Gilbert.

Cedric clung onto Robert's leg and tugged. 'No, no… don't fight. If the guard hears he'll throw his bucket contents down onto us. Or worse.'

'You come seek me when you're ready, 'lil girl.' Gilbert sneered.

Robert opened his mouth to retort, but deciding there was no point, felt his way back to the wall.

'So, when do we get fed and watered?' Robert rasped.

'Hmmm,' Cedric paused for a moment. 'It's hard to measure the passing between day and night down here, but I don't believe there's anything with the regularity to term it as a feeding *time*. A bucket of the worst pottage you'll ever taste is lowered… perchance once daily. The time betwixt feedings feels sometimes greater and sometimes lesser, yet perhaps the speed of its passing depends on the depth of our mood.'

'What of water? I've tasted nary a drop for more than a day.'

'Ah, well water's different. You hear that dripping?'

Robert nodded. The distinct drip sounded every couple of seconds which he'd assumed was a measure intended to torment the incarcerated. He strained to listen for the source.

'There's a well yonder - beyond the wall. Water leaks through the rock and drips down the wall in the corner. When you have thirst, you must take water from the wall.'

Robert bowed his head and massaged his temples with his thumbs. He wasn't going to be lowered to licking dirty water from a stone wall, let alone the same stones the other prisoners suckled on. He decided could manage another day without a drink. Robert briefly wondered if it would be preferable drink his own passed water than drink from the wall; he shook such thoughts from his head.

Cedric patted Robert's shoulder as if sensing his cellmate's thoughts.

'Peace, friend. You'll only be here until trial. Although I suppose they'll defer it to the royal court if you're here for something more serious.'

'Aye, I am. That could mean months.'

'Nay,' Gilbert snorted, 'nary would they keep ye so long. Prisoners takes up room and needs feed. Magistrate will hang ye and royal court confirm sentence thereafter.'

'Costs money to hold a man waiting trial,' Cedric said with a tinge of bitterness. 'The courtesy of long incarceration be only preferred on those with coin to pay the goaler.'

'So, how long you been here?'

'Oh, me? Well… as I told, it's hard to tell the passing of time; perchance five or six weeks. But I'm a special case.'

Robert inclined his head in curiosity, waiting for Cedric to decide to continue.

'I took a loan from the sheriff. Used the coin to buy from him the right to mill village bread and manage the communal oven. I were unknowing that the sheriff sold similar licence to two others. Three millers are two too many for a village of a hundred souls.'

Robert thought for a moment, then nodded. 'I see. The sheriff profited from the three of ye knowing that at least one, probably two of you would default.'

'Exactly!' Cedric clapped. 'Now he can declare my newly built mill forfeit and taken as payment for dues. I expect he will muscle the other millers out of business and install his own fee-paying tenant miller.'

'Bastards all o' them,' Gilbert spat. 'I'd crush the skull o' every highborn snotfly I met if I could get outta here.'

'Anyway…' Cedric cleared his throat. 'I suppose I am to remain here until such time as the sheriff has secured title to my land and property. Pray, what injustice do they have you here for, Robert?'

Robert pondered how much he wanted to tell his companions: they might turn approver against him, twisting his words in the hope of better treatment for themselves. It was also possible that one or more of them had a connection to Sampford Spiney and sympathies with the Spiney family.

'They got me for murder. I didn't do it.'

'Ah, a pure o' heart innocent. Just alike me!' Gilbert chuckled.

Cedric sighed. 'Innocent or nay is a matter of indifference. Standing accused is half-way to dangling from the rope. If you've witnesses to vouch for you, mayhap you have a hare's chance against the hound. If not, perchance you have coin to barter your way free, but I warn thee they'll take you for all you got because you've no other choice.'

'I'm not buying my freedom. I'll walk out of here with no smirch.' Robert's voice become hoarse. His dry throat closed over, forcing a succession of coughs.

'You should go to the wet wall,' Cedric said.

Robert grunted. He wasn't thirsty enough to lick stone yet. He rested his elbows on his knees and hung his head, replaying the morning's events. His thoughts dwelt on Alice. He wished he'd had some passionate moment with his wife before rushing off; he imagined what they might've done together. Eventually his thoughts turned to the events at Sampford Spiney and his journey to Lydford. He tried to fathom who might have committed the deed he was accused of: it had to be one of Spiney's own household, didn't it?

The hatch above groaned as it was pulled open. A dim light emanated through the square hatchway but didn't dare to extend its hazy fingers even as far into the void as the first rung of the ladder. There was a shuffle of movement on the opposite side of the cell as Gilbert shifted or stood. Nate's muttering became quicker and increased slightly in volume.

A blurred shape descended through the hatch; visible for just a second as it passed in front of the light source. Rope gently rasped against the rim of the hatchway. Wood thudded against wood as the object knocked against the ladder.

'The feed bucket,' Cedric breathed into Robert's ear.

A ruffle of movement came from Gilbert's half of the cell. The ladder creaked where he leaned on it. His breathing came heavily. 'C'mon, c'mon,' he muttered.

The occasional thump of wood against the rungs marked the bucket's progress. Finally, the bucket clattered as Gilbert snatched it. The rope recoiled upwards with a lazy hiss as it was dragged against the hatchway, then the door slammed down, and a bolt clicked into place.

The bucket rattled, accompanied by Gilbert's grunts and smacking lips.

Robert stood. 'You pig, have you your snout in the feed? That's for all four of us.'

Gilbert barked something unintelligible through a mouthful of food.

Robert felt Cedric's hand grasping his forearm.

'Peace, friend. Gilbert takes his fill first, then I. Nate gets what's left. I think we can let you go second: before me.'

Robert ripped his arm free of Cedric's hold. 'I'm not eating that swine's seconds. Neither are you - not even that simple bastard in the corner.' Robert stepped forward and felt for the source of the wet chewing noises. His hand contacted slippery, grimy skin stretched tight over a dome of bone: Gilbert's bald head. Robert's fingers quickly searched a grip, but the head ducked out of his grasp.

The bucket thudded onto the ground. Robert accidentally kicked it as he moved forward, looking to grab his quarry, his arms sweeping in an arc like a man threshing straw.

'You fool, you spilled the pottage!' Gilbert sputtered. The voice came from low: he was crouched or prone.

Robert fell upon the sound. His knees struck upon soft flesh. Air burst from the lungs of his quarry in an almighty gasp. Robert's hands found a linen shirt, the material stiff with soiled matter.

Gilbert slapped at Robert's arms. Robert's tightened his grip on the shirt. He'd expected Gilbert to be tall and muscular, but the man beneath him was podgy, sweaty and soft.

Gilbert's squirmed but couldn't move out from under his assailant. He released little cries of frightened exertion; knowing he was already bested. His flailing arms were easily forced to the ground and pinned under Robert's knees.

'You're a fat bastard, aren't you?' Robert said, putting his face close enough to Gilbert's that his beard brushed Gilbert's nose.

'Get off!'

'Next bucket cometh down: you don't partake, to account for you pigging this lot. Henceforth, I share the food out evenly. Agreed?'

'You can't just come 'n impose yer own rules on us. We takes turns. We got our order.'

Robert applied pressure with his right knee, pressing it down on the chubby man's arm.

Gilbert cried out.

'I've half the mind to drown you in your own night soil, but fate smiles on you, for I'm reflective upon such circumstances as brought me here and I remain reluctant to compromise my chances of freedom, so I'll merely hurt you until you see things my way.'

Robert applied more pressure with his knee.

'Ah! Okay! We'll do as you say.'

'Good.' Robert patted Gilbert's cheek then stood up. He turned about and felt for the bucket. He picked it up and sniffed it: peas pottage. The bucket wasn't heavy; a brief exploration showed it to be a quarter full. There was no spoon. He reached out for Cedric, finding the cloth of his brais. He put the bucket into Cedric's hands. 'Here, take what you will then give the rest to Nate.'

'Won't you eat?'

'I told you: not seconds.'

***

There were two periods of sleep before the hatch next opened. Already Robert was unsure if it was day or night and or if he'd been imprisoned for a day, two, or even more. Another bucket descended. Gilbert made no move to retrieve it but panted in anticipation from his half of the chamber.

Robert waited at the bottom of the ladder. He couldn't see the bucket even when it neared his head and could track it only by the sound of it clacking against the ladder. He found the bucket and unfastened the rope, which began to ascend as soon as it was free of the bucket's weight.

The contents didn't smell particularly pungent. Robert put his hand in and felt tough bread. Searching further he found a waxy smooth substance: cheese. He broke the bread into four parts and the cheese into three. He tossed a piece of bread over to Gilbert.

'Here. You should be grateful I spare you anything,' Robert said, his voice came dry and raspy and his tongue felt swollen and heavy.

He moved to Cedric, then Nate, pressing bread and cheese into their waiting palms. Nate ceased his muttering to rabidly stuff the food into his mouth which he chewed with the enthusiasm of a starving hound.

Robert bit into his bread. It tasted of mould, but the first food he'd eaten for what may have been days was as welcome as a harvest banquet. He swallowed with difficulty, trying three or four times before the morsel of bread could pass down his dry gullet. It was time to try the water.

The dripping directed him to the correct section of wall. Robert brushed his fingers over damp stone. A drop splashed onto the back of his hand. He sucked it. The water tasted of rust. After a moment's hesitation, he put his lips to the wall. The rock was cold, wet, and flecked with grit. He dared to lick the wall and was rewarded with more dirt than water. He felt for a damper section. His hands found a smooth stone. He licked it, tasting metallic water, he lapped at the stone. Robert continued sucking at lapping at the wall until his tongue was sore; still his thirst had not been quenched. He dabbed the last of his bread against the stone, turning the crust over in his hands so it soaked up as much moisture as possible then stuffed the sodden hunk into his mouth.

Robert compressed the damp bread between his tongue and the roof of his mouth; it released its moisture like a sponge. He sucked the bread to disintegration, then proceeded to eat the cheese. The handful of cheese stank of sour milk when held close to the nose. It was soft and somewhat creamy, but no less mouldy than the bread. Robert ate it all in what felt like a very short time. He finished up by licking his fingers, then listened jealously to the sound of Cedric chewing and swallowing. He banished a fleeting thought of how easy it would be to take food from the others. He wondered if that was how Gilbert started out: resisting the urge to steal from his cellmates until hunger became too great. He similarly banished sympathetic thoughts toward his portly companion, recalling the crime the man stood accused of.

'How long am I down here now?' Robert croaked.

'Maybe a day, I think,' Cedric said, 'maybe a day and a half.'

XI

The days were counted by the meals. It was impossible to accurately gauge the passage of time and so it was mutually accepted to equate one meal to one day. The food was certainly not cooked for their benefit alone; Robert assumed that what they ate were the leftovers from the guards' and servants' meals. If there weren't enough leftovers from breakfast, the bucket included the remains of the next meal, which Robert attributed to the seemingly differing mealtimes; they could be eating as early as midday or as late as evening prayer.

The prisoners passed their time arguing over petty things: taking up too much room, making too much noise, being too quiet, allowing one's urine to seep to a part of the chamber not reserved for defecations. Despite Robert's attempts at sharing the food equally there were disagreements with Gilbert over the portions and the distribution, including even a suggestion that Robert retained more food by way of residue elements sticking to his fingers as he handed out the food. Even Cedric argued over the food at times; Robert didn't begrudge it, the novelty he'd provided as the new prisoner had worn off and disputes over trivial matters seemed to help time pass more swiftly between the bucket descents.

When they weren't bickering over some triviality, the prisoners reminisced over idle matters: the best meal they'd ever eaten, the worst meal, the most beautiful girl they had laid with, and the ugliest. All discussion focused on the past and avoided the present and future. Early on Robert tried to discuss the first thing they would do when released, but the subject was met with a long silence, broken only by Nate's mumblings. When they talked or argued, it was to escape for the few moments they could. Robert sensed that each of them shared his own fear - that they might never be released. They were, after all, in an oubliette: a place to put people to forget them. Robert tried to quietly ignore thoughts that his future might be nothing more than endless black and the ever-present stench of slowly decaying faeces. Even hanging would be a preferable fate.

Gilbert was retelling a story from his childhood: he'd stolen a loaf from a baker and was about to be discovered by the infuriated baker. He had to eat the entire loaf, including crumbs, as quickly as possible to destroy the evidence. It was a story told three times already, many details changing each time. It didn't matter if the entire tale was a fabrication or if Gilbert changed it just to keep it fresh, either way, it occupied the time.

'Just as he grabs me by the scruff 'o me neck, I notices I've dropped a morsel 'o bread into the fold of me jerkin, so as quick as ye likes I-'

The hatchway bolt snatched back, ending the story. The trapdoor creaked open. It was early for food. The prisoners stood, waiting for the bucket to be lowered, but instead came a voice.

'Gilbert Mason. Come up.'

The instruction was met with silence.

Robert held his breath. The guard had never addressed them before, but now one of their number was being called out. Was such a summons a good omen or ill?

'Gilbert Mason! Be he alive down there?'

'Yes, yes damn ye! I'm alive!' Gilbert snapped. The ladder squeaked as the large man ascended, huffing with each rung ascended.

Once Gilbert reached the top and cleared the hatch, Robert thought he glimpsed a black silhouette of the bald man's dome as he looked back down at his erstwhile companions, but before anything could be said the hatch slammed shut and the bolt slid into place.

'Will they free him?' Robert said.

Cedric sniffed. 'Never heard of anyone being just being freed from Lydford, have you? Expect he's going to trial.'

God protect him and us, Robert thought. He made the sign of the cross. Devout only at times of peril, he briefly wondered if his silent prayer might serve as a hex from a vengeful god irritated at being hailed only at such times. He licked his cracked lips and clasped his hands together in prayer. *God, if you see me through this, I'll listen at church to what the parson has to say and try to give alms whenever I can.* He grimaced. It was a bad prayer and blatantly barely half meant. Robert decided he would listen at church; he only ever went to avoid the fines for non-attendance, but maybe it was best to be attentive to one's immortal soul. He let his hands drop to his sides: he'd think of a better prayer later.

'Amen,' Cedric said.

Robert glared in the direction of his voice, irritated that Cedric might have sensed Robert's moment of devotion.

'Amen,' Robert muttered. Maybe Cedric's prayers were more powerful than his own.

'He's in God's hands now.'

'Aye, and being as he's guilty as sin, I expect he'll be cowering in the very presence of the Almighty afore long.'

Cedric retreated to his spot against the wall. Robert moved to take his adjacent space but paused, deciding he might as well make use of the additional room. He felt his way to Gilbert's wall and lowered himself, sitting with his back against stone.

'Couldn't wait to put some inches between us?' Cedric said lightly.

'Bah! I expect you're as tired of my stink as I am of yours.'

Robert rested his right foot atop his left knee and felt the soles of his foot; the blisters had burst but the skin was still raw in places. He'd tried to avoid stepping in excrement to help prevent any open cuts on his feet becoming infected, but it was a near impossible task: despite making their mess in a corner the foul matter seemed to permeate the whole floor.

'Do you think he'll plead innocence?' Cedric said.

Robert shrugged. Realising the motion went unseen he decided to let silence be his answer.

'What about you?' Cedric pressed on.

'What do you mean?'

'Will you plead innocent?'

'No, I was rather looking forward to being hanged.'

'The hanging man hangs,' Nate hissed, 'he hangs he hangs he hangs!' his voice trailed off as he uttered the words over and over.

Cedric sighed. 'I meant, what will you say? Are you truly innocent?'

'There's not much I can tell. I'm innocent. I know not the culprit, but I have my thoughts on the matter.'

Robert directed his gaze to the patch of void where the hatch was. He wondered if the guard ever listened to the prisoners' conversations. Sound seemed to resonate up through the cell, so he expected the guard could hear if he wanted to. Maybe some fools had seen themselves to the noose by speaking too loosely in the oubliette.

'You should think of what you will say,' Cedric said, sounding eager. 'If you go to your trial unprepared, you'll swing for sure. Try it on me. Pretend I'm the judge. How do you plead?'

'I plead for you to shut up. You're starting to make as much sense as that fool in the corner.'

'Alright, if you don't want to prepare, at least tell me who you think did it.'

Robert rested his head back against the wall. He'd given much consideration to the identity of the killer, but always came back around to the same suspect: Henry. He wasn't entirely sure the younger Spiney did it, but patricide didn't seem beyond him: he certainly had a cruel streak. Henry had hastened to accuse Robert for the crime rather than try to root out the true murderer. Was he in a hurry to inherit his father's lands? Robert fathomed that the only other person who might have benefitted from William Spiney's death was Robert himself: If he were a juror, he'd be convinced of his guilt.

Was it somehow possible that in a drunken stupor he had snuck over to Spiney's lodging and slain him? Robert recalled that he once sleep-walked out of camp when in France, but that was after several jugs of a particularly strong moniack. It was inconceivable that he could commit a murder while drunk and return to bed without a mark of blood on him and without waking the others.

'You won't speak on it?' Cedric said.

'I'm thinking.'

'Well… who is the most likely murderer?'

'Ah, well that'd be me. I was trying to think who else could've done it.'

'And?'

'And thinking about it makes me tired. I will sleep.'

'Hmmm, well you should dwell on it. If they've taken Gilbert to trial, you could be next.'

'Or you.'

'No, not I.'

Robert groaned and scratched his beard; it felt silky and matted. He was glad he couldn't see what he looked like, but his imagination conjured images of the most dishevelled beggars and even lepers.

'No, really,' Cedric pressed on. 'Why would it be me? My crime is one the manorial court could deal with. It's a matter of unpaid coin, not violence.'

'Except you failed to answer the summons of the manorial court - you said so yourself. That's why you're enjoying incarceration here.'

'True enough. Even so, default would be settled by distraint, not the county court. I'll be kept here until I die. My punishment for refusing to pay a corrupt sheriff.'

Robert sighed. 'You seem to be accepting your fate well enough. You and Mad Nate here together 'til death do you part? Are you sure they didn't hang ye already and this be your hell?'

Cedric grunted a note of laughter then became quiet. The cell, never entirely silent, settled back into the constants of dripping and crazed mumbling.

Robert tried to sleep. In truth he wasn't tired, but he didn't want to dwell too long on who was truly responsible for the crime; the wondering, theories, and thirst for revenge would make him crazy: better to wait until he was free, then he could pursue the matter with vigour. Where *was* Guy? Robert wondered. Even if his seneschal had relaxed in Plympton, downing cups with his brother, Alice should have sent word to them to hurry to his rescue.

***

Robert woke up with the sound of the latch above sliding back. He leaned forward, instantly alert. He wasn't sure how long he'd been asleep; sometimes he'd felt as though he'd slept for hours but on conferring with his cellmate found it to be mere minutes.

'It *has* to be the feeding,' Robert said.

'Robert Wood!' The guard snapped.

Robert looked to where Cedric sat. Neither spoke nor breathed.

'Robert Wood: come up!'

XII

Robert blinked as he tried to focus his vision. The guardroom was dimly lit by a few rushlights, glowing embers danced around in his vision, blurring everything else. The hatch slammed back into place and the latch was pushed across. Robert realised he hadn't bid farewell to Cedric. A hand clapped on Robert's shoulder, startling him.

'This way.'

The guard kept his hand on Robert's shoulder, gently yet firmly guiding him through the doorway and up the steps toward the hall and whatever judgement awaited.

Robert's feet no longer hurt, but the hard, cold floor felt strange to walk upon after days of standing in rotten straw and human filth. He touched the wall beside the stairwell and let his fingers trail along the grainy surface as if afraid he would be plunged back into darkness at any moment. It was painful to remain upright; back, calves and leg joints ached with their renewed use. Daylight burst through thin rectangular windows along the staircase. Robert paused to feel the warmth on his face but was unable to open his eyes against the bright light.

'Keep going,' The guard growled as shoved Robert's shoulder.

Robert continued to ascend, moving cautiously as the nerves in his legs trembled in their waking. He silently scolded himself for not stretching regularly in the cell to keep his muscles active. He'd not expected to become enfeebled so quickly. He dared not open his eyes beyond narrow slits. Spots of light danced in his vision, he kept his eyes closed for several seconds at a time, only peeking for brief moments as he tried to readjust. He felt his way along the wall and was forced to trust that the guard would guide him by the shoulder from any missteps.

'How long was down there?'

The guard pushed Robert's shoulder. Although not tolerant of any halting, the guard was at least abiding of the slow pace of progress, which Robert attributed to likely experience of many prisoners with atrophied limbs and poor vision from long incarcerations.

The twenty or so steps and short corridor walk to the hall took a few minutes; enough time for Robert's vision to revert sufficiently for him to focus without wincing, although the colours and blotches which swam in his peripheral vision refused to be blinked away.

Lyford's hall was the finest Robert had been in, if small by the standards of the nobility, it was at the very height of a dream for a lowborn commoner. The room was at least as wide as Robert's longhouse and the ceiling beams were high enough that they might only be touched by the uppermost of four men standing on each other's shoulders. The walls were painted with biblical scenes - mostly those of judgement. One wall was dedicated to a depiction of men falling into the fires of hell. The wall behind the dais showed Jesus on the cross with lamenting disciples kneeling before him and angels peeking through clouds to blow golden trumpets.

A well-trodden line of carpet ran from the doorway almost to the opposite wall. A lord in a voluminous robe and feathered cap sat in a high-backed chair at the centre of a dais overlooking a long, sturdy table. His collar and cuffs were lined with squirrel fur, denoting a man of status. A large wolfhound rested its head on the lord's boot.

Four seats along the table were occupied by officious looking men in gaudily pompous dress. Robert recognised only one of them: the sheriff, Sir John Herle. The table was covered in scattered parchments, not unlike the table at the Sir John's residence. Robert's eye lingered on a wide dish of fruit perched at the table's edge.

'Ah, what have we here?' said a balding, middle aged official, raising his eyebrows as if he'd only just noticed the dishevelled prisoner standing before him. He lifted the corner of a parchment and made a show of scanning it for information. 'Robert Wood. Ah, yes… the murderer.'

The noble on the dais sat upright, disturbing his dog who looked up at him expectantly before lowering its head again. The Lord toyed with a lock of brown hair that dangled from under his cap. Clasps of polished bronze or gold on the lord's robe glinted in reflected light. His pupils darted up and down as he examined the accused man.

'Has he pled guilty?' the Lord said. His hand flopped open; the index finger lazily pointed at Robert.

The balding official picked up the document and scanned it again and shrugged. 'No, Sir. At least, no plea is recorded.'

'Oh.' The lord shifted on his chair, frowning and blinking. 'Well... I suppose we better ask him. You there - I've forgotten your name. How are you pleading?' The finger continued to wave vaguely in Robert's direction.

Robert cleared his throat and looked straight into the lord's eyes. 'Innocent, m'Lord.'

'Oh...' the lord looked about as if confused. 'Well, was he caught in the act?'

Robert opened his mouth to answer before realising the question wasn't for him: after stating his plea he was off no immediate interest.

The official glanced over his parchment again. A younger man in simple attire got up from his seat at the bottom end of the table, shuffled to the official, leaned over and whispered into his ear.

'Ah!' the official exclaimed as if he'd just remembered something important. 'He was brought in by the son of the slain who captured the accused... Robert... Wood? Yes, Wood... Captured him in the vicinity of the crime; armed and behaving suspiciously.'

Robert clamped his teeth together and remained quiet: it would not serve him to interrupt or speak out of turn.

'Oh...' The lord blew out a puff of air and fanned himself with his hand. 'So, not caught in the act of murder then?'

'Apparently not, sir,' the official said.

'Has he been tortured?' the lord asked, squinting at the accused.

Robert looked down at himself, only now taking stock of his appearance: his bare feet were black from dirt and encrusted blood; faint prints marked the floor where he'd walked. His hose and shirt were stiff with grime, and where not torn were stained in various dark shades. Both hands were blackened to the wrists. He could not present a more destitute visage if he'd begged from a city gutter for a year.

'No, sir,' the official said in an almost jovial tone. 'We refrain from torture. We sit in fair judgement.'

It was only then that Robert realised there was no jury: at any trial there should be a jury of twelve. There were two benches for a jury running along the flanking wall, but they were empty.

'If I may, sir…' Robert spoke loudly, bowing his head briefly.

The lord shifted in his seat with an alarmed expression on his face. He adjusted his robe and spread his open hands in a magnanimous gesture. 'Go on then. Say your piece, yet with haste, yes?'

'I see you've no jury. As m'Lord said: you sit in fair judgement, to which end a jury is required. I would save you both the time and expense of detaining me and assembling a jury.'

'Sit in fair judgement? I?' the Lord said incredulously. He looked at his underlings one after the other then back at Robert, then gasped and raised a triumphant finger. 'Ah, he thinks of me as the judge! Does he not? The judge, by God!'

The Lord laughed and his minions chuckled and smiled along with him.

'My God, dear fellow,' the Lord wiped an invisible tear from the corner of his eye as his laughter subsided. 'I'm not the judge. I'm the coroner. We're trying to thin out the cells ahead of the judge's arrival… To save money and time, as you say, yes? So, we have the Sheriff here and my own good self: the persons required to hang someone should they be caught in the act or have confessed. You've neither been caught in the act nor pleaded guilty, and I suppose for reasons of not wanting your neck stretched are declaring innocence, so pray tell how you wish expedite the process and expense for us?'

'I ask the right of trial by combat as proof of innocence or guilt.'

The Lord's eyebrows lifted. He regarded Robert for a second or two, then clapped his hand to his chest and giggled, filling the chamber with his yapping sound as his head lolled around in his mirth. The officials added their laughter after a few moments' hesitation. The dog sat up and barked at his master.

'Trial by combat?' The Lord said finally, again wiping away an imaginary tear. 'Oh, I say, you are a funny fellow. Are the any other archaic practices you'd like to call upon?'

'Tis my right,' Robert said, his voice rebounding off the walls.

'Is it?' the Lord flinched. His face contorted in bewilderment.

'It is, sir,' the official said, 'although we've not seen such a thing in these parts for… well, I'd have to check the records, but I'm want to say that it has probably never happened.'

'Well, I shan't allow it,' the Lord snapped. 'It's barbaric and archaic. We're not Welshmen or foul heathens… No, I shan't allow it.'

'Ah, sir…' the official cleared his throat. 'It's not really the coroner's decision. The accused may challenge the plaintiff, under certain circumstances.'

Sheriff Sir John Herle held up his palm. He waited some moments while the room's occupants turned their attention to him, then stood, inclining his head to the official and then to the lord.

'I know you are newly appointed to your post of coroner, my Lord. I believe I can assist, if I may… Master Robert stands accused by young Henry Spiney, correct?' He turned to Robert for affirmation.

Robert nodded curtly.

Sir John gave a thin smile. 'Henry Spiney is a boy of what? Twenty years? His hands doubtless as smooth as the day he were born. Yet Master Robert served as billman in a our most just and noble army, winning himself coin on the battlefield by the unhorsing and capture of a knight of some means. Unless I am very much mistaken, there is not a sinner's chance in the sulphurous pit of Hades that Henry Spiney will accept a trial by combat.'

'He cannot refuse me.' Robert dared to speak without permission and failed to curb the snarl in his tone. 'Tis my right to challenge him.'

Sir John raised his palm again and held it there until the tutting and muttering officials became silent. 'Indeed, Master Robert. However, if there is undeniable proof of culpability, the accused may not ask for trial by combat.'

The officials nodded their agreement.

'There is nary a thread of proof let alone that which might be termed undeniable,' Robert growled, 'there be no proof at all!'

Sir John rapped his knuckles on the tabletop three times and fixed Robert with his light blue eyes. 'Indeed, Master Robert. However, is it not probable that when confronted with a battle Henry cannot win, witness will quickly be found to swear that you committed the dark deed? Perhaps found among those men whom I understand escorted you here? Is it not probable that young Henry will pay for the word of his bondsmen and perhaps your men as well? One of the men from your tithing brought you here, did he not? Villeins are so easily bought, do you not think so, Master Robert?'

Robert couldn't find a reply. He knew Sir John spoke truly. There would be no combat: it had been his only chance at freedom and the sheriff had snatched it away. Most of a jury would be made up of men from the place of the crime and Henry Spiney could pay them off at will. The noose was as good as about Robert's neck. He looked the doorway: it was still open. The guard stood two paces behind him. Robert considered that if he acted quickly enough, he might surprise the man and be on his way. The fancy passed almost as soon as he considered it. Robert would suffer no man to say that he ran; in any case he wasn't in fit state to flee - even the slovenly guard would catch him before he reached the corridor.

Everyone was watching Robert; mostly with amused expressions. The sheriff's countenance was sombre, and his eyebrows knitted together as he studied the accused.

'I have a suggestion,' Sir John said, 'I don't believe the evidence against Master Wood is, as it stands, sufficient. As I've portrayed, I don't think it likely that we will see fair trial. Perhaps we can allow the accused a chance to prove his innocence.'

The coroner leaned forward from the chair and inclined his head.

Sir John basked in the attention and confusion of his peers. A faint smile played on his thin lips.

The coroner made an irritated hand motion for the sheriff to continue.

'My Lord, we're expecting the judge to travel from Branscombe in around a week from now. Master Wood has been, until now at least, an upstanding member of his parish. I would have him paroled and given a week to find whatever proof he can of his innocence and locate the true murderer, if indeed it not be Master Robert himself. It would seem the fairest way, would it not?'

The Coroner studied Robert and wrinkled his nose as if he only now caught the scent of the offensive blend of malodours emanating from the accused. 'Let him go? Look at him: he's nothing but a base villein. He'll steal away, then we'll have to hunt him down again.'

'That's my problem as sheriff, not yours.' Sir John raised his voice and rested his hands on his hips. 'If he runs, it will be as outlaw. It will be legal for any man to slay him on sight. We'll give him a week to return with proof of innocence and the guilty in bondage.'

Robert clenched his clammy fists. He dared to hope he might have a chance, yet he couldn't fathom why the sheriff suddenly stood for him: a guilty conscience for deceiving him over the bailiff position?

The Coroner shrugged and sat back in his chair. 'Well, let it be on your head, Sir John. It's your right to set him free if you see fit.'

'It is.'

'Oh, just one other thing,' the Coroner leant forward, gripping the arm rests he peered down onto Robert as if he might suddenly spring into action. 'I want a scribe to go with him and record everything he does so we can be assured he doesn't buy witnesses to have some poor villein hung in his stead.'

The officials murmured among themselves. Sir John rapped the butt of his dagger on the table for silence, then studied each shocked face along the table length before pointing the dagger at the young, plainly dressed official at the end of the table.

'You, recall to me your name?'

'Me? Uh… Edmund, Sir. Edmund Chance.'

'Right. Edmund, you go with Master Robert. And you…' Sir John turned to Robert, 'you're to provide lodgings in your home for the clerk and feed him as you feed yourself. You will present yourselves here within a week of today or be declared outlaw. Do you agree?'

Robert nodded. He looked at the clerk who diverted his own gaze down at the table, pulling a leather-bound book in front of him and flipping it open he pretended to study it.

Edmund looked to be his mid-twenties and as thin as a reed. He wore no wedding band. Thick brown hair was cut in a straight line around his head just above the ear, with the back and sides shaved. An Adam's apple protruded prominently from a scrawny neck. His face was thin face, almost gaunt, with a pointed chin but thick lips and large, dark eyes. His blue doublet might have been fine when new but had become frayed and had a patch on the elbow and the sleeves were short: the doublet wasn't seemingly made for him, but rather gifted or inherited.

Edmund raised a shaking hand. Sir John ignored it and rapped the table to divert Robert's attention back to himself.

'Understand, Master Robert, that you are being granted unprecedented licence to clear your name. It is only because of your relative status in my manorial court, and that you have been, unto now, of good character. I know much of your… bullish reputation: I want none of that. Do you understand?'

Robert nodded.

'Do you have anything to say?'

'I'll not be travelling as if a vagrant.' Robert raised his arms to indicate the rags he wore. 'I shall need clothes, shoes, a good horse, and I want my sword back. The gaoler has it.'

Two of the officials put their heads together, whispering and frowning at Robert. The Coroner giggled.

'You have means, Robert,' Sir John snorted. 'Buy such as you need in the village.'

'the gaoler has my purse. I dare say it's devoid of coin by now.'

Sir John leant on the table with his fists. He stared at Robert from under knitted eyebrows. 'I'm offering you a rare chance and you complain of your wardrobe? At my pleasure I could have you tossed back into the dungeon and... oh, what is it, Clerk? Put that damnable hand of yours down!'

Edmund lowered the limb. His chair grated on the floor as he pushed the seat back and stood. He bowed his head in meek apology. 'Forgive me, sirs. I... I can't help but wonder: if the accused should not return within the week and be declared outlaw... what is to refrain him from uh...'

'Murdering you like he did William Spiney?' Sir John rasped with a wry grin.

'Uh, yes... something that way.' The Clerk bowed again and then lowered himself into the chair.

'Nothing I suppose. But if you don't go, you'll be back to whatever stinking furrows your family labour over. Does that adequately answer your question?'

'Yes... yes, Sir. Thank you.'

The Sheriff sighed. He looked from the clerk to Robert. 'Very well. I'll have a pair of horses from the stable prepared. Should they not be returned, their value will be indebted by you. Sword and purse will be restored to you. I believe the gaoler turns a small profit in selling shoes and various items of clothing confiscated from the condemned. I'll ensure that he finds you a pair of shoes and a suitable tunic.'

Sir John looked at the guard and jerked his head toward the door.

Robert was escorted by the guard into an anteroom with a narrow window and a small rectangular stool. He was made to wait there until the guard returned with a basin of water. Robert washed his face, hands and beard as best he could. The water soon turned grey, then black, making the use of it serve to only redistribute the dirt over himself.

Peyter, the hook-nosed gaoler came to the doorway. One of his eyes winced as the other bulged; it was uncertain what emotion the expression conveyed, but it was clear it was some shade of displeasure. The gaoler sniffed and held out Robert's sword. The belt was wrapped around the sheath and the purse hung over one of the sword's quillions.

Robert snatched the offering. He drew the blade. The gaoler bristled at the doorway. Robert examined the weapon and slid the sword back into the scabbard. Inside the purse he found the piece of cloth his wife had embroidered with the image of a flower when they were courting. There was no coin. He held the purse open and stared at the gaoler.

Peyter smiled weakly and tucked a greasy strand of hair behind his ear. 'Few pennies short is ya? I gots to cover expenses. We can only hold so many and we gots to feed ya.'

'There were more than four shillings in my purse.'

'Hmmm. Mayhap there were. Looks empty now.' Peyter showed his rotting teeth and gave a short laugh but kept his hand on the rim of the door, seemingly ready to push it closed should the former prisoner lunge at him. 'There also be the matter of cost in clothing. You could say that you had your money's worth in your stay here.'

Peyter clicked his fingers and a ragged underling advanced from further down the corridor with a bundle which Petyer snatched and thrust toward Robert. The gaoler backed out of the room and closed the door the moment Robert accepted the offering.

Robert unravelled the bundle; a pair of shoes fell onto the floor, wrapped in what turned out to be an unlined riding cloak. The thin grey material of the cloak could be looked through when held up to the window light. There was no trim and a few holes; it would suffice to cover his filthy clothes but was likely the poorest item of attire the gaoler could have mustered.

The shoes appeared worn but practical until Robert inspected the left shoe; the front half of the sole flapped uselessly, making it unusable for walking, but it would do in the stirrup. Robert squatted onto the tiny stool and grunted as he pulled the leather tight over his feet, fearing the boots might tear apart with the effort of squeezing his feet into them, but after a short time his feet were compressed into the shoes.

The clasp on the cloak had broken off so Robert secured it with a knot. The cape wouldn't close around him fully, leaving the middle of his filthy shirt exposed. Robert knocked on the door and picked up the bowl of filthy water, holding it steady with both hands. As the door creaked open, Robert upended the bowl over the feet of the guard.

The startled guard cried out. Quickly recovering, he bared his teeth and his hands closed into fists; he met Robert's gaze and stepped back, glowering.

'Apologies, friend,' Robert said, 'I'd meant to pass you the water, but my hands are feeble from incarceration.'

The gaoler watched from the end of the corridor. Robert had intended the dirty water for him, but the guard likely deserved no less.

'Yer horses be waiting. Begone if yer ready,' Peyter said.

Robert had to make exaggerated steps with his left foot as he walked in order to avoid tripping on the flapping segment of sole. He steadied himself on the wall as he descended the steps, but he was soon in the afternoon sun, standing on the far side of the bridge from Lyford goal. He closed his eyes and lifted his face to the sun, enjoying the warmth which seemed to heal and cleanse him. He remained comfortably absorbed in the sun's glow for a short while, his peace only disturbed by the incessant ringing of hammer on metal from the village.

The clerk waited nearby, mounted on a donkey with a blanket thrown over it's back for a saddle. An almost identical beast stood beside it. A villein offered the rein to Robert. As soon as Robert took possession of the donkey, the villein skulked off without a word.

The donkey remained passive as Robert mounted it, taking care not to dislodge the blanket as he did so. He looked over at the scribe who stared straight ahead while clutching a satchel to his chest with one hand and the rein with the other.

'Don't look so bloody scared,' Robert growled, 'hungry though I am, and as like a frightened rabbit you may seem, I'll not devour you.'

Edmund's eyes turned toward Robert, his face following stiffly a second or two later as if worried the motion might unbalance and unsaddle him. He nodded, causing his fur trimmed cap to slide down over his eyes. He lifted a hand to correct the hat, but failed to let go of the donkey's rein, tugging the bride and sending the beast turning in tight a circle. Edmund flailed and lunged forward, gripping the donkey's neck to stop himself from falling off.

'This may become more damnable than my journey here,' Robert growled, his tone then softening. 'Let us be gone before the beast gets the better of you.'

XIII

Edmund's donkey frequently stopped at the roadside to munch lush clumps of grass or to sniff the decaying remains of a rotting vegetable fallen off a cart. Other times the donkey halted just because it preferred to stand motionless, staring at nothing, perhaps lost in some musing, which despite his best efforts, Edmund could not shake the beast from.

A length of frayed rope served as a rein. Edmund flicked it against the donkey's neck and made such noises as he felt were encouraging to the movement of the creature, but which provoked little reaction beyond a flick of the ears. Attempts at equine communion descended into muttered grumblings. His cheeks burned red.

'If you can't keep up, ye shalt need catch up,' Robert shouted over his shoulder. He allowed his mount to trot at its own lazy pace along the path toward Tavistock.

'You can't leave me!' Edmund called out.

Robert halted his donkey. He turned the animal so that it stood sideways on the track. He watched the scribe kicking the flanks of his mount and tugging on the poor animal's mane; this last gesture finally stirred the ornery beast: it snapped its large teeth at the rider, shook its head, then returned to stubborn passivity.

As much as Robert would willingly leave the fool behind, he realised that the young man was almost certain to run back to Lydford and report Robert as an outlaw. Robert sighed, then nudged his mount into a walk back to the clerk.

Edmund ceased his futile actions as his ward neared. He sat up straight in the saddle, making an obvious effort to appear confident despite his predicament. He pursed his lips, seeming to brace himself for whatever sharp words Robert had for him.

Robert halted beside Edmund and held out his palm. He said nothing, trusting that his blank expression and unwavering eye contact aptly conveyed that the clerk was beneath worth of any withering remarks.

Edmund looked down at Robert's hand. His puffy lips silently worked as if he were trying to speak before his brain could decide what he wanted to say.

'Hand unto me the rope,' Robert said. He maintained eye contact for some moments after the makeshift rein was pressed into his grasp, then urged his mount onward. One tug of the rope was enough to spur the donkey into motion. Robert kept the clerk and his mount in tow. Edmund's donkey allowed itself to be led without a hint of obstinacy.

They rode in silence for a time. Robert closed his eyes, revelling in the sensation of freedom, and the taste of clean air as he sucked it into his lungs, holding it for a few moments before slowly releasing it. He listened to the birds; seldom had he paid attention to their song, but now their tune became the sweetest music. It didn't matter that he was as filthy as the basest of beggars, with grime covering his skin like an oily dye, he was free from his incarceration.

Robert's thoughts unerringly drifted back to the cell despite his relish of the outdoors. It had only been a few days imprisonment, but that noxious oblivion had turned his senses against him, making enemies of sound and scent while suppressing the sense he relied on most. He shuddered at the thought of how long it might have taken him to become like Mad Nate; he'd always thought himself strong, but the black confines of the oubliette unerringly sought its victims' vulnerabilities.

A whistled tune shook Robert from his thoughts. He recognised the opening notes of '*Little St.Hugh*'. Robert turned, glaring at the clerk who immediately desisted his song. Robert's musings wandered back to the black cell. He heard dripping - exactly as it had been in the dungeon. He looked about for the source of anything which might be causing the sound. The ground was dry; it clearly hadn't rained in days, there was no well, waterfall, or any other visible water source, but still the sound persisted. Robert forced his concentration on other sounds until the clap of iron hooves on the path began to simulate water drops hitting the cell floor. He halted his donkey and held his breath. Wind rustled leaves and birds continued their song. From his peripheral vision he saw the clerk open his mouth to speak.

Robert raised his hand for silence. He nudged his donkey into motion; straight away he thought he heard a drip. He clenched his jaw and squeezed his hands into tight fists. Was the cost of freedom his sanity?

The terrain rose into hills on either side of the track. Atop a steep mound to the west was the gibbet where violent or notorious criminals were left to rot. Crows weaved over the hilltop. Robert stopped his mount again and shielded his eyes from the sun with his palm as he looked toward the hill's summit. He could make out the L-shape of the gibbet's post and the black shape of a body dangling under the frame's arm.

Robert released Edmund's rope and kicked his mount's flanks, spurring it up the incline. The hill plateaued and was devoid of foliage, so Robert kept up his pace until he reached the gibbet.

Crows perched atop the iron cage took to flight, squawking their protest at their meal being interrupted. The cage was cylindrical and a little wider than a man. The body inside was slumped with its bald head rested against the bars. Chubby legs in soiled and tattered hose dangled through gaps between bars. One arm protruded with palm open and fingers splayed as if begging for a coin or piece of bread.

Robert studied the piggish face: A wide, stunted nose and chubby lips. Black imprints from the knots of the rope used to hang him circled the neck. The dead man had soiled himself and released his bladder - Robert wondered if it was before or after death. The body was fresh enough that the area around the groin still appeared damp.

'Poor 'ol Gilbert won't like that one bit,' Robert whispered. He sighed and patted the bar nearest Gilbert's pale head. Robert turned his donkey and headed back down the hill, taking a diagonal route when the decline increased. He found the clerk near the bottom; pleading with his mount to move as the beast nuzzled something in the grass.

'Yah! Yah!' Edmund shouted at his ignorant mount. He jolted in the saddle on noticing Robert nearing him. 'Oh, my! You frightened me. I thought you a bandit. Y-you didn't say if I should follow or stay…'

Robert passed close by Edmund and snatched the rein out of his hands. He gave the rope a sharp tug, then they were moving on again at a slow walk.

'Where did you go?' the clerk said.

'I had to visit a friend.'

'Oh.' Edmund murmured, stammered, then chose to remain silent.

They rode with only the clap of the hooves and gentle tones of nature breaking the silence until after a while of listening for it, Robert thought he could hear dripping.

'Scribe, speak to me of yourself,' Robert said, not bothering to look around at Edmund.

'What?'

'Where do you hail from? How became you a scribe? Tell me anything you think useful or of interest.'

'Useful, sir?'

'Just bloody talk.'

'Uhmm.' Edmund clicked his tongue against the roof of his mouth for a few moments before continuing. 'Well, firstly I'm not a scribe. I'm a clerk.'

'What's the difference?'

'Well, sir... the difference is considerable, but I don't suppose it will mean anything to you or be of interest.'

Robert turned. His eyebrows knitted together, and nose wrinkled. 'Are you saying I won't understand? Do you hold me stupid, boy?'

'No! No.' Edmund waved his palms quickly in front on him in exaggerated surrender. 'I-I just meant...'

'You rectified me then decline to be declaring reason for your correction. You must think me a fool.'

'No, sir. Please... I just didn't want to tire you with the detail...'

'Bah!' Robert turned back to the track ahead. 'Where are you from?'

'Launceston, Sir.'

'Stop calling me sir. I be neither knight, priest nor lord. How'd you end up a scri- clerk for the sheriff.'

'I was a third son, Sir… uhm, Master. Sorry. Third son. My father worked the land for the then sheriff… Sir William Bonville. When he took office, he had several young boys apprenticed as clerks. He saw me working the fields with my father and fancied that I appeared clever. He offered my father the chance to have me apprenticed in his service and I've worked for each sheriff since.'

'Keep talking.'

'Well, Master Robert, there isn't much more to say on the matter. Did you wish to hear something specific?'

'By God's cap! Just talk. Anything. Talk until I tell you stop, then remain silent until I tell you begin talking again.'

'Oh, well… let's see. I… hmmm. Oh, dear, Master. Now that you insist I speak, I must admit it vexing hard to think of a matter to talk on…'

'Why did the old Knight think you smart? Because of your friar-like hair and pale skin?'

'Oh, well he really didn't say. Perhaps I had an air of-'

'It's because you appear weak and sickly. He didn't want you working his land because you present as too feeble to be of use. Better to stick a quill in your hand then have you fall ill and die useless in the fields.'

Edmund didn't answer. After a few seconds Robert looked around at the clerk: he rode with his head slightly bowed. He watched Robert with the eyes of a dog afraid that it's master might strike it just because it was there.

Robert sighed. How could someone so meek survive even in a lord's hall? He thought for a few moments of something to lighten the mood.

'Well, perhaps it wasn't that you looked pathetic. Perhaps you were just one of the boys he wanted to bugger during their supposed apprenticeship, eh?' Robert smirked at his jape.

Edmund bowed his head further and averted his eyes. Robert shook his head and yanked the donkey's rope.

'This way, Clerk. We're going off the track and up over the moorland from here.'

There was little to mark the trail by which they left the road other than Robert's local knowledge, intermittent patches of flattened grass, and an occasional hoof print. He led them up over the open moorland, travelling about a mile West of his outward journey. Wind whistled loudly over the hilltops, drowning out the phantom sounds that haunted Robert. The sun was occasionally masked by clouds for minutes at a time, causing the temperature to drop almost instantly so that Robert pulled the threadbare riding cloak more tightly around him, just to then cast it back off his shoulders when the clouds cleared.

The trial become more obvious where the grass grew thicker; a narrow defile of flattened green showed the way. They took a detour around a small hamlet and its outlaying pastures and farmland; although Robert didn't know anyone who lived there by name, he was damned if he was going to let a single soul more than necessary observe him in his poor state of dress. They picked up the trial again on the far side of the hamlet as it led down toward the River Tavy.

'Tell me something more,' Robert said.

'Well, I was thinking of something to say and I remembered an interesting story-'

'You probably deal with much of the Sheriff's communications, accounts, and his writing, correct?'

'Oh, uhm. Yes. I do.'

'The sheriff had me make my sign a document a fortnight ago. Told me it was related to an agreement I understood was between us regarding the office of bailiff. Turns out it likely wasn't. I don't suppose you'd have seen it and have recollection of it?'

Robert turned to study Edmund's response, frowning and setting his jaw firm to warn the clerk against deceptions or half-truths.

The clerk blinked several times. He averted his gaze to some point on the horizon as if whatever he stared at there might better jog his memory.

'Office of bailiff? Well, I don't see every parchment or page of every book, but I have no recollection. The bailiff position went to the one you... I mean, the other fellow, did it not?'

Robert fixed Edmund with a hard stare for several seconds. He thought the lad turned a shade or two lighter, if such was possible, and he thought he saw him gulp.

'He offered it me and then give it Spiney. There's some trickery. He had the parchment with my mark upon it and I believe it to read something other than what he told me it read.'

Edmund pursed his lips and made a sucking noise as he thought. 'Master Robert, I don't want to uhm... that is to say, how could you... I mean...'

'Just spit it out, damn you!'

'Well, Sir... Master. With respect, did you not read the document before signing?'

Robert returned his focus on the route ahead. They were travelling on a gentle slope down to the Tavy. The river's gentle trickle became audible although it was obscured from view by undergrowth. The track had vanished, but the point they were heading for was a muddy clearing which marked a ford where the river was just a few inches deep during warmer months. A sparse scattering of hazel trees lined the river, with their flimsier branches swaying lightly in the breeze.

Something at the ford caught Robert's attention; he'd thought it was the motion of the leaves at first, but as he focused his sight, he could pick out something behind one the trees. Robert squinted: there was a horse standing the shade of a large hazel tree. He could see no evidence of a rider. As they came nearer to the ford, Robert could see that the horse was tethered to a low branch. It was a bay: a plough horse.

XIV

'Wait here.' Robert swung down from his saddle. He handed his mount's rein to Edmund but had to glare at the clerk before he accepted it. 'Don't drop it. I'd sooner the beast drag you than for you to let it loose.'

'What's happening? Is there something amiss?' Edmund looked about, having picked up on Robert's state of alert.

'I'm going down to the ford. Remain here lest I summon you.'

Edmund gulped and nodded.

Robert strode toward the crossing. His eyes searched the tree line for any indication of danger. The only sign of life was the podgy farm beast standing in the deepest shade of the thin tree line. The trunks and much of the ground about the horse were cast in black shadow. The animal was unperturbed by Robert's approach, standing motionless with only its tail flicking lazily. Robert's gaze passed over the branches above and along the water route; there was no sign the horse's owner. Boulders littered the terrain on the far side of the river, a few were large enough to conceal a man, but none close enough to offer any advantage of surprise to a would-be assailant. Robert gripped his sword sheath; partly to keep it from tripping him as he walked, and partly so it would be ready to draw if there was an ambush.

Water trickled between moss covered rocks and over smaller smooth stones with a sound like a gentle summer shower. It was possible to cross the ford without risk of wetting one's feet, but Robert stepped slowly and firmly onto the first rock - careful to create as little noise as possible.

The draft horse stared at Robert with placid, blank eyes. Robert approached it slowly with a palm outstretched. He patted its nose and looked the beast over; it was unsaddled, without even a blanket flung over its back. Robert made his way down the horse's flank, running his fingertips along the beast's side. He scratched the horse's rump.

'Good boy,' Robert muttered, wondering if the owner was a farmer who had tied the horse in shade so it could take water from the riverside. He looked uphill to the hamlet. The fields were being worked. It was the harvest season, and the summer festivals were mere days away. Two draft horses were visible in the fields; hitched to carts as wheat sheafs were loaded in. There was at least one stable in the hamlet, as well as several trees suitable for tethering a horse within watchful distance of the farmers.

Something disturbed a stone somewhere behind Robert. The stone clattered over a series of other water-smoothed stones before splashing into the water.

'I knew it was you,' Robert said gently without turning around. He kept one hand on the horse, the other still held his scabbard. 'I fancied I recognised your horse.'

'Ruuuaahh!' The guttural roar charged down on Robert upon a clamour of kicked pebbles and a rush of splashing steps.

Robert span to his right, sweeping his sword from the scabbard as he turned. He hoisted the blade in time to block the downward stroke of a heavy axe, catching the wooden axe handle in the nook of his sword's crossguard. The curved axe head stopped inches from Robert's brow. Robert put his left hand against the flat of his sword blade and braced against the force of the strike. He used the crossguard to push the axe aside, diverting the direction of attack enough to unbalance his assailant.

The attacker shifted stance, managing to resist the deflected momentum, he hooked the inward curve of the axe around the edge of Robert's sword, forcing Robert to hastily pull his blade free - back into a defensive guard before the axeman could use the hook to rip the sword from his grasp.

Robert side-stepped a couple paces to his right to put more distance between himself and the obstacle of the docile horse which stood oblivious to the nearby violence.

Rowan the Large snarled, baring large square teeth with equally spacious gaps between them. His face was already beaded with sweat that soaked into his pointed beard. He brought his axe back ready to swing again.

Robert lunged, poking his blade at the huge man's chest as the axe was being hoisted overhead. Rowan stumbled back out of reach, losing his balance, he dropped the axe and fell onto his buttocks into three-inch-deep water. He scrambled backwards, eyes fixed wide on his quarry, trying to put distance between them while his left hand blindly felt about for his weapon.

Robert lazily swung his blade at a dandelion, lopping off the head. He turned his attention back to Rowan as the giant's hammy fist closed around the axe shaft and the big man struggled to regain his feet.

'I'm in nary a haste to slay you, you pig,' Robert said, adopting a mid-guard stance from which he could quickly bring his sword to defend from high or low attack. 'I've a fancy to make you suffer a tad.'

Rowan yelled and swung the axe in an arc at Robert's mid-section. Robert moved into a rear-guard stance; the sweeping backstep was enough to put a few inches distance between himself and the thirsty axe head without even having to employ his sword. He allowed himself a mocking wink at his assailant.

Rowan frothed at the mouth like a berserk from old legends, wielding his weapon in a clumsy reverse stroke. Robert took another wide step back, choosing to avoid the attack altogether rather than parry so to better wear the opponent's strength and resolve.

'Perchance you're in need of a longer axe,' Robert said, smiling.

Rowan cried out in rage. His nostrils flared; mouth and bloodshot eyes were wide, and knuckles whitened by the tense grip on his weapon. He hefted the axe in an overhead arc and rushed the two steps needed to close the distance with Robert. The strike, predictably, aimed downward between Robert's eyes.

Robert blocked the strike and sidestepped into the attack, ramming his shoulder into Rowan while simultaneously hooking the axe blade with his crossguard, ripping the weapon from Rowan's grip as the big man stumbled. The axe clanged against pebbles, splashing up a small spray of tiny granite stones and water. Robert flicked his sword blade around to rest on Rowan's shoulder.

'Cease. That's it. Stop,' Robert said. 'I'll cut yer damned neck should you as much as cast your gaze on that axe.'

Rowan dropped to his knees in the riverbed. Panting, he looked up at Robert and bared his teeth defiantly despite his submission.

Robert touched the edge of his blade against his opponent's neck. He took a moment to catch his breath. The fight had been brief; just a few seconds, but the excitement and effort of the struggle left him with starving lungs, a thundering pulse, and shaking hands.

'Who set you upon this foul deed, bastard?' Robert seethed, saying the last word through clenched teeth. 'I should by rights slay you now, alas you be of more use to me alive.'

Rowan didn't reply. His pupils were wide against his reddened sclera. His cheeks and nose were flushed as if he'd been drinking. His shoulders heaved. His breath came as a violent snort; each exhalation spraying spittle which collected in a foamy mass on his black beard. He glared his hatred at Robert.

'You bastard,' Robert said. He pressed the sword against Rowan's neck so that the villein would feel the grain of the sharp edge threatening further violence. 'That Spiney bastard compelled you to wait upon me, did he not? Say it. Then say it again afore witnesses and I'll let you live yet.'

Rowan roared. He surged from the riverbed, lunging with blackened fingernails at Robert's neck. Robert's trembling hand fumbled and lost grip on his sword. Rowan was inside his defence before Robert could do anything about it.

Wet, clammy hands slapped against Robert's face and neck. He was unable to resist the force and impetus of the huge man's bodyweight. He fell. Sharp stones bit into his back. He glimpsed azure sky, quickly replaced with Rowan's snarling face. The breath was pounded out of him as the brute slammed onto Robert's chest. Fingernails dug into Robert's cheek and neck. Cold water sloshed into his ears and over his face. Rowan's crazed onslaught found form and purpose; fingertips pressed into Robert's throat.

Devoid of breath, Robert gasped helplessly for air. The grip was such on his throat that he feared his attacker might rip his oesophagus out with his bare hands. He tore at his assailant's shirt. His hand found Rowan's face but all he could do was to rake his fingertips over the man's eyes and nose without finding any purchase. He was going to die.

Coloured dots flashed in Robert's vision. He couldn't focus. His throat made a pathetic, dry rasp, quickly drowned out by a high-pitched whine of fury which could have only been Rowan's. Robert's right hand slapped the water, grasping at wet stones while his left hand slapped pathetically against Rowan's shoulder. He felt a palm-sized stone come into his grasp; his fingers tightened around it and arced it toward Rowan's head. The rock struck with a dull thud: still fingers tore at his throat. He slammed the blunt rock into his opponent again. Then again. On the fourth strike the fingers around Robert's neck loosened. Robert sucked in air. He dropped the stone and instinctively cradled his neck. He couldn't swallow enough air to satisfy his starved lungs.

The brute still sat astride his chest, holding the left side of his head while rivulets of blood seeped between his fingers. The big man moaned and winced.

Robert knew his enemy would recover in moments, sitting astride Robert's chest, the giant villein still held advantage. Robert fished around for his lost rock. He found another smaller but sharper stone and stabbed it at Rowan's head.

Rowan made a low, pained cry as the stone dug into his temple. Robert stabbed again, and again. His vision was blurred; water splashed into his eyes with each attack. All his strikes hit, but the attacks were wild; sometimes striking bone or skull and other times the resistance felt more fleshy. Each successive strike was a fraction weaker than the preceding one. He glimpsed Rowan still holding his head. Again, and again Robert jabbed with the stone until he felt his attacker's weight shift to one side. He pushed the giant in the direction his weight tilted, and the man collapsed face first into the water.

Robert kicked and pushed his way free from Rowan's body, only to then thrust himself upon the fallen giant as he lay face down in the water. He hoisted the stone above him with both hands and drove it down repeatedly onto the back of Rowan's head, dashing the back of his skull. Rowan's black hair was matted with blood, dying the surrounding water dark red, before filtering away into fading maroon tendrils with the current.

Robert kept stabbing. He felt skull fragments dig into his fingers and became aware of his own screaming rage. He looked at the jagged stone in his hands; it was almost the shape of a spearhead, and thick with sticky blood and hair. His fingers were likewise stained. He dropped the stone into the water and sat back, gasping for breath.

It was a minute or so before Robert recovered all his senses. Every nerve quaked; he hadn't felt that way since he was in France twenty years before. He looked at Rowan the Large; unmoving except where the current caused one of his hands to gently wave in the stream. Robert rolled him over onto his back. Rowan's jaw hung slack and his eyes were cocked and without focus.

'Bastard,' Robert spat. The villein would take whatever secrets he had about the Spiney affair to hell with him. 'Bastard!' he snarled. He stood on shaky legs and looked about for his sword, finding it in the riverbed.

A protesting cry from one of the donkeys caught Robert's attention. In the excitement of the fight he'd had forgotten the clerk. Edmund was trying to encourage his animal to movement by striking its ears and kicking his heels into its ribs. The beast walked in a circle, honking. Edmund had released Robert's donkey which stood immobile, passively observing the clerk's efforts.

Robert ran back up the hill, sword in hand, waving at the clerk. 'Where do you think you're going? Stop you fool!'

The clerk kicked harder at the donkey and made a frightened yelp as Robert drew near.

'Bloody desist! You saddle-goosed wandought!' Robert snapped, coming to a stop short of donkey and rider. He dug the point of the sword into the ground, resting on the hilt. 'What are you trying to do?'

'You... you slew that man! I saw it!' Edmund stopped kicking the donkey but still tugged at the rope, which only succeeded in making the donkey bite at him again.

'Verily, that be all you were seeing?' Robert seethed. 'did you not see the bastard meant to kill me with his axe? Like as not he'd have killed your own self afterwards as a witness. Will you stop bothering that bloody animal!'

Robert snatched the rope from Edmund's grip and spent a few moments calming the donkey. Edmund sat with his back straight as a rod and his lips pinched together as he gripped the donkey's mane.

'It were self-defence,' Robert said. He rubbed the donkey's nose then stepped back. He plucked his sword from the ground, wiping the tip between finger and thumb before sliding it back into its sheath. 'Do not fear that I intend thee harm, Scribe. I slew that bastard in self-defence: you know as much, yes?'

'If you say so.' Edmund didn't move a muscle. He watched Robert like a rabbit frozen with fright.

'What ye mean: if I says so? The bastard were hiding in ambush! Are you bewitched, man?'

The clerk blinked but didn't respond.

Robert sighed and tried to adopt a nonchalant countenance. 'Remember to me your name, Clerk? Nay, it doesn't matter; I shall cause no harm, I swear it. I beseech you, tell me how you beheld that fight.'

'Edmund.'

'What?'

'You asked reminder of my name: it is Edmund. And to answer your other question: I saw a horse tied to a tree and I saw you go down and make as if to steal it. I saw its presumed owner attack you with an axe and then you slew him with... what, a knife or your hands? I know not. I was fervent in my attempt at flight by that time.'

Robert wiggled his index finger in the air. 'There be a few things you don't know. That... man, he was one of Spiney's men. A real bastard. He was among my captors who brought me unto Lydford - and he were the last pleasant of the lot. I recognised his horse - that's why I went alone and with caution. It was tied there as a distraction so he could ambush me.'

Edmund winced and pursed his lips. After a moment's thought he nodded and relaxed his shoulders a little. 'I suppose it would explain why the horse owner was concealed behind a tree with an axe.'

'Yes, just so!' Robert grinned and jabbed his finger at the clerk. 'Might yet be the old sheriff was right: you can think better than the basest of muck pilers!'

Edmund's mouth twisted like he'd swallowed something that tasted awful.

Robert walked over to his donkey and picked up the rein.

'What are we to do about the... corpse?' Edmund called out.

'I'll go back and search it in a moment, but I don't think there's anything on his person unless there be a small purse or pouch secreted someplace. Rowan the Large *was* a muck piler, and not like to have a slither of a coin to his name.'

'No!' Edmund blurted, his voice high pitched and worried. 'I didn't mean you should rob his earthly remains. I meant... we can't leave him there. We should notify the hamlet to send for the constable...'

'The corpse stays. We go. You've got ink and quill - make up a sign that reads *robber* and we'll tie it about it his neck. If I can find a length of rope, we'll hang him from his hiding place.'

Robert led his donkey down to the ford, leaving the clerk's protesting stuttering behind. He looped the beast's rein around a low branch and walked to Rowan's body. He kicked the corpse with his good shoe and decided was little point in searching it; the white shirt was soaked through to the skin, making it clear there was nothing hidden underneath or tied about the neck. He'd no wish to rifle Rowan's hose: if there was anything hidden there it could remain on the body.

Robert searched among nearby trees and found a folded blanket and a flask laying in the long grass. He picked up the flask and shook it; there was a small measure of liquid. He unstopped the vessel and sniffed it: water. He upended the contents down his throat. The mouthful of liquid was warm and bitter, but welcome all the same. He tossed the empty flask into the stream.

Edmund had managed to encourage his donkey down to the river but failed to make the beast stop. It moved to the water's edge, forcing Edmund to flail at low hanging branches that snagged his clothing. The donkey lowered its head and drank as its rider sputtered from a face full of twigs.

'I must protest, Master Robert!' Edmund cried out, his normally pale features were flushed. 'We shall be in grievous strife with the law should we fail to raise the hue and cry. We'll be considered murderers. We could be hanged!'

'Uh-huh.' Robert scratched his beard and mounted his donkey. 'Let's ride on. Suppose you needs me to lead your beast.'

'Master Robert, did you listen to anything I said? We could be strung up as murders.' Edmund shook his head, causing the ends of his hair to flick into his eyes.

'I've nary an idea what you're panicked about. I'm the one what slew the bastard. Scribe that notice if you like but be quick about it.'

'No!' The violence of Edmund's shout seemed to surprise and frighten himself; he wobbled in his saddle and his eyes lolled about until he steadied himself by grabbing the donkey's mane. 'I shall do nothing of the sort: I'd be aligning myself with your mischief if I did. I'm going to the hamlet to speak to the head man of the tithing and report this appropriately. You can cut me down if you want, but that's what I'm doing.'

Robert watched the young man with his flushed face catch his breath. Robert shrugged when it became apparent that there was nothing else forthcoming, but when opened his mouth to speak, Edmund cut him off.

'And I'll walk to the hamlet. This donkey is hell sent!' Edmund kicked his leg over the creature's back and slid down from the saddle. He marched up the hill, swinging his arms with exaggerated determination.

Robert watched him go. He smirked to himself, scratched his beard and rode to Edmund's donkey, picking up its rope.

XV

Robert and Edmund travelled a circuitous route around Sampford Spiney, approaching Woodtown from the West, keeping the bracken speckled hills between them and the sight of the buildings and farmland of the Spiney family hamlet. Edmund had become competent enough in his handling of the donkey to lead the stubborn beast himself. Robert insisted they travel in single file, mumbling that in places the track wasn't wide enough for two.

Robert was irritated at Edmund for the delay at the hamlet where he'd fought Rowan the Large. The head of the tithing had initially wanted Robert held and taken back to Lydford for murder but became more pliable to reason when Robert's hand when to sword hilt. The couple of coins Robert prised from Edmund had the head man accepting the claim of self-defence as truth despite the deplorable condition of Rowan's skull. On the promise of a few more shillings later, the men of the tithing agreed to hang Rowan's body from a tree as warning to other would-be robbers along the well-known shortcut between Lydford and Sampford Spiney. Handshakes followed by a clash of foaming tankards sealed the bargain and they left the hamlet as friendly acquaintances, ignoring Edmund's protests that the coroner should be summoned. The clerk had to satisfy himself with writing a statement of the events around Rowan's death which the head of the tithing promised to hand over to the sheriff.

'Should we not stop at the church to give thanks for our safe travel?' Edmund said, observing the pointed crenelations of the church tower peaking over the nearest grassy rise.

'No.'

'Oh, then we'll pray when we arrive at your abode?'

'You do that.'

Robert sensed the clerk bristling. It was, he supposed, impossible for someone who lived a cloistered life of learning to escape the most stringent of religious leanings.

'My wife has set a shrine in one of our outbuildings. She prefers to call it her chapel. Even had the sexton from the church yonder to bless it. You may pray there.'

'Gratitude,' Edmund said, his voice raising in relieved merriment. 'May I ask what you intend to do once we arrive?'

Robert grunted.

'My apologies. I don't wish to pry. I meant regarding your plans to show your innocence; we have but a week. We've used the best part of the day in coming here and our only produce thus far is a second slaying.'

'I'll do nought today. I shall wash, eat a good meal, burn these rags, drink beer, and then bed my wife. Tomorrow we'll begin.'

They skirted along edge of the woods just west of Woodtown. Robert pulled his cloak over his shoulder as the temperature dropped under the shade of the trees. Thick undergrowth made the woodland difficult to penetrate on horseback except by the game trails leading into the Royal Forest of Dartmoor which were largely followed only by poachers. Rushing water from the River Walkham could be heard. Edmund had to encourage his donkey into motion when the unruly creature found interesting things to sniff and nibble among the natural debris of the woodland floor.

'So, you've a mind that I murdered Spiney, eh?' Robert said, as the track into Woodtown came into view.

'What? Forsooth no. I mean… I am impartial, sir. I observe and record only, not judge.'

'Hmm. Be well you remember that.'

'Verily did I not forget it.'

Edmund urged his donkey forward so that he rode alongside Robert. He stared at the side of Robert's head until Robert finally flicked an irritated glance at him. Edmund's expression was emotionless, but his eyes keenly observed Robert as if trying to discern something about him.

'What?' Robert snapped.

'Why do you assume that I believe you guilty? Do you think I will prejudice your investigations?'

'Prejudice? I know not, but I know you think me guilty.'

'Because you killed the other man?'

'Aye, in part. Also, because you be afraid of me; that's not so rare in itself, but you said something about me showing my innocence.'

'I don't understand.' Edmund shook his head.

'You said *show* my innocence. Not prove it. If you thought me truly innocent, you'd have said prove. Showing my innocence is akin to some trick to create the pretence of innocence.'

Edmund frowned for a moment and then nodded.

'Verily, you may speak true. I apologise for my assumption. I will be more... neutral.'

They joined the trail into the hamlet. John Sherman's hut was the first to come into view, then the sheep pens, stable, and the spinners' cottages, and the cabbage and wheat strips behind them.

'I would ask a favour of you, Clerk,' Robert said.

'Yes?' Edmund said when it became clear Robert was awaiting some response before he would continue.

'If you have fellowship with the clerks and scribes in Sir John's service, I would ask that you write, asking to confirm the content of the paper I signed.'

'I can do that,' Edmund said with a nod.

'My thanks. There were two. One was burnt, but I believe the other remains, and I think the content differs from the one which was read unto me. Ensure you stress confidentiality. I think the answer you receive may be the key to all of this. I shall have a reliable man courier the letter.'

Edmund cocked his head to one side, frowning in thought. He straightened himself when he realised Robert was watching him.

'Apologies, Master Robert. Do you believe Sir John is somehow behind all of this? I can't say I see how it would benefit him.'

'He's up to something. The timing of the slaying is curious. I don't want to say more now, but it's either him or Henry Spiney; or perchance the both of them together.'

Edmund whistled and shook his head. 'Henry? Patricide? It's a terrible sin.'

'Even so, it happens or there wouldn't be a word for it.'

'Master Robert, if you believe Sir John conspires against you, why would you trust me, his servant? Twas the Sheriff that appointed me to this task.'

'Aye,' Robert sniffed. 'I been thinking on it - that be why I'd not asked you afore to send the letter. I recall your visage when the Sheriff told you accompany me; twas plain on your face that there was no prior plotting that you were involved in. Aside; you serve the post of sheriff, not Sir John himself. Come Christmas there be a new Sheriff.'

'I see.' Edmund nodded thoughtfully. 'You speak truly. I've no loyalty to Sir John beyond my duty. He doesn't even know my name.'

'Bah!' Robert snorted. 'You're a scribe. You've no need of a name.'

'Clerk,' Edmund mumbled.

The pair rode at a lazy pace along the track. They passed the shearer's cottage; the door was closed and the sheep in the pen unattended. One of the spinners' husbands stood up from toiling the fields and covered his brow to watch the approaching riders. Chickens skittered about the path.

The riders dismounted outside the stable. A stench of manure permeated the air. A carthorse and a riding horse occupied separate stalls with sodden straw on the ground; two other stalls were empty. Robert guided both donkeys into pens and gathered up hay that was stacked at the far side of the barn to distribute to the four animals.

'Water the horses and donkeys, will you? I'm going to find my wife. Come into the house when you're finished.'

Edmund seemed about to protest at being designated menial work but then nodded and turned to face his task with slumped shoulders.

Robert marched toward his house. After a few paces the flailing sole of his shoe caught on the ground; he stumbled a couple of steps before he could right himself. He muttered a curse, then waved a greeting at Muriel as she emerged from her home with an armful of yarn which she dropped, running back inside at the sight of her dishevelled master.

Robert turned the iron ring on the longhouse door and thumped the door open with the base of his fist. He stepped inside and glanced left and right, not seeing any sign of occupancy.

'Wife! I return!'

A muffled voice came from the loft. A moment later a head popped through the interior window. Alice's hair was unkempt and her neck bare. She blinked twice and rubbed a palm over her eyes.

'Husband? Is it truly you?'

'Aye.' Robert slid the tattered shoe off his left foot and tossed it into the cold ashes of the firepit.

Alice's head disappeared back through the window. Floorboards creaked.

'Wait up there, wife!' Robert bellowed. 'I shall be up directly.' He ripped the shoe off his right foot.

Alice reappeared at the window. The weariness in her expression was replaced with sharp focus and determination. 'No, you won't, Husband dear. Look at the state of you. I will not abide you in the bedchamber in such a state. Wait there and move not a step. I will dress and be down - then we'll have you bathed.'

Alice moved around the loft, muttering to herself as she dressed. Robert dropped the cloak from his shoulders and pulled the shirt over his head, discarding it into the firepit. Dirt and dried sweat coated his torso. His chest hair stuck flat to the skin. He found his fingernails blackened; the toenails likewise: he felt a fool to appear before his wife in such a state.

Alice's footfalls rushed down the stairs. She ran barefoot into the chamber, wearing a simple woollen dress and her hair tied up in a bun from which several strands were escaping. She flung her arms around Robert's neck and kissed him roughly on the nose and then again on each cheek. She pulled back from him, holding his arms tight as she examined him.

'Oh, my dear husband! What in the name of the Lord did they do to you?'

'That'd be a long tale, wife. I know you need not ask, but I say for the sake of assured honesty between man and wife: I laid not a hand on that bastard Spiney, as God is my witness!'

Alice frowned and hurriedly crossed herself. 'Husband, you need not swear such oaths to me. I never for a moment believed you capable of harming poor William.'

'Regardless, I wanted to speak it. Verily, I thought you worried halfway to death. You may worry no longer.'

Alice nodded vigorously. 'I have barely slept at night. That is why you find me abed at this uncommon hour - so I might catch a few moments sleep between my hours of tears for a husband I feared lost to me.'

Alice put her head against Robert's chest. Her arms encircled and squeezed him. She released a long sigh and leaned her slight frame against him. Robert run his fingertips up and down the back of her dress and made a shushing sound to soothe her.

'I should make myself so perilously absent more often to find you so welcoming on my return.'

Robert chuckled, but Alice looked up at him with scorn and pinched his chin between her thumb and forefinger.

'Don't you dare, Husband, or you might come home to find me worried fully to death.'

Alice made to move away but Robert pulled her back into his embrace. He held her for a time, feeling her gentle breath on his skin. He kissed her forehead and they parted.

'Now, we will bathe you, Husband. Oh… I have some of your filth upon me. It is as well that it is only simple dress. Go and fetch a barrel outside. I will have the spinners fetch water and I'll put the largest pots to boil so you might enjoy a warm bath.'

Robert nodded and turned as the door opened. Edmund stopped on the threshold, jolting at the sight Robert standing shirtless before him. Edmund turned his head aside and coughed into his fist. Alice made a startled noise.

'Ah, panic not dear. This is just a clerk… or scribe, I forget which, whom I am under the charge of. What's your name again, lad?'

'Edmund. Edmund Chance.' He bowed to the waist.

'A pleasure,' Alice said, her tone was sharp enough that Robert looked around at her. 'A clerk you say? How joyous. You can tell me all about it later. Perhaps you wouldn't mind helping fetch water for the bath my husband so desperately needs. I will need to make myself more decently presentable since we apparently have a guest.' She jostled both the men out of the house with one hand while fussing with her hair with the other.

The door was closed upon the men. Robert turned to Edmund and shrugged. 'She's usually more welcoming. Her one sin is pride - you've caught her in a commoner's dress.' He spoke in a quiet voice, casting a guarded look at the closed door, then continued more loudly, 'You go fetch water from the well. I'll bring a barrel.'

**

The water in the barrel was warm and felt good against Robert's skin. The bath soothed his ravaged feet and eased aches from tired joints. He held his nose and submerged his head. His knees and back were pressed against rough wood, but he welcomed the sensation of the water comforting and cleansing him. He resurfaced, feeling instantly rejuvenated.

'Oh, look what you've done!' Alice scolded.

Water was flowing over the edges of the barrel. Robert raised himself, resting his arms on the barrel rim. Water soaked into the ground, saturating the rushes and turning the compressed dirt into wet mud. Robert squeezed water from the tip of his beard and swept back hair which had stuck to his forehead.

'Forgive me wife. I forget myself.'

'Indeed you do, Husband, but I will forgive you on consideration of the perils and horrors you have surely suffered.'

Alice submerged a square of cloth into the water and pressed it against Robert's cheek, rubbing away grime. She washed his whole face, neck, chest and then his back. Bathwater already cloudy when he had entered it quickly turned grey.

Robert closed his eyes, resting his forehead on his wrists upon the rim of the barrel as his wife cleaned his back. He'd briefly outlined his misfortunes while the bath was prepared. Alice had listened, her hand covering her mouth through much of it. He spared the details of the squalor of the cell and made no mention of Gilbert and his fate, nor Mad Nate.

'I had given thought that my brother might secure my release. Did he remain in Plympton?' Robert yawned, the exertions and stresses of recent days soaked away into the dirty water. He felt he might sleep for a fortnight if he could.

'I sent for him as soon as I heard you were taken by Henry Spiney. On his return, Eustace went straight to Henry to plead reason, but Henry wouldn't receive him.'

'Hmm, not surprised. They'll hold this against our family for generations unless the true culprit is caught.'

'Yes, dear.' Alice's rolled up the sleeves of her linen undershirt so she could submerge her arms and scrub Robert's lower back. 'Eustace travelled to Lyford, but they turned him away saying he'd have to wait until the sheriff and the bailiff could decide what to do with you. He left Guy in lodgings there to await news; did you not see him upon your release?'

Robert raised his head, turning about in the barrel to face his wife. 'I did not. I suppose my release was... sudden. I was going to have Guy courier a note for me. We will have to send someone back to Lyford to fetch him.'

Alice ran her fingers through Robert's scalp, picking out detritus and sculpting his wet hair to her taste. 'I'm sure he'd have news of your release and return on the morrow.'

'Aye.' Robert rested his head on Alice's shoulder as she toyed with his hair. 'So where is my useless brother? Is he returned to Plympton or retired to some Tavistock tavern to sing bawdy songs and slap wenches' buttocks?'

Alice tapped Robert's temple with her fingertips. 'Don't be speak so ill of your kin. Your brother is not a tavern wastrel.'

Robert looked up at Alice with one eye. 'Yes, he is, and well you know it.'

'If you must know he has been managing your estate. He is about here someplace. I'm sure he will come inside to welcome you home as soon as he knows you're returned: I daresay word of your homecoming has spread.'

'Hmmm,' Robert imagined of a mob from Sampford Spiney pounding at the door and threatening to fire the place. He glanced at his sword propped against the wall. 'Managing the estate, you say? Mismanaging more like. Have you seen the condition of the stable? And what of the sheep? Who is looking after them?'

'Shhh,' Alice laid her lips gently on Robert's forehead. 'Don't worry yourself about such things. John Sherman has been taking full care of the sheep.'

'What?' Robert stood so quickly that water again sloshed down the sides of the barrel.

Alice recoiled as water soaked the hem of her woollen dress. She threw up her hands and glared at her husband.

'Robert!'

'That bastard is still on my land?'

'Yes, of course! He lives here. He's been good help. He has taken responsibility for taking full care of the sheep. He's even fed and watered the horses.'

Robert slid one leg over the side of the barrel, then the other. Mud and rushes stuck to the bottom of his feet. He strode to his sword and pulled it free of the sheath which he tossed to the ground. 'I'll be getting him off my land this very instant.'

'Robert, you're naked!' Alice blocked the door with her body, placing her hands on each side of the doorframe.

'Move aside!'

'I shall not! What will you do? Slay him or just beat him out of Woodtown? They'll say you're crazy or devil possessed. Think about your predicament, Robert.'

Robert ground his teeth, averting his eyes from his wife's pleading face. He threw the sword down on top of the discarded scabbard.

'I thought the bastard betrayer had gone over to Spiney. He probably thought me already dancing at the end of a rope so he might stride around my estate as if nothing were amiss.'

'You may recall, dear husband, that all members of a tithing are required to bring to justice any other member accused of a crime. If John didn't join Henry in taking you to Lyford it may have been that the whole tithing would be fined.'

Robert sighed and put his hands on his hips. He nodded and forced a meek smile at his wife. 'You speak true, but John Sherman went beyond his duty. It was a persecution. But you're right: I can't confront him at this time.'

Alice moved to her husband, taking his hands in hers. 'If you want rid of him, evict him legally, or increase the rent on the property so he cannot pay it.'

Robert nodded and kissed the tip of Alice's nose. 'You're right, as always. Anyways, I need speak to him. He was the first one hereabouts to hear the hue and cry. Might be he knows something more.'

Alice squeezed his fingers. 'Be peaceful about it, dear husband.'

'Always. Come, it's nearing dusk. Let's prepare bedding by the fireplace for our guest. We'll all sup together then I'll take you up to our bed and show you truly that your husband be returned.'

Alice pinched a knuckle full of his chest hairs, giving them a small tug accompanied with a reproachful pout.

'Husband, your... clerk is our guest. We should share the bed as is common courtesy.' She put a finger to Robert's lips, stopping the protest on his tongue. 'We have not the strength for it, Husband. I haven't slept well in days and I can see you haven't. We will have time aplenty for being man and wife once good Edmund has returned to Lyford.'

Robert sighed, deflated. 'Ah, and my brother too. Four in a bed made for two!' Thought of sleep made him yawn again; he was more tired than hungry. He smiled at Alice: she always knew what was right. He kissed her again on the forehead.

Alice smiled faintly. 'What will you do first in this... inquisition into the death of William Spiney?'

'Well, best way I can see is that tomorrow morn I shall go over to the Spiney estate and see for myself the truth of it all.'

XVI

Robert rose at daybreak and set out early to inspect his estate. He found that the spinners had been more occupied with managing their strips of land than working his wool; the output had been little more than half of what he'd expect over the days of his departure.

The woodpile outside the house was depleted sufficiently that Robert had to spend time felling two trees on the edge of the estate, then debranching them ready to be sawn into logs. The task aggravated his spine; still stiff and aching from confinement. He'd been pleased that the clerk had insisted on sleeping by the fireplace, but annoyed that Eustace hadn't followed the example. Robert resolved to play on his discomfort to oust his brother and any other would be bed-guests over the coming days.

The sun had been up for more than three hours by the time Eustace emerged into daylight. He stood in the doorway with his cap tilted to one side, doublet open, and shirt unlaced. He stretched and yawned with a mug of ale in hand.

Robert struggled with an urge to march over to his brother and drag him to the nearest horse trough for a prolonged dunking. He leant on the wood axe he had been using and watched his brother rub his eyes, belch, and take a step before noticing Robert, whereupon he jolted, spilling some beer.

'Oh, morning Brother,' Eustace smiled, raising his flagon in salute. 'I welcomed you back last night, but I think you were asleep when I came up. It wasn't even sundown. I am told you suffered an arduous time.'

Robert nodded. 'Most arduous, Brother. At least I had you to manage the estate in my absence.'

'Ah, yes.' Eustace took a sip of beer, wrinkled his nose, and emptied the remainder on the ground. 'Spoiled. Last nights' beer. I was just going to discharge my bowels. We'll talk shortly, yes?'

Robert nodded, his eyes following Eustace's unsteady walk to the trench that Robert and one of the spinner's husbands had recently dug for the latrines. Robert sighed, shook his head, and walked to the house, resting the axe beside to the door. He went inside where he found Alice stirring a pot over the fire pit while the clerk sat on a stool brought in from the solar. They were in conversation but stopped as he entered.

'Husband, good morn,' Alice dropped the ladle into the pot and stood to embrace him.

Alice wore her simple dress and a linen coif, indicating that she intended to spend the day labouring in and about the home; she would wear a circlet or headdress if she were likely to encounter anyone outside the home other than the spinners. Robert wondered why she didn't dress up for the guest, reflecting that perhaps she decided to appear humble since their visitor was a pious man of no particular means.

'I saw you out working,' Alice said. 'I stopped Edmund from going out to disturb you. I thought you might wish some time for yourself to reflect or pray as you toiled.'

'Thank you, wife,' Robert grunted. 'I was managing such work as my brother should've seen to these past days.'

'Oh, are you still singing that tune?' Alice said with a sigh. 'He has been vigorously employed I assure you. He's not used to managing Woodtown. You know he's much more comfortable in Plympton.'

'I've left the axe outside. When he returns from his fouling you can tell him I expect him to saw and chop those trunks I've felled. The saw is in the stable. One of the spinner's husbands will help him with it.'

Alice stepped back and regarded him with narrowed eyes. 'Don't be mean. You know Eustace is not a such a man as is suited to rough labours. Where are you going, Husband? Do you still intend to go to Sampford?'

'Eustace is strong enough. He can labour when it suits him - rare as it is. And aye, I intend to go to Sampford Spiney directly.' Robert beckoned Edmund. 'We'll go now, Clerk.'

Robert went to his chest and retrieved a blue doublet with the sleeves removed which he put over his shirt. He tied his sword belt around his waist and turned toward the door.

Alice stopped him, placing both hands on his chest.

'Husband, perhaps a dagger is enough for protection. The sword speaks of violence.'

'I always wear the sword. If I intended violence, I'd take the bardiche. Folk are used to seeing me sword armed. If I go without it'll strike some as peculiar.'

Alice thought for a moment and then nodded.

'Have they put that bastard Spiney in the ground yet?' Robert snarled his deceased foe's name.

'Husband! On the morrow. I... wished to ask of you if we, or at least I, should attend his service.'

'We should not. Neither you nor I. John Sherman can represent Woodtown. They can bury those bastards together for all I care.'

Alice glowered at him as she crossed herself and muttered something under her breath.

'Master Robert,' Edmund said, hovering behind Alice. 'I've made the letter you asked for. You said you had a man to bring it before the sheriff?' Edmund held up a roll of parchment with a string tied around it.

'Has Guy returned?' Robert said without acknowledging the clerk.

Alice shook her head. 'He must be riding this morn. I expect we'll see him before vespers.'

Robert stepped past Alice and snatched the parchment from Edmund's fingers. He unrolled it and looked over it, squinting at the lettering before passing it to his wife.

'Is there a family seal we might apply?' Edmund said, his eyes wandered the floor.

'String will suffice,' Robert snapped.

Alice rolled the parchment and wound the string back around it. She offered it back to Robert with a nod.

'Give it to that brother of mine, dear,' Robert said. 'Tell him ride to the sheriff's estate with it and await the response. He's not to open the response on pain of... pain. I'll deal with the wood myself later.' He pecked his wife on the cheek and marched outside with Edmund rushing after him.

'Don't do anything rash!' Alice called from the threshold.

Robert waved farewell without looking around. He walked the path toward Sampford Spiney, paying no heed to the spinners' husbands who paused their field toil to stare at him as he walked by.

'Will we not ride, Sir?' Edmund said, his breathing already beginning to sound laboured as his thin legs hastened to keep pace with Robert's purposeful strides.

'I can't abide watching you try to master that donkey. Aside from which, I'm not certain Spiney will tolerate us tying our mounts to his posts.'

'Do you think there will be trouble?'

'If I'm lucky.'

***

The stablemaster and one of the household servants stood behind the gate outside the manor at Sampford Spiney. The servant, a cook Robert fancied by the stained apron, held the gate shut with both hands. The stablemaster stood beside him, wearing a doublet of red and white; the colours favoured by the Spiney family which they wore in pretence of the coat of arms which they aspired to be ordained to bare.

'I'm here on a matter of law,' Robert told the two men for the second time. They continued to glare back at him.

The steward rushed out of the manor house carrying a wooden staff. He stopped behind the gate and thumped the butt of the staff into the dirt.

'You've the very nerve of the devil to show yourself here, Robert Wood,' the Steward growled.

Robert looked over his shoulder at Edmund. 'Best you tells him. And tell him well or we'll be in straits to proceed.'

Edmund blinked. His jaw stammered. He sputtered, then finally ceased trying to form words as Henry Spiney emerged from the manor house closely followed by his mother.

Henry was wide-eyed. His pupils flicked between the two intruders. A disgusted sneer creased his face. He carried a long dagger in one fist and a metal buckler in the other. He wore a red and white doublet which Robert imagined belonged to his father.

Mathilde, in mourning, wore a veil secured around her head by a black cloth circlet.

'Surprised to see me alive, little Spiney?' Robert said, tucking his thumbs into his belt.

Henry made to push past his servants, but Mathilde shouted at them to keep the gate secured. The cook held the gate firm even as Henry tried to push him aside. The steward put his hand on his master's shoulder and murmured soothing words into his ear. Henry's gaze dropped to Robert's sword. He ceased struggling with the flustered cook over mastery of the gate.

'Honestly, Spineys,' Robert said, smiling broadly, 'if I desired violence, a gate would deter me not, so don't worry yourselves over the security of that little sty you hide behind.'

Henry pointed his dagger at Robert. 'Why are you returned? You should be awaiting the Royal Court's justice. My father is not yet in the ground and I shall not stand to have you here desecrating his memory, you vile murderer.'

Robert sniffed and turned to Edmund. 'Scribe, tell 'em.'

'Uh, I... uhm, my Lord and Lady,' Edmund bowed his head as he spoke each title. 'I... I'm in the service of Sir John Herle, Sheriff of Devonshire. I'm tasked to assist Master Robert with an... inquisition? Yes, inquisition into the murder of your good husband and father, God rest his soul.'

'What is he jabbering about?' Henry snapped.

'Get to the point, Clerk,' Robert said out the corner of his mouth.

'Forgive me, Sir, M'Lady.' Edmund bowed again. 'I bear legal papers with the Sheriff's seal...' Edmund unfastened his satchel and produced a cream parchment with a red wax seal affixed to the bottom. He held it aloft with a trembling hand. 'Master Robert has licence to conduct such enquiries as he sees fit within the confines of the law until seven days past the dating of this document - that being of yesterday's date.'

Edmund walked to the gate, offering the document for inspection.

Henry slipped his dagger into his belt and snatched the paper, casting his eyes over it as his retainer and the steward read it over his shoulders. Their frowning heads moved from left to right as they read the content.

'Whatever does this mean?' Henry said, tossing the parchment toward Edmund who scrambled to catch it as it drifted down toward the dirt.

'It means,' Robert said, 'that you can't stop me from entering your land, questioning your family, staff and even yourself if I see fit, which I warn you: I do. I also wish to observe the corpse.'

Mathilde gasped and shook her head vigorously. The retainer took her arm and whispered in her ear.

'The corpse?' Henry sputtered. 'You mean my father! No, you shall not desecrate his holy peace with your presence. We all know who slew him. We should've hanged you here. I shall protest strongly that you have been permitted to walk as if free instead of hanged in the first instance at Lydford.'

Robert closed his eyes and nodded as Henry spoke, making a show of yawning when the young man finished speaking. 'Well, like it or nay: you can't stop me.'

'I can too!' Henry snapped. 'What punishment do you think I will endure for banishing you from my lands? Imprisonment? Hanging? Not so! They'll fine me a few shillings, that's all. And by God, I'll pay such a fine a hundred times over before allowing you onto my land.'

Robert cast a sharp look at Edmund, who gave a slight shrug. Robert hadn't considered such a refusal once the correct provenance had been shown, but he knew Henry was right: there would be only slight penalty, if any at all.

Henry made a scoffing laugh, folding his arms across his chest. 'Begone, murderer, afore I have you shackled. Be warned: I shall send one of my men to Lyford to insist that you be returned to gaol and trialled forthwith.'

Robert allowed a flicker of a smile. 'Another of your men to Lydford? Funny thing, that be. Pray, what happened to your man, Rowan the Large? I don't see him among you.'

Henry narrowed his eyes. He whispered something to his head retainer, who nodded and turned on his heel, heading back toward the house.

'You've disgraced poor Alice,' Mathilde said, her wavering voice tinged with sadness as much as bitterness. 'After you've been hanged, I hope she will find a gentle soul to wed her. She's still of marrying age and shouldn't be left to ruin by the ruffian she was tied to.'

Edmund stepped close behind Robert, breathing on his neck. 'Master Robert, I fear the steward has gone to summon such help as he can to assail us. We should depart.'

Robert gave a sharp shrug of his right shoulder, making the clerk step back.

'Where be Rowan the Large?' Robert stood on tiptoes and swivelled left to right, cupping his hand over his brow as he made a pantomime of searching. 'Has anyone seen him? He does stand out.'

Henry's cheeks burned red and his mouth twitched with barely contained hatred.

'Have you seen him?' Robert jabbed his finger at the cook who quickly shook his head. He repeated the question as he pointed at the stablehand who only frowned in response, and again to Mathilde who clutched her hand to her chest, looking frightened and bewildered in equal measure.

'Begone,' Henry spat, glaring.

'Do you know where Rowan the Large is?' Robert said, turning to Edmund.

The clerk visibly stiffened. His eyes widened. He looked from Robert to the small gathering behind the gate and back again. He licked his lips and blinked rapidly.

'Well… I know,' Robert said, turning back to his hostile onlookers. 'Last I saw, he were swinging in the gentle breeze with a sign hanging about his neck declaring him a villainous robber and would-be murderer.'

'So?' Henry snarled, 'he is nothing to me. What of it?'

Robert nodded, pacing back and forth in front of his audience, enjoying his theatre. 'Well, Spiney… your man Rowan waylaid us on our journey from Lydford. Waiting in ambush like a cowardly robber.'

'So?' Henry spat. 'The villeins who reside on my estate can't be herded about and watched over like sheep. I expect he wished to avenge his former master. I hold no fault in it.'

Robert stroked the end of his beard as Henry spoke and nodded gently when he'd finished speaking. He tilted his head from left to right as if weighing up Henry's words. He ignored the reappearance of the steward flanked by two villeins armed with staves who marched to join their landlord.

'My confusion, Henry,' Robert said, his conversational tone drawing suspicious looks from the assembly, 'is that Rowan was in your company at Lydford, yet you returned without him. I can't imagine he parted your company without permission - nay, without orders.'

'Prove it: if you can.' Henry said, smiling as the three retainers fell in behind him. Henry jostled the cook aside and opened the gate.

Edmund coughed into his hand and took a few steps back. Robert cast a sharp look at him.

'I don't have to prove it, Spiney,' Robert said as the men filed out of the gate, forming a line behind their master. 'The guilt of your man Rowan is proven. Unless you intend to murder both myself and the Sheriff's clerk, word might yet reach the sheriff to the extent that your man, seen by many in Lyford in your company, waited for news of my release to hide in ambush for me. A jury can decide the truth of it: perhaps after you enjoy stay in my former accommodation.'

The villeins held their staves ready. The steward kept his dagger in his belt but stood sideways on with his finger tracing the lining of the sheath. The stablehand gently swung a wooden farming flail back and forth while the cook could only clench his fists.

Henry held the dagger and buckler idle at his sides. He frowned at the patch of dirt between his feet.

'Henry, careful,' Mathilde warned.

Robert kept his hands away from his sword. His imagination had already played out a scene of the men rushing him: he would slay one in the same motion he drew the sword, then dispatch the others in quick succession, leaving Henry to last. His opponents were unconfident and their courage already wavering. Robert knew that if he showed too much aggression or confidence they might back down. If he remained placid, maybe one would feel motivated to violence, spurring the others on, then he would be justified in dispatching them without fearing accusations of murder.

'Wait!' Edmund shrieked, thrusting his hand high in the air like a priest invoking Christ. 'I am unarmed. If you should slay me, you will surely face justice. If you kill only Master Robert, I will speak against you and see you all hanged.'

The henchmen looked at each other, unsure. The stablehand stopped swinging the flail. Henry's shoulders slumped.

'I have a proposal,' Edmund said, speaking quickly. 'Allow me to speak to all those on the estate. Master Henry will not set foot inside your hall. I have no stake in the matter and will report and record all I hear truly.'

Henry scowled at the ground, seeming to consider the offer. He nodded once and opened his mouth to speak.

'Unacceptable!' Robert bellowed. 'I'm not standing idle, waiting for a damned scribe to ask questions pertinent to my continued existence.'

Edmund clasped Robert's forearm. His fingertips dug into Robert's flesh.

'Master Robert, please!' Edmund hissed, 'I'm trying to serve your cause without us being killed or your having to hamsoken the entire Spiney family.'

'I'll not wait like an obedient horse,' Robert said through clenched teeth.

Edmund looked over his shoulder at the assembly, some of whom still appeared poised for action. 'Trust me,' he whispered, 'I will ask all them all - the entire estates' residents to gather in the hall so I might perceive who are the witnesses for further inquisition. This will leave the grounds deserted save perhaps a few children.'

Robert shook his head, not understanding. Edmund further dug his fingers into Robert's arm and lent in close, his bulging eyes boring into Robert's, their noses almost touching.

'The estate will be empty. You may investigate the physical while I conduct inquisition. They'll never talk to you, so it's the best path. Nay, the only path.'

'Very well.' Robert shook his arm free from the clerk and rubbed the sore flesh as he addressed the gathering. 'I accept! The Clerk conducts such inquisition as necessary. I shall return to my estate to await his findings.'

Henry exchanged glances with his steward.

'We accept!' Mathilde cried out from behind them. She squeezed her way between her son and his head man, lifting the front of her dress as she moved. 'Better to endure this than such slaughter as Robert Wood surely intends upon us! We accept.'

Mathilde panted and a small trickle of sweat ran down her temple, whether from the sudden burst of movement or from being overwhelmed by emotion Robert was unsure.

'Mother!' Henry snapped.

Mathilde turned on her son. Her expression halted his outburst.

'Very well. Accepted,' Henry said at last.

'Walk back toward your home,' Edmund whispered, 'it may take me some time to inter all into the hall. They should not think of you as sniffing about. Return only once you are confident all are inside.'

Robert nodded. He looked the clerk in the eye, trying to take the measure of him, deciding that perhaps the old sheriff was right in seeing something in the skinny, thick-lipped, sickly looking oaf.

'Ask them good questions, Clerk,' Robert snorted.

XVII

It grated Robert's pride to be seen retreating down the track to Woodtown, seeming to leave a stranger to deal with his affairs. He walked nearly halfway to Woodtown when he turned off the trail and knelt behind a bush where he could observe the Sampford estate. A bell rang to summon the field hands who were then directed into the manor grounds. The elevation of the land and the wall surrounding the manor prevented a clear view, but Robert could see people going to the manor. He was soon satisfied that the clerk had successfully gathered the whole Spiney household and tenants, and so Robert again ascended the path.

The manor gate creaked noisily at Robert's touch. He winced and silently cursed the gate and its maker. There would be no excuse if he was found snooping around; he decided that if was observed from a window or found by some retainer or labourer, he would plainly state his intent and continue about his business until ejected by force.

Robert walked to the stable, taking care to tread on the grass rather than the patchy track where his footfalls would make greater noise upon stones and dry earth. William Spiney's body had been found by the stable; Robert knew there was unlikely to be anything significant remaining, but it seemed the prudent place to begin.

The stable housed several palfreys and lower quality horses in individual stalls. A horse snorted as Robert entered the stable, the others paid him no attention. There was little of note; tools hung from wall hooks in a corner above an anvil. Hoofprints marked the ground all about and bundles of fresh straw were ready for being put into the stalls. There was nothing to suggest a murder had taken place.

Robert walked around the outside of the stable and found nothing of interest. He stopped to think, stroking his beard as he considered what he was actually looking for. He was confident that the murderer was a member of the Spiney household.

William Spiney took his morning ride at, or shortly after, dawn. The hue and cry was raised not long after the sun had cleared the hills; almost certainly it was very shortly after the slaying. It didn't seem likely that the murderer would've rushed into the manor house due to the risk of being seen by one of the household. Robert considered that they may have vaulted the chest high wall, hidden around the side of the manor, or may have even been the one who initiated the cry. Robert grunted in frustration that time was spilling away while he was wasting it on his musings.

'What am I looking for?' Robert muttered to himself. He had few facts of the slaying to base his search on. He decided if the murderer was one of Spiney's own household, they shall have needed to quickly be rid of the weapon to avoid being seen with it, but what was the tool of the killing? A hammer? An Axe? Had it been recovered? He knew so little.

Robert looked back to the stable. There were several items capable of causing serious injury, but would there have been time to wipe them down? The killer may have used rope to avoid leaving bloodstains, but strangulation was slow, leaving too much chance of being caught. It had to be a bladed or bludgeoning weapon. There were plenty of rocks and stones scattered about; he didn't have time to examine them. Even if a rock had been used, what would finding it prove? Robert decided he had to rely on the device of William's demise being a tool or weapon: a hammer would likely prove the killer a labourer or smith. If shears, and he would love it to be shears, it might implicate John Sherman.

'Where are ya?' Robert muttered to himself. His eyes passed over everything but saw nothing of note. Colours blurred together as his searching became frantic. Time was running out and he was finding nothing. He tried to focus. He slowed his breathing and closed his eyes. If he was the killer and had mere moments to conceal his guilt, where might he secrete the weapon? He considered that the killer may have thrown the weapon onto the roof or into one of the bushes beyond the wall where it might be retrieved later. His eyes settled on the stone trough right outside the stable.

The water was murky; scum, leaves, and swimming insects adorned the surface. It would be an ideal hiding place, and capable of concealing a weapon of good size. Robert knelt by the trough and rolled his shirt sleeve up to his bicep. He plunged his hand into the stagnant pool, grimacing as his hand slid over the slick, greasy stone basin. He touched on a few small stones and something matted and slimy which he shook off his submerged fingers. Then he felt something that moved and felt like metal. His exploring digits quickly found it again; with elation he realised what it was before he even raised it. He lifted the item triumphantly from the trough: a dagger.

It was a bullock dagger. Nearly a foot in length including the handle. The blade was thin and narrow: designed to easily slip through the visor of a downed man-at-arms to pierce his eye and skewer the brain. The Quillions were two small rounds the size of acorns. The handle was of solid wood with a simple engraved pattern of diagonal lines which crossed to form rough diamond shapes. The hilt ended in a steel cap with a maker's mark: a circle with a line through it. There were no notches in the blade, no rust on the metal, and the grip was unworn. Robert wondered it had been purchased for the single purpose of committing the murder.

The dagger was an archer's weapon; similar to the bullock dagger Robert carried himself. He couldn't recall anyone else owning one; most people carried only a common knife that was practical for everyday use, Robert decided that if someone used a bullock dagger to kill William Spiney, it was in a deliberate attempt to cast suspicion on Robert himself. He tucked the knife into his belt. He allowed a flicker of a smile; he'd made some progress. Next, he had to confirm that a bullock dagger was indeed the instrument of murder.

Robert walked out the manor gate. As he closed it, he cast his gaze across the windows, all of which were had the shutters open. The back of a coifed head was visible through one opening, but nobody seemed to have observed him. He followed a dirt trail around the side of the manor. The path was flanked on each side by a line of trees and shrub which gave some protection against wandering eyes. The route led toward the fields and hovels of numerous commoners, and to Robert's next destination: the church.

There was no need to rush or skulk along the churchyard trail - nobody could challenge him for visiting the church, and if they did, his presence was easily explained away, yet he could still feel his heart thud in his chest. Robert walked past haphazard headstones bearing crudely carved names. The church door was closed. The latch clacked loudly as Robert turned the iron ring. The studded wooden door and its hinges groaned in concert on opening. Robert grimaced and silently cursed all carpenters, smiths, and anyone else involved in the construction of doors. He stepped inside and carefully pushed it shut; his muscles only relaxed once the latch squeaked back into place.

The interior of the church was cool despite the warmth of the day. Light cascaded through coloured glass windows illuminating floating dust particles. Granite walls were brightened with various biblical scenes painted with varying degrees of skill. Unlit lanterns hung from the timber rafters. The central aisle was flanked by neat rows of benches. A thick carpet led up to the altar where a well-placed brass cross was illuminated by a cone of holy light from a high window. Below the altar lay Robert's objective: a gilded coffin.

Robert's footsteps sounded loud even on the muffling carpet. Robert hoped the Parson was in the Spiney manor; being an intrusive and eternally judgemental man, he almost certainly was busy sticking his nose into the Clerk's work; even so, the thought of being caught sneaking about William's coffin created a strange stirring in Robert's gut: he had no had cause to weasel about like a thief before and doing so sat uncomfortably on him.

The coffin was lacquered and brightly painted. It lay on a wooden trestle with the lid just above waist height, ready for the funeral service on the morrow. Robert placed his thumbs on the edges of the flat lid, hoping that it wasn't nailed down. He dug his thumbs under the lid and was able to lift it.

A foul odour escaped the coffin: that of a body left unwashed and unscented for too long mixed with other unpleasant odours which Robert couldn't immediately place. He averted his face and held his breath while the smell dissipated through the church, then he removed the lid altogether and rested it against the nearest pew.

William was dressed in his finest blue velvet doublet with matching belt. His shoes curled to excess at the toes, the leather was unwrinkled and not a grain of dirt marked the soles. A half-length cloak of red, with white fur trim, was folded back over his shoulders. A grey chaperon adorned his head, lined with squirrel fur and bearing three pilgrim badges which Robert suspected were gifted rather than earned. William's pale hands clasped a fresh bunch of lavender.

The face of the deceased was white and the lips dark purple. Robert took a moment to look on the face of his opponent and then crossed himself. He'd never had warm feelings for William Spiney: Like Robert, he had succeeded as a merchant to become a landholder, but the Spineys had never had to go without meals or toil a whole day for a crust of hard, green bread. Until the farce over the office of bailiff they had cordial relations and their wives had been friendly, but there had always been a rivalry. The Spineys considered the Woods imposters - mere villeins who had somehow cheated their way to moderate means. Of course, they never said such to Robert or his family, but it was felt with every perfectly pronounced word and in every tired gaze and sigh Robert's company seemed to elicit from them. Now that Robert regarded the peaceful, almost inhuman countenance of his adversary, there was no jealousy or ill feeling. Robert allowed a grim smile: such finery as the corpse had, he was still dead before his time and would appear before his Lord naked as the lowest of men.

There was no visible sign of wounds. Robert took a quick look around to make sure he wasn't being watched before he unclasped William's cloak and began to unbutton his tunic. He glanced up at the largest window and the brilliant, shining image of Christ on his cross looking down on him - perhaps in judgement at the desecration.

'Apologies, Lord,' Robert muttered as he returned to his labour of unfastening William's clothing.

Robert quickly found the fatal wound: a black line two fingers wide at the front of the neck, just to the right of the

Adam's apple. The wound was thin; about the width of the bullock dagger. He removed the weapon from his belt and measured the distance of the wound between finger and thumb, then transposed the digits to the knife blade while trying to keep them the same width apart. The wound measured as wide as the blade at almost halfway along its shaft. The dagger tapered quite sharply toward the end so he was satisfied that more than a third of the dagger had gone into the victim's throat; a wound which would surely have left the victim choking on his own blood for some time before dying.

Pulling up the under shirt, Robert found two stabs in the ribs on the right side. The blade had slipped between the ribs. The punctures were not wide: either not penetrating deeply due to resistance from bone and internal organs or because the attacker was panicking; stabbing quickly and not making forcing the blade in far enough for a quick kill. There were no other apparent wounds on the torso. Robert decided that he'd found enough. He tucked the dagger back into his belt and began to tie up the neck of the shirt. He'd almost finished buttoning the tunic when he heard the handle on the church door turn and the lever squeak upward from the catch.

XVIII

The church door swung open. A figure paused in the doorway: it was Henry's steward. He opened his mouth but didn't say anything, seemingly unsure how to proceed.

Robert stood motionless beside the uncovered coffin. There was no point making an excuse or trying to defend his actions; desecrating a corpse inside a church was a crime so unthinkable there wasn't even a name for it. Robert supposed that may shortly change.

'Well, you caught me. What of it?' Robert growled.

The grey-haired steward stepped over the threshold and pushed the door closed behind him. He winced. 'What of it? *What of it?* you ask?'

Robert stepped aside from the coffin as the Spiney family's head retainer walked stiffly toward the open casket. He stopped a few steps short and gulped, as if afraid of what he might find. His eyes flicked to Robert and then back to the coffin. He took the last hesitant steps and peered inside. The tip of his short, grey beard twitched. He closed his eyes and turned away, bringing his fist up to his mouth he gnawed on his knuckle and released a sound like a suppressed sob. His face creased and twisted in apparent agony. His eyes flashed open, blazing at Robert.

'What have you done is sacrilege!'

'Ah,' Robert nodded, 'so there be a word for it.'

'What?' The Head Man's quaking fingers went to the knife at his belt. He seemed to think better of it as he touched the blade. His arm rose to point a trembling finger at Robert. He took a step back; slowly shaking his head. 'You had best explain yourself! And with haste!'

Robert exhaled at length as he glanced at the coffin. He shrugged and flapped a hand in the direction the deceased. 'I needed to see how he died. Wouldn't need reducing to this recourse if it weren't for his bastard son.'

The steward stepped back and thumped into a pew, startling himself. He shook his head as he regarded Robert through thin, accusing eyes. 'To think you had my sympathy when the young master had you dragged to Lyford the way he did. Now I see you're the very lowest of curs.'

Robert tucked his thumbs into his belt and nodded. 'I thank you, sir, for your sympathies. Mayhap it was that which kept me warm through the cold, wet night whilst tied to the tree, and through the blinding darkness I endured for days thereafter. Yes, I thank thee all the way to hell for your sympathies, Sir.'

The men stared at each other. Robert took note of the other man's tense, bristling stance and twitching fingers that seemed eager to close around the dagger hilt. He noticed the Steward's suspicious eyes examining him the same way.

Robert forced his stance to remain passive. He gestured at the studded oak door. 'Leave in peace if you wish. Scurry to your master. I'll stop you not.'

'Peace? You *are* crazed. Why did you do this to poor William?' the Steward's voice croaked with emotion.

'Do what?' Robert frowned at the body as if only just noticing it. 'You mean desecrate his coffin? Or put him in it in the first place?'

'You confess it then? You slew him?' The Steward glowered.

'No, damn ye! Although for the trouble it caused me, I may as well have done the deed. Ah! I said I would, didn't I? Aye, I did. Words spoken in haste crossed with anger.'

'By God, man! Did you do it or not? Speak the truth now or I'll see thee dead!' The steward sprayed spittle as he snarled, but refrained from drawing his dagger, instead knotting his balled his hands into fist.

'Calm,' Robert said, holding up open his palms. 'Both you and I know nary a drop of blood will you spill on consecrated ground, or you'd have your blade in hand already. Now, what's your name? I forget.'

'John Sage,' the Steward said through gritted teeth. 'Answer my question or I swear, by Christ that I'll raise the hue and cry and see you hung this very day.'

Robert squared his shoulders, puffed out his chest and looked the Steward in the eye. 'No, John, I didn't kill your former master. I'll not speak false and say I mourn him, but kill him I did not. I swear it on mine own soul and that o' my good wife, Alice.'

John Sage maintained unblinking eye contact for some moments after Robert finished speaking. He nodded, still shaking. 'I dislike you, Robert Wood. You art a bully, a braggard, and common brawler, but you have personal honour, at least.'

Robert dug his thumbs back into his belt and gave a curt nod. He lowered his gaze; his newfound respect for the steward leaving him embarrassed at being caught rifling William's corpse. 'Well… I think it best we put the body, uh… that is, William, back as it… he were.'

John Sage narrowed his eyes at Robert and jutted his chin toward the coffin. 'Make good your own foul deed.'

Robert shrugged and moved back over to the casket. He finished buttoning the tunic and fastened the cloak's clasp. He quickly brushed down the front of the fabric and stood back, inclining his head as he examined the body's appearance, then he picked up the coffin lid.

John helped Robert manoeuvre the lid into place. Finally, the two men stood silently before the altar. John knelt and crossed himself. Robert waved his hand vaguely in emulation.

'So, what secrets did befouling William's earthly remains reveal?'

'He were stabbed unto death…' Robert drew the bullock dagger from his belt, 'with this.'

John Sage's eyes widened at the blade held upright between them.

'Not by I,' Robert said, 'I found it. In the horse trough afront the stable. I needed to open the coffin to see if the wounds match the blade.'

'So, that's the evil weapon…' John Sage gulped. 'Do you know who did it?'

'Nay. Not yet.' Robert put the dagger back into his belt. 'Could only been one o' your household. Or perhaps John Sherman.'

John Sage tilted his head. 'The Sherman? Why he?'

Robert scratched his beard and sniffed. 'Well, in part I'll admit it be my wish he be the slayer, but he was already about when the hue and cry was raised. He was over keen to assist your master in holding me guilty. I'm not swearing by his guilt, but it were either he or one of your own.'

John Sage nodded. His brow furrowed in concentration. 'I think it was not he, which worries me.'

'Why? Do you have a suspicion who it might be? Speak up if ye do.'

'Not that...' John held his hand up and took a step back from Robert. 'I mean it is as you say: if not John Sherman, it is like as not someone from Sampford Spiney.'

'Like as not?' Robert's raised voice bounced off the walls and into the rafters. 'It's more than like as not. It must be!'

John Sage held up both palms. 'Peace. I just... know not whom or why.'

'Henry Spiney. For inheritance. That be both who and why.'

'Nay!' John shook his head violently as if to exorcise the concept from his mind. 'I'll not hear of it. It's not he.'

Robert tried to suppress a scowl, wondering incredulously how the loyal buffoon could be so blind to the possibility.

John glowered back, seeming to sense Robert's thoughts. 'I know he's no saint, but it's not patricide. Henry never showed any eagerness to ascend to his father's place. You saw how vengeful he turned after the slaying.'

'Bah! Saw it? Aye, but a trick that could've been. Acting a grieving son.' Robert narrowed his eyes. 'Are ye protecting him? What do you know?' Robert grabbed John's collar and twisted it.

John clasped Robert's forearm and tried to push him away but the younger and stronger man held firm.

'Tell me what ye knows!'

'Nothing!' John's hot breath hissed against Robert's cheek. 'Naught more than you. Let me go. People know I'm in here with you.'

Robert released his grip and pushed John's shoulder. 'People? Nah. Lies. You knew not that I was here or you'd have not come alone.'

John Sage brushed down the front of his doublet and straightened his collar.

'A farmer's son you walk in. He ran up to the house to raise the alarm. Lucky for you, I was the first man he saw. I came alone to avoid the same unpleasantries you endured after the slaying. And this is how you greet me for it.'

Robert chuckled mirthlessly and sat heavily onto the nearest pew. 'Don't pretend you're a friend o' mine John Sage. You came alone because you want the same as I: to find the bastard who killed your master.'

John bowed his head and crossed himself. He sat on a pew on the opposite side of the aisle. The two men looked at each other in silence. Robert sensed a grudging respect between them as unlikely allies. Robert felt his old pain in his right hand: the bones often still ached from his twenty-year-old injury. He shook his hand and flexed his fingers.

John pointed at Robert's hand. 'I hear you hurt your hand on campaign against the Dauphin?'

'Aye. Resulting from an ambuscade near Troyes. A Burgundian smashed me hand with his stave.' Robert mimicked the motion of an overhead strike. 'Never could draw a bow after that. Fingerbones too weak. Picked up a bardiche taken from the same fight. Carried it with me all through France. It now sits in my solar. Expect maybe one day soon I'll have cause for using it again.'

John Sage leaned forward, perching on the edge of his bench, his hands braced on his knees. 'You think that makes you special, don't you? Being a fighting man a score years ago.'

Robert's back straightened. He regarded John Sage coolly. 'Special? About this place, aye. More'n a mere muck piler anyways.'

John slapped his knee and shook his finger at Robert. 'Yes, I knew as much! I bet you had no idea that I fought on those same lands ten years afore ya! With King Edward's sons - all three! Siege at Nantes you say? I fought at Limoges as a young boy no older than you were like to have been at Nantes.'

'You?' Robert eyed the older man, suspicious. At around fifty years of age John still carried himself well, although not physically muscular as archers often were, he was athletic with a quiet confidence in his stances.

'Aye.' John jabbed his finger into Robert's shoulder. 'The difference between the like of you and the like of me is humility. I don't dwell on or boast of past deeds nor wear a stolen battlefield remnant at my waist like a robber knight. Muck pilers you oft say of the villeins? Well, how many muck pilers were with you in Brittany?'

Robert didn't answer but shifted uncomfortably on the bench.

'I'd brave to venture that you were a muck piler too, Robert Wood. A lucky muck piler who was the first to put his hand on a fallen knight and claim him as prize. It makes you lucky, not better.'

'Wasn't luck. Unhorsed him myself I did.' Robert rubbed his shoulder where the steward had poked him.

'Be that as it may, 'twas was only that one moment in time which separated you from the likes of those out there who toil the land or tread on your wool.'

'What's your meaning, old man?' Robert stood so that the steward would have to look up at him, but Robert found himself glowering at John's shoes and feeling like a boy scolded.

'My meaning, Master Robert, is that your arrogance got you into this trouble and if you continue as you have been, you'll be responsible for your own undoing.'

Robert walked over to the altar, scuffing his shoes along the tiles as he went. He looked up at the stained-glass window. Christ's image still appeared perceptively all-knowing and mournfully judgmental. He wondered if everyone felt so judged when they looked up at it, and whether it was by intent of the glass smith or through divine provenance.

'I'll think on your words, old man. Even though you're Spiney's man, I don't hate you.'

'Nor should you.'

Robert heard the bench creak as John Sage stood. The hobnails on the bottoms of his shoes clicked the floor tiles back to the church door.

'I'm going back to the house afore I'm missed. You should leave by the transept door and be sure not to be seen. Oh, and Robert…'

Robert turned slightly at the waist and looked over his shoulder at the steward.

'If you or your clerk find the truth of this slaying, let justice do it's work, not your angry sword.'

Robert gave a single nod and turned back to the altar. He heard the door open, then shut. He looked back up at the image of Christ and clasped his hands together.

'I suppose this is all your doing. To teach a wayward soul humility. Bah! Well, I'll take your lesson.' He glanced at William's coffin. 'I won't attend your funeral, bastard, but I'll come to church on Sunday and say a prayer for ye. Bastard.'

XIX

A farmer and his wife mutely observed Robert from the shade of a copse of trees at the edge of Sampford Spiney. They watched him walk out of the churchyard and past the Sampford manor. The man put his arm around his wife's shoulder and whispered something into her ear as Robert passed them by. Robert stopped, looking back at them until they turned about and headed back to their farm. Robert shook his head, mumbled 'muck pilers,' and headed back to Woodtown.

'You knows when you're past feeding don't yah?' Robert said, looking down at his midsection. It was after midday and his stomach groaned for sustenance. He patted his belly as he walked. As trees gave way to open terrain his longhouse came into view. A thin plume of smoke rose from the firepit chimney. Alice would have breakfast waiting for him. He sighed upon realising that he'd likely have to wait for Edmund to return before he could eat. Robert consoled himself with the thought that Alice will have already finished midday prayer, so he'd not be compelled to partake - if she complained about his missing prayers again he'd tell her he'd attended church, which he decided was true enough. She might question why he'd enter the church after he'd refused her suggestion of attending the funerary service on the morrow. He contemplated possible responses, all of which involved lies or omissions. He'd no desire to lie to his beloved and even less to tell the truth about his desecration of the corpse, and so decided he'd say nothing of his church visit.

Robert became aware of footfalls some distance behind him. Was the farmer following? Had the muck piler alerted someone to Robert's presence? He walked on, betraying no sign that he'd noticed the thudding steps. He watched a kestrel circle the fields behind the Spinners' hovels. The afternoon sun was warm on his face and he had to wince against the sun's brilliance to observe the bird. He unfastened the top button of his sleeveless doublet and tugged open the laces on the top of his shirt.

The footfalls quickened. Hardened leather clumped on mud and stone.

A dozen yards, Robert reasoned. He kept his gaze forward and swung his legs gaily, taking pains to walk as if he'd not a care in the world.

The gait increased in volume and frequency: the pursuer was running - charging.

The sudden rapidity caught Robert off guard. He snatched his bullock dagger from its sheath. In his haste he snagged his shirt sleeve on the hilt of the dagger he'd found in the horse trough, slowing his defence by a breath. The attacker was almost upon him when he spun about with blade at the ready.

'Whoa! What manner o' pie is you baking?' Guy Wynter said, holding up black gloved hands in defence.

'Bah!' Robert growled, lowering the knife. He slapped the air in Guy's direction. 'A pie o' the like you'll break your teeth on if you tried a taste of it. What did ye mean rushing me so?'

'I was not wanting to make no hue n' cry to announce me self on account that you was moving 'bout Spiney estate in caution.' Guy removed his riding hat and fanned himself with it. Yellow stains showed on his shirt underarm where the doublet and sleeve separated.

Robert put the dagger back in the sheath and gave Guy a questioning look.

Guy gestured toward Sampford Spiney. 'I come'd up here after arriving at your homestead. Mrs Wood told me you'd not far gone n' headed up to Sampford n' asked of me to follow on, n' make certain you was kept safe.'

Robert frowned. 'Why didn't you make yourself known?'

'I waved as I walked up. You was closing the gate afront the Spiney manor. Intent on watching the windows and silent pacing you was. I could see you wouldn't be thanking me fer callin' out. By time I caught up you were in church. Thought best wait outside.'

Robert thought for a moment then nodded. 'Very well. But why'd you not waylay the Spiney man who came into the church? And why wait 'til I am halfway to home afore you rush up to me like a rapscallion intent on robbery?'

'Oh, I was in the graveyard, concealed well by the Nave side. The time I saw the Spiney man 'twas late to do a thing. I thought mayhap you'd arranged meeting with him.'

'Ah, yes… and I came out the other door, so you can't have put eyes on me until I was past the graveyard.'

'Aye, like that, Master. Apologies if I been addle-pated.'

'Nay, it be fine.' Robert clapped his hand on Guy's shoulder. The retainer grinned, flicking away the sandy fringe which fell across his eye.

'I'm glad to see you returned,' Robert said.

The duo walked side-by-side to Woodtown. Guy idly kicked a stone from the path which skidded across sheep-gnawed grass.

'Glad you be back to Woodtown you be belonging,' Guy said, still fanning himself gently with his hat. 'I should've been aside you when they tried to take you. My apologies for it, Master.'

'Nonsense,' Robert barked, 'we'd have both ended up in a Lyford cell if you'd been present. Matters have proceeded well as can be expected under such grim circumstance.'

'I waited for yous at Lydford, on Mrs Wood's order. Had to drop the guard a farthing each day for word o' you. I think he didn't want to stop gettin' his coin, so when I asked for news the day o' yer release the guard said nawt. Did you's get the bread I gave over for you?'

Robert grunted. 'No, I did not. I expect the guard enjoyed it. How did you come to learn of my release?'

'Rowan the Large.'

'Eh?'

'Spied him lurking. He were also askin' for news. I 'spected he came to hear o' your release afore me. The last day I thinks to me self: I didn't see Rowan the Large since yesterday. So, I questioned the guard more… close like, n' then he tells me truly.'

Robert hummed his acceptance of Guy's narration. He walked on in silent thought. For Rowan to have waited ahead in ambush he must have known of Robert's release before Robert left Lydford. He wondered how long it had been between the Sheriff granting parole and Robert walking free from Lyford Gaol. He supposed it might've been long enough for the guard to get word to Rowan in exchange for a reward, but he couldn't shake off the feeling that the sheriff somehow had a hand in it.

'Is all well, Master?'

'What? Yes... yes. I was just thinking. I've much to dwell on, Guy.' He clapped Guy's shoulder again. 'After all this is done, we'll buy you a good costume. It's high time we got you built a cottage here too. You've been in my service a year and still sleeping in the barn loft or on the rushes by my fireplace. The head man of my estate should sleep in a bed. I bet the Spiney head man does, and if he doesn't, he should. What say ye?'

Guy blushed and bowed his head. His fringe slipped over his eyes again. 'I don't deserve such honour, master. I'm but a simpkin in your service.'

Robert laughed and pushed his knuckles into Guy's shoulder.

Thrusting open the front door of his house, Robert breathed in the welcome scent of frying salmon. Saliva quickly filled his mouth.

Alice looked up from beside the firepit where she nudged salmon around a pan with a wooden spoon. She smiled warmly as the two men walked in.

'Welcome back, Husband, Guy. I trust you bring good tidings.'

Robert returned the smile and unfastened the rest of the buttons on his doublet.

'As good as can be expected. This smells ready to eat. I'll pour beer.' He walked toward the larder, stopping in the doorway when Alice called out.

'Oh, no, husband! We must wait until good Edmund returns. We can say prayers together while we await him. I'm sure he won't be long now.'

Robert sighed and sank against the doorframe. He lazily turned his head to Guy who still hovered by the threshold.

'Twas worth the try, Guy, but I knew she'd make us wait.'

XX

'Be you well fed?' Robert said. He watched Edmund slide his eating knife over the wooden plate, scraping up the last remnants of salmon and parsley sauce.

The clerk licked the knife, made an approving hum, then pushed the plate a few inches away from him across the tabletop. He smiled his thanks at Alice and picked up his cup and swallowed the last mouthfuls of beer.

Robert perched on the edge of a stool, steadying himself with an elbow on the table corner. Guy sat beside Robert. The pair had been intently watching the clerk eat, having shovelled their own meals down their gullets as quickly as they could despite disapproving looks from Alice. They at least abided by her insistence that they not bother Edmund for further details of his enquiries until after he'd finished his meal.

Alice picked up the empty plate and carried it out of the solar. Edmund wiped the blade of his eating knife on a square of cloth from his satchel, then wrapped the knife in the cloth and put both into the bag.

'A fine meal your wife presents,' Edmund said. His smile faltered when he noticed Robert's glaring eyes. He looked to Guy and finding his countenance equally unwelcoming he looked back to Robert. 'I have made many notes, Sirs. Look.' He opened his satchel again and removed a dog-earned bundle of parchment which he placed on the table. He leafed through the pages, showing that eight or ten sheets were covered in elegant straight lines of curved and flourishing lettering.

Robert drummed his index finger on the paper. 'Does any of this nonsense aid me? You were in there for hours. What findings do you have?'

'Well…' Edmund smacked his lips, savouring the aftertaste of the meal. 'I wouldn't say hours. It was Sext when I began, and the church rang Nones just a-'

Robert sliced his hand through the air in a cutting motion and flashed his teeth.

'Do not divert with idle blabber, Clerk.'

Edmund nodded and sighed.

'Very well. I shall summarize: if that would suffice.'

'Speak it,' Robert grunted.

'I perceived that little of what I was told as untruth. The tales they all told complimented each other where necessary. William Spiney was accustomed to a morning ride about his estate and the surrounding land and normally rode alone.'

'Aye. Common enough knowledge. Continue.'

'Yes, verily, Sir. On the morn of his death, he rose slightly earlier than usual but not so early as to be unusual. The stablehand hadn't yet prepared a blanket for under the master's saddle and went to fetch one. It was on his return that Master William was found slain.'

'An unlikely tale. Must've been the stablehand who did for him.'

Edmund held up a finger. 'Not so. A household servant swears that the stablehand came into the house to obtain the blanket and was made to wait a short time while one was fetched. This is also sworn as true by the cook who laid eyes on the waiting stablehand and exchanged words with him.'

Robert grimaced. 'I suppose it an unlikely triumvirate of murderers between servant, cook and stablehand. One of 'em would've given up the other two to the gallows. For now we shall have to take it as truth. What about the Spiney sapling? Can any swear to where he was?'

Edmund arched an eyebrow and shrugged slightly. 'He was abed until the hue and cry was raised. He has a chamber in the house which he occupied alone. None saw him egress the room, but I have the word of his mother, the steward and a servant, that he came down upon hearing the cry, having seemingly not long awoken.'

'Hmmm.' Robert scratched his beard. 'Might be easy enough to slay someone and return to the bedchamber if he was cunning. And lucky.' Robert pulled a face as he considered the possibility. It seemed too neat that Henry might have murdered his father and returned to his room unnoticed past the waking household.

'There would be more to it than caution and luck,' Edmund said. He leant back and laced his fingers together, resting his hands on his chest and smiling smugly. He endured being stared at by Robert for a few seconds before his smugness dissipated and he was compelled to continue. 'There was, you see, a substantial amount of blood seepage; both on the slain and the ground about him. It would seem unlikely that the killer will have escaped without bloodstain. I have the sworn word of five witnesses that there was a clear imprint of the front half of a shoe in the lifeblood of the deceased.'

Robert raised his eyebrows and looked across to Guy who nodded faintly and smiled.

'Good... Good!' Robert slapped Edmund's shoulder. 'What else? You're holding back, I can see. Stop trying to impress me with your wit and say what you know.'

'Well, I asked to see the shoes and boots of the entire household. I examined all and found no trace of blood. I concede that of course the blood may have been cleaned, but it is a hard labour to remove such a stain from leather or hide. I think the murderer made the print while crouching or kneeling beside William Spiney in order to stab the ribcage.'

'How can that be known to you? You're trying to make a poetry out of the mundane now, Scribe.'

Edmund held up his index finger again. 'Thusly: As the pooling of blood was mostly from around a neck wound, it would seem that William Spiney lay choking in his own blood when he was stabbed in the ribs. Blood, I understand, flows more freely while the body retains the spirit. As the rib wounds produced less blood it is a sign to me they were the freshest when the heart stopped beating. Furtherance: Although my experience and knowledge has limit, I have thought that when attacked, the assailed will hold up hands or fists in defence. There was no indication of defence from the victim, such as wounds to the arms or hands, therefore the attack was unexpected and by someone known to William. Someone unused to killing, hence the clumsy stabs to the ribs instead of to the heart.'

Robert shook his head. 'No, that is your wit playing artistry with half-facts.'

'Not quite, Master. We know the murderer was a novice because the attack didn't kill outright. We shall demonstrate. Would you two men please stand aside from the table?'

Robert sighed and exchanged looks with Guy. Robert shrugged and stood, followed by Guy. They moved to the centre of the solar, standing in front of the unlit fireplace.

'Good,' Edmund said, still sitting. 'Now, Master Robert: You have two daggers I see - would you take one and please make as if to attack your man there, feigning a stab toward the neck. And you, Sir... apologies I know not your name.'

'Guy.'

'Guy, react naturally, please.'

Robert shrugged again. 'Ready?' he asked Guy.

'No, no!' Edmund said, waving his finger. 'Not ready. Be unready, Guy. It is an unexpected attack. Please, put your hands behind you or behave as you if are greeting good Master Robert.'

Robert rolled his eyes. 'Alright then. Guy, are you unready?'

'Aye. Unready.'

'Please, Sirs, do this with solemnity. Please.'

'Very well,' Robert said. He swept his dagger from the sheath and in the same motion thrust it toward Guy's neck, taking care to ensure the attack was wide of the mark.

Guy stumbled back, knocking the table as he tried to parry by slapping one hand against Robert's arm and hooking his other arm around Robert's wrist.

'That's enough,' Edmund said. 'You see, you can't help but prepare for the attack. You know it is coming and react in accordance. The attack was completely unexpected.'

'Could the killer not have hidden n' attacked with surprise?' Guy said as he and Robert moved apart.

'Yes,' Edmund conceded, 'but the attack was frontal, allowing the opportunity for defence.'

'That be fine,' Robert said, 'but it doesn't assist us any. I need know who not how.'

Edmund drummed his fingers on the table. 'I'm hoping the one may lead to the other. I also know the assailant favoured the left hand.'

'you can't know that,' Robert said.

'Ah, but I can…. Please, Guy… lay down as if you are slain. On your back.'

Guy looked to Robert for guidance.

'Do it,' Robert sighed, 'let's see what mummery he has for us now.'

Guy lay on the floor. Edmund rose from his seat and prompted adjustments to Guy's posture to align with how the fallen body of William Spiney had been described to him.

'Now, the shoe mark was here…' Edmund slapped his foot down a few inches from Guy's ear and knelt beside him. 'Now the stab wounds to the body are here.' He knelt and poked Guy in the ribs, tutting when Guy slapped his hand away.

'I see your wisdom in it,' Robert said, scratching his chin. 'With the left foot positioned by Spiney's left ear, the dagger must've been in the murderer's left hand or the angle would be too awkward. Yet the throat wound was on yonder side.'

Edmund raised his finger. 'Indeed. When standing, a dagger thrust from the attacker's left side will strike William's right. The killer stabbed the right side of William's throat, and when Master William fell, the murderer knelt on William's left side, stabbing the ribcage twice, then fled.'

'So, he favours the left?' Guy sniffed. 'Many people here abouts use both 'ands. That why we got two.'

Edmund sat on his stool and showed his teeth in a brief smile as he rocked his head from left to right as if weighing up Guy's reasoning. 'True. True. Tis not final proof, but merely progress. Wait… Master Robert, how did you know where the wounds were located?'

'Ah, I discovered it while talking with John Sage, Spiney's head man. Anyhow, I found something more.' He took the murder weapon from his belt and slammed it down on the table.

Edmund fell backwards over his stool in fright at the sudden motion, his head and shoulder thudding into the wall. The ruckus brought Alice dashing past the privacy screen into the solar, clutching the front of her dress to not trip on it.

'Whatever is going on?' Alice demanded.

'Progress!' Robert snapped. 'That there be the tool of the murderer. I found it in a horse trough but a few yards from where the bastard lay slain.'

Edmund rubbed the back of his head. He righted the stool and sat upon it, picking up the dagger tenderly between thumb and forefinger. He held it near to his face and examined it closely, turning it over in his hands while the others watched him intently.

'Well, there's no evidence of blood,' he said finally, setting the dagger back down on the table. 'Yet it would not be hasty to make assumption of this being the tool of the slaying.'

'It is the tool,' Robert said firmly.

'Oh? Why so sure?' Edmund asked, intrigued.

Robert shook his head and waved a dismissive hand. 'I know the blade matches the wounds on the body. That's all I'll say on it.'

'Be rid of it,' Alice snapped, pointing out the window. 'I want it not in our home. It's a thing of evil.'

Everyone looked at the blade until Robert gingerly picked it up and handed it to Guy.

'Conceal it in your barn loft.'

Guy nodded, taking the weapon and bowing his head respectfully to Alice as he passed her by.

Alice stood with hands on her hips staring coldly at Robert. She swept the coif off her head which she wrung in her hands. Her blonde curls bounced around her neck as she stormed out of the room.

Robert caught Edmund's questioning look and groaned. 'She's devout. I should've known wiser than to bring that thing to table.'

Edmund licked his lips and nodded slowly. 'Indeed, Master Robert. However, in these dire circumstances wouldn't it be wise to keep such an item close? It might yet be the key to all of this.'

'To tell thee true, I believe me forsaken. Tis a mere five days afore I face Lydford justice again.' Robert regained his stool. He dug his elbow into the table and rested his chin on his palm.

Edmund slowly reached out toward Robert's shoulder, then seeming to think better of it put his hand down on the tabletop.

'Well, Sir, I would vouch that we've done well for a day's toil. From my inquisitions I have been able to remove from suspicion the majority of the Spiney household. We also know the murderer favours his left hand and we have the dagger used in the slaying.'

Robert grunted and kneaded his eyes with his thumb and forefinger. 'Aye... aye. You speak truly. I just feel melancholy that the truth is yet unknown to me. I thought it would be easier.'

Edmund smiled meekly. 'Perhaps you thought you'd bash a few skulls, thump a few tables, and the murder would offer himself up?'

'No.' Robert bristled defensively, then frowned in thought. 'Well, perhaps something akin to that. Aye.'

'Well, perhaps I'll take time to pray. I may continue my inquisition on the morrow. There are still a few who interest me.'

'Who?'

'Ah, let's see... John Sage, Henry and Mathilde Spiney, and one or two of their servants.'

'Not Sage. Wasn't he.'

'Oh?'

'Wasn't he,' Robert said more forcefully. 'I know it. You should speak with John Sherman. I'd suspect him.'

Edmund cocked his head. 'Ah, I haven't heard that name. Pray, who is he?'

'One 'o mine. John the Sherman. Last hut southbound of here. He was at Sampford Spiney same time as they took me for the killin'.'

'Nobody has spoken his name. Why would nobody mention him?' Edmund flipped through the pages of his notes, his brow furrowed in consternation.

'Peace, Clerk. John Sherman is beneath notice that be why. But I noticed him. I'd also point suspicion at Sir John Herle and Rowan the Large.'

Edmund looked into Robert's eyes. He sucked in his puffy lips to form a thin straight line and his fingertips pressed into the tabletop, turning his knuckles white.

'Master Robert, I can't question the sheriff, as well you know, and if Rowan the Large was the murderer... well you have served him justice before the pie is baked, haven't you?'

'Perhaps,' Robert said, stifling a yawn. The combination of afternoon heat and the taxing of his mind had begun to tire him. 'But we have the dagger - as you said it may be key. I will wait for my brother to return with such news as we may glean from your fellow clerks, then we shall find where this dagger was made. It appears newly crafted. I think perhaps the smith who made it might recall the man who bought it.'

Edmund winced but made no reply.

'It's a bullock dagger,' Robert said as if to a child. 'I know you think a smithy might make many daggers. A bullock dagger isn't commonplace. I doubt he'd have made three in the last year.'

'Ah, very well.' Edmund smiled. 'Then we know our next steps.'

XXI

The lych bell rang. Its deliberate, strident strokes announcing the progress of William Spiney's funeral procession. The chimes resounded from Sampford Spiney down to Woodtown.

Robert squinted up at the church from the window in his solar. Movement on the nearby path caught his attention - John Sherman walk hurriedly by; not daring to look at the house as he headed toward the churchyard. The two spinners were further up the path, their husbands remained behind on to work their field strips.

Alice had taken heed of Robert's warning and stayed home. She remained sulkily subdued, pursuing her chores with an uncommon silence that betrayed her annoyance at the loss of face her failure to pay final respects to their esteemed neighbour would entail.

The bell ceased ringing. The final chime lingered for seconds after it struck. Robert turned from the window, excused himself from Edmund's company, and went outside to take stock of his estate.

Guy walked with Robert and together they examined the sheep. Robert had purposely waited until John Sherman was absent because he didn't trust himself to keep control of his temper in the presence of the snivelling betrayer. Robert noticed Edmund walking away from the house and shouted to him, demanding to know what he was doing. Edmund shouted back that he was taking a stroll on the assumption that the favourable weather might help enlighten him on how to proceed with his inquisition.

Robert was quietly impressed with the clerk; he had exceeded the sheriff's instruction to observe and record, assuming the role of the lead inquisitor with a confidence previously unseen. Robert resolved not to praise him too heartily though, lest the indulgence go to the young man's head.

It was near the ringing of Sext when Eustace rode into Woodtown. Robert grimaced on realising that his brother had ridden directly through Sampford Spiney not long after the hamlet's funeral attendees had returned. He decided not to accost his brother over the error, reflecting that he might have foreseen that his brother would always take the easiest path, and that he should have warned Eustace to skirt around Sampford.

Eustace rode past Robert and Guy. He stood in his stirrups waving his feathered cap and smiling broadly like he'd won some great glory rather than having merely completed a task as a courier.

'Go see to his horse,' Robert muttered.

Guy spat out the piece of twig he had been chewing and jogged to the stable.

Robert waited for his brother at the side of the path near the longhouse. Eustace handed the horse over to Guy without a word, pausing only to fetch a leather scroll case from the linen saddlebag. He walked toward his brother, still smiling broadly, then bowed at the waist with a flourish, sweeping his hat behind him. He held the pose for a moment before rising.

The sound of clapping from behind Robert drew their attention. Eustace bowed to his sister-in-law and then lifted his hat in an extravagant arc to replace it on his grinning head.

'Well met, Eustace!' Alice cheered, ignoring Robert's irksome look.

'Brother. My good lady...' Eustace nodded politely. 'I return with your... well, I know not what. Shall we see?'

Eustace unbuckled the scroll case but before he could remove the parchment, Robert snatched it. Eustace's face dropped. He glanced into the empty container which he cradled with both hands. His shoulders slumped and arms dropped to his sides. His bottom lip stuck out a fraction as he made a disappointed noise.

The scroll seal was intact. It bore the sigil of Sir John Herle along with an inscription. Robert couldn't read the words, but he knew such things were always in Latin.

'Robert!' Alice seethed. She strode to her husband with her hand held out for the paper. 'Don't be so uncouth! You sent your brother on this errand and there's not a word of thanks for him. Now, give the parchment. You need Eustace to read it for you -

if your good brother is favourable to doing so after the cold greeting he has received from kin.'

Robert held the letter over his head, beyond the grasp of Alice's beckoning fingers.

'This be for my own self and the clerk. I don't desire any other to peck their nose into it except by invitation.'

Alice stepped back. Her mouth dropped open momentarily before she regained her composure. Her nostrils flared and eyes widened.

'Husband, you go too far. Apologise to your brother this very moment and return unto him the scroll.'

'I shall do no such thing!' Robert lowered the parchment now that Alice was no longer reaching for it, but he was careful to keep hold of it with both hands. He turned to Eustace and forced a wide smile. 'I thank thee, Brother, for performing the menial task. Did you lodge comfortably with the sheriff and dine on venison at his table?'

'Oh…' Eustace shrugged. 'The sheriff wasn't in residence. It was comfortable enough, yes. A bed to myself and a ready supply of mead from the Abbey of the Benedictines.'

'Aye. That's why it took you so long in the returning, eh? Well, at least they affixed a seal on the scroll to stop you sniffing at the content.'

'Now, that's not fair, Brother!' Eustace raised his voice and straightened posture. 'I had to wait on the clerks. It was late to ride when they gave me the message, so I'd nothing to do but wait 'til morn.'

'Aye. Well, I'll not inhale your breath lest it burn my eyes, but the hour of your return tells that you either became lost or laid abed late due to an overindulgence.'

Eustace compressed his lips together, making them turn white. Alice shook her head in disgust at her husband's behaviour and went to Eustace's side, putting a comforting hand on his shoulder.

Robert turned to leave them, intending to seek out Edmund, but then noticed the clerk waiting at the side of the house. Edmund turned away when Robert looked at him, his cheeks burned red, seemingly embarrassed at witnessing a family dispute.

'Come,' Robert barked at him as he strode past the clerk and into the longhouse.

Robert sat at the table in the solar and beckoned Edmund sit beside him. He broke open the scroll's seal and unfurled it. His eyes wandered over the page, trying to make sense of the strange scrawling. He recognised a couple of letters but not enough to distinguish any words. He'd always found it interesting, almost magical, that sounds could be formed from a mark scored into leather, paper, or hide. It was a secret that only the fortunate and the privileged had been allowed access to, and although it had always fascinated him, he somehow always felt that the actual learning of such a monumental undertaking was time best spent on looking after his business.

'May I?' Edmund gestured to the scroll.

Robert put the letter on the table and pushed it toward Edmund. The ends of the parchment rolled inward when Robert removed his hand from the paper.

Edmund picked up the parchment and turned it so that light from the window fell up on it. His eyes moved from left to right and he hummed and grunted quietly to himself as he read. Finally, he rolled the letter up and placed it back on the table. He opened his mouth to speak but was stopped by Robert who held his hand up for silence at the sound of the door opening and then closing.

'Who be it?' Robert called out.

'Guy. Should I come or go?'

'Come.'

Guy entered the solar with his cap in his hand. 'If you don't mind my telling, Master, methinks yer wife be mighty angry.'

'Such is the natural state of a wife, my man. Once you be wed, you will find this to be so. Even more so if she be devout.'

Guy nodded and leant against the fireplace.

Edmund's eyes flicked between the two men until Robert gestured for Edmund to speak.

'Well, Master… it is somewhat… perplexing. I have the answer for your question, but I fear the answer may raise only further questions.'

'Well, speak it, by God's cap!' Robert gestured with a flurry of his hand for Edmund to hurry his report.

'The scroll says that the document you made your mark on was a land grant. It increases the demesne of Woodtown by four furlongs to the south and west and includes the right to deforest such land as falls within that realm.'

Robert stood and frowned over the clerk's shoulder at the open scroll. 'This can't be. There was no such agreement.'

'A forgery?' Guy offered. 'I hear tales that folks of means might tend toward such a thing.'

Robert shook his head. 'Nay, not a forgery, but trickery all the same. I see now that I was misled into signing two papers of differing content, but why a land grant?'

'Aye,' Guy agreed, staring out the window. 'What's benefiting the sheriff to be giving away land? Do he even own that land?'

'Well actually…' Edmund said, his finger searching the document for the appropriate point. 'He does. It is part of the land that Sir John purchased from Plympton Priory two years past. There is a fee to be honoured. Twenty marks for the land to be paid on St. John's day.'

Robert was stunned to silence for some moments. He steadied himself with his hand on the shoulder of the scribe. He scrutinised the document, frantically willing his eyes to be able to interpret the writings and hoping he might find the clerk had read it wrongly.

'Read it aloud. In full. But quietly.' Robert went to the privacy screen to make sure his wife hadn't come in unheard. He didn't want Alice to be worried by the details of this new predicament.

Edmund read through the entire letter. It was addressed to him from a clerk named John and merely summarised the supposed agreement rather than replicating the wording of the original legal document. Robert had him read it through twice more.

Robert paced the four strides from table to far wall and back again. He repeated the journey, running a trembling hand through his scalp.

'I must say, Master Robert,' Edmund ventured, 'it seems to me a peculiar agreement for you to be unaware of. I see not why the sheriff would sell you land you did not wish to purchase.'

Robert stopped pacing and looked at the clerk with a bewildered expression. 'You don't see? I do. I see most clearly; like the morn sun has risen upon me.' Robert shook as he spoke.

Guy pressed his back to the stonework. Edmund shuffled his stool back the few inches he could before it met the wall.

Robert's breathing became fierce. Blood had rushed to his cheeks and spittle flecked onto his beard as he struggled to contain his rage, giving him the appearance of an overboiled pot.

'The bastard...' Robert pointed out the window at some conjured yet unseen focus of his anger. 'He desires not twenty marks. Bah! He wouldn't take a single coin from me when I thought 'twas paying for bailiff.'

Edmund swallowed and licked his lips. 'Then, Sir, I fail to see the direction of his endeavour. Bastardly as you say it may be.'

Robert sighed with exasperation and slapped his hand onto his forehead, brushing his hair back. 'The direction of his endeavour is toward Woodtown. A land fee to be paid the same day as the quarterly tax. What would be the penalty should I fail to pay due taxes on the quarter day of St. John?'

Edmund frowned, taking a moment to think before answering, not wanting to risk angering the volatile merchant with an incorrect answer.

'I... suppose, the sheriff might levy the cost from you in terms of property or land to the value of the tax and the twenty marks land fee too, if not paid.'

'Right!' Robert wagged his finger in Edmund's face. 'And wouldn't you think twenty marks a high valuation for a mere four furlongs?'

'That was my thought,' Edmund said carefully, 'but I haven't surveyed the quality of the land. There was mention of woodland.'

'Bah! The land is worth not half that… and less than a month betwixt my mark on the paper and the fee's due? He never intended fulfilment of the debt. Twas designed to be defaulted.'

'Then still I… oh, oh!' Edmund's eyes widened. He put a hand over his mouth. 'I see.'

Guy stepped forward from the fireplace, looking inquisitively from his master to the clerk.

'Aye,' Robert said sourly. 'He wants Woodtown and my wool trade. Just like he stole the baker's land 'n trade.'

Guy pulled a face. 'A knight such as he having want of Woodtown? What with all the land what he's got?'

Robert began pacing again. 'John Herle is a known land thief. Anyway, it's not the land so much. It's the trade. I've grown this trade over the last few seasons. Done well this last year including tenant rents. Expect to do even better next year.'

'But if that was his intent, should he not write a hundred marks for the land? You might raise twenty,' Guy said.

'Nay. He knows that between managing this place, a large house in Plympton, and with a brother who's naught but a wastrel and a wife with a taste in finery to make a Burgundian Duchess appear cheap, that I'd not have a deep purse for savings. A hundred marks will be suspicious on paper. If I was to appeal on grounds o' trickery a hundred marks would prove him false. Twenty? Well, that is near belief.'

'He cheated his own muvver-in-law out of her lands, 'n robbed her sons of their inheritance,' Guy offered. 'Such is common knowledge.'

Edmund tapped his lip thoughtfully. 'I've heard such gossips and more similar. I dwelt little on it.'

'Dwell on it now, Clerk,' Robert grumbled.

'So, you've not twenty marks?' Edmund said, averting his gaze when he drew a glare from Robert.

'Half of it. He wouldn't take coin off me when I met him, knowing I'd likely find purpose for it afore St. John's feast day.'

'I understand not why he had you set loose from gaol,' Guy said. 'Easier to take what you got if you be locked away awaiting Royal Court.'

'If this is all true,' Edmund said slowly, 'perhaps, what with the previous accusations of Sir John obtaining land by deception, he would seem too guilty in trying to obtain the improved land and business of one left rotting in Lydford gaol.'

'Yes!' Robert slapped Edmund's shoulder. 'You've the right of it now! And I'll bet he was the one who had Rowan the Large told of my release from gaol so he might waylay me. It would be much easier for him to claim his dues from my widow.'

'How'd he know to talk to Rowan the Large?' Guy said, 'I'm not mindful that they'd be acquainted.'

'That's where Henry Spiney's role is revealed,' Robert said, smiling. 'He's worked a plot with the sheriff: The sheriff gets land I've improved and my trade and Henry get his father's. I am surer now than before that Rowan the Large killed William Spiney... on the instruction of Henry Spiney and Sir John Herle.'

The three men stayed quiet for a time as they considered their thoughts on the matter.

'We still need to prove it somehow,' Edmund said finally. 'Assuming of course that your theory is true... and I concede, it has the taste of truth to it.'

'The dagger is still the key,' Robert said, 'we need to find the maker, then if God is on our side, we'll get to the truth of it.'

'The maker of the dagger?' Guy said, his expression confused.

'Yes, Guy. The one I bade you conceal.'

'I know that smith's mark.'

'What?' Edmund and Robert said together.

'I once bought something crafted at same the forge. It be down Sutton way.'

'Sutton? Why didn't you say afore?' Robert said. He clapped his hands upon Guy's shoulders and playfully shook him.

'I knew not that it was of import nor that you wished to know, Master.'

'Ha!' Robert grabbed Guy's cheeks, squeezing them gently between his forefinger and thumb. 'You're a wonderous fool, Guy! Courtenay's loss, you are! Courtenay's loss and my enduring prize!'

Robert released Guy, who stepped back smiling weakly and rubbing his cheek. He glanced nervously at Edmund who shrugged one shoulder and smiled kindly.

XXII

Robert called his brother into the solar and had Guy roll in the barrel of the stronger ale from the larder. The brothers, together with Guy and Edmund, sat drinking beer and listening to Robert's stories. Mindful of John Sage's advice, Robert held back from reminiscing too much about his months in France; instead regaling his captive audience with stories from his childhood; most of which made Eustace blush.

Whenever Alice came into the solar Robert would talk of some occasion in their early courting days or speak of how heavenly she looked at their wedding. At first Alice didn't react to the obvious attempts at mollifying her, but she smiled when he related the tale of when he first set eyes upon her.

'I returned to her father's shop every day for a week, buying goods I'd not a need of, just to catch a glimpse of her afore I finally plucked a measure of courage to ask permission to court her. Her father knew my intent from the first day but said nothing as he was making a good business off my returns. Ha!' Robert slapped his knee, caught up in the mirth of his own tale.

The other men said little. Edmund protested that he had few stories of his own to relate, although Robert pressed him into speech. Edmund's mundane tale of a mislaid ledger was met with silence and forced smiles. Guy told a short story about a boy cleaning a garderobe gutter at Tiverton Castle. The young lad got himself stuck in the chute; his cries for help only being noted when one of the Lord's family received a frightful lamentation from below when they sat upon the latrine to attend their business. Eustace had tales involving drunken encounters at taverns and stories of his sharp wit in dealing with foreign merchants in Plympton - none of which anyone seemed to find particularly interesting or amusing, but Robert listened with a tolerant smile even though he'd heard versions of most of them before.

Alice served a supper of mutton and vegetable pottage with hard bread. After they had finished eating, Robert pulled her onto his lap. She laughingly resisted with a slap on his forearm, but he held her tight and so she took his cup and fed him his beer; much of which soaked into his beard. Robert squeezed her thigh and ignored her half-hearted protests over such base behaviour in company.

One of the hamlet's fullers, a middle-aged called Aubrey who was afflicted by some blistering skin disorder on his face, came by the window to offer good tidings and was handed a tankard of ale. He joined the conversation at the window, telling a couple of raucous tales of his own which amused everyone to the extent that his cup was refilled three times. Even Alice smiled at most of his stories, although she hid her humour behind her hand at some of the lewder parts.

The church bell rang for vespers. Edmund was already dozing with his head rested on the table. A small pooling of drool formed at the corner of his mouth. Alice climbed off Robert's lap, pulling her wrist free of his lingering grip. She lit two tallow candles, shuttered the window, and announced that she was readying for bed. Robert watched her until she departed the solar; only then realising he'd done nothing to mask his leering grin.

'My good companions…' Robert said, frowning at how loud his voice suddenly sounded. He stood and made to adjust his belt up before realising he'd removed it hours before. 'I shall likewise retire. I invite you all stay. Guy, fetch firewood enough for the night from the woodpile and such straw as you might require for the three of you to make bed upon. Tonight, I shall have my chamber for my wife and I alone.'

'You'll make me sleep on the floor?' Eustace said in surprise tinged with horror.

'Aye, or you might ride back to Plympton. I fancy there be a nice goose feather bed waiting for you.'

Guy snickered into his cup, ignoring the indignant look from Eustace.

Robert held onto the table. He rested his weight against it, involuntarily shifting the table a few inches so that the far end pressed against the wall. Edmund didn't stir.

'Easy, Master,' Guy said, grinning.

'I wasn't head rushed 'til I stood,' Robert announced. 'Best not stand, lads: it be the standing that affects the balance.'

Eustace hoisted his cup in salute and brought it to his mouth, then recoiling from it, he lifted it to his eye, frowning into the empty vessel and shaking it to make sure it was indeed empty. 'I'd have sworn there was beer,' he muttered. He looked longingly at the barrel and yawned.

'Didn't take much to put your clerk to rest,' Guy said, nodding toward Edmund's unconscious form. 'He sipped so delicately I don't fancy he finished his third cup.'

Robert staggered into the privacy screen. Stumbling backward he was caught by Guy before he could fall.

'Should I help you to loft, Master?'

'No. Unhand me.' Robert concentrated on standing firm, stretching his arms to his sides to aid balance. He felt in full control of his senses, it was navigation that proved difficult. It had been a long time, perhaps more than a year since he'd last enjoyed a bellyful of beer. His tolerance was less than he expected. He winced at Eustace, trying to gauge his brother's level of drunkenness: he looked tired but decidedly sober, at least while sitting. Perhaps, he decided, Eustace was a little too well versed in consuming quantities of alcohol.

'I must protest, Brother,' Eustace said.

Robert swiped his hand through the air in Eustace's direction as he navigated his way around the screen and into the central chamber. He noticed Alice looking down on him from the loft window. She pursed her lips and slammed the window shut. Robert puffed out air: she hadn't spoke against their drinking so she couldn't very well be mad at him for being drunk.

Deciding to relieve himself before going up to his bed, Robert went outside. Not wanting to walk to the latrine trench in the dwindling light for fear he might topple in, he relieved himself a few yards from the house, humming as he did so. He waved at Muriel as she carried a bucket from the well to her hut. She swung her unladen arm to counter the weight of the filled bucket. She didn't return Robert's wave and averted her face as he urinated.

'Yup, well... pox on you, Muriel,' Robert mumbled as he struggled to tie the front of his hose before abandoning the task;

he'd be removing them shortly. He went back inside, secured the door and trudged up the steps to the loft.

Alice was already in bed, laying on her side with the woollen blanket pulled up over her shoulder. A tallow candle burned at the bedside on a lead plate. Robert sat on the edge of the bed and pulled off his boots.

'I need to take what money we have to pay the sheriff,' Robert said. 'It won't be enough. Might be I'll need to borrow a little.'

Alice stirred, turning onto her back. 'Is that what your letter entailed? Did the sheriff ask a fee to quell the charges?'

Robert paused his attempt to peel off his second boot. He hummed for a moment before responding. 'Something of the sort. Best I count what we have.'

'Leave it for morn.' Alice sat up and lay her hands on Robert's back, running her fingers along his broad shoulders. 'It's late. Is Eustace still in his cups?'

'He'll not bother us. He's to sleep afore the fireplace.' Robert closed his eyes, enjoying the sensation of his wife's fingers through his shirt.

'Oh, Robert!' Alice dug her fingertips into his shoulders. 'That is ill mannered of you. It is bad enough our other guest insists on sleeping like a servant.'

'Bah! He'll be fine. I wager he'll be happier sleeping aside from a half-full barrel than in this plain bed.'

'Lay back on the bed with me, dear,' Alice said quietly.

Robert felt himself stirring at his wife's words. He closed his eyes and let Alice gently pull him down to the bed.

'Wait.' Robert forced himself to sit upright. He pulled off his remaining boot which thudded on the floorboard. He rose to his feet with a reluctant groan and walked to the corner of the room where his wife's clothes chest lay. He tugged it, dragging the large wooden box across the floor. The iron braces of the chest squealed against the floorboards.

'Robert! Desist that at once! Come abed: you are making much fuss.'

'Verily,' Robert grunted as he pulled again, eliciting another grinding protest from the chest. 'This will be but a moment, dearest. I must know what we have to pay the sheriff.'

'Husband…' Alice was sitting up on the bed in the long plain linen underdress she usually wore to sleep and her cloth coif. She looked pleadingly at Robert. 'Please, just leave it 'til morn. Your wife awaits you.' She pulled at the neck of the dress to reveal a shoulder. Her pale skin seeming almost ghostly in the dim light.

Robert watched her, enthralled. He remained rooted in place with his palms on the chest as he struggled to control his balance and his suddenly urgent breathing.

Alice removed her coif and untied her hair, letting the wavy golden locks fall around her shoulders. Although they had been married years, Robert seldom saw her hair unadorned and hanging freely.

Robert stood up from the chest and glanced over to the corner of the room and back to his wife.

'Just a moment, my dearest. I shall have to put the chest back in place anyhow. If I can but count the coin I may put my thoughts at rest.'

Robert went to the corner and knelt, prising up a loose section of floorboard. He put his hand into the concealed compartment and withdrew a small cloth pouch fastened with leather thonging. He laid the pouch down and untied the bindings. The pouch unfolded, revealing a small pile of coins. He blinked at the pile and squinted, his sight straining in shadows of the recess. He reached for the candle, but he already knew there weren't as many coins as there should be. He fingered the coins one by one into a second pile, then sat back on his haunches and closed his eyes.

'Eustace?' Robert said, his throat suddenly dry.

'He needed the coin for expenses in Plympton. Export fees and household costs. It's not like here in Woodtown, as well you know. You were in Lyford at the time. We… I thought it best to wait before telling you because you have so much consternation already.'

Robert remained facing the corner. 'There's less than three pounds here. He's removed four or five pounds for... expenses did you say?'

'Please, don't anger. You will imbalance your humours. Your brother will ensure the money is repaid by year's end. He promised so.'

Robert chuckled humourlessly. 'You ill believe that as well as do I. Such coin as whatever Eustace owes in Plympton is due in payment for honeyed wine, low ladies and dice games lost, not fees and taxes.'

'It won't happen again, Robert. Please don't be cruel to him. I... I offered him the coin when he explained the predicament. He didn't ask it. He protested even. If you have anger, it should be for me.'

Robert bowed his head and rubbed the knuckles of his fist against his forehead. His throat felt suddenly sore and his nose stuffed with mucus. His eyes moistened and a single teardrop fell onto the board between his knees.

'Robert, what are you doing? Have I grievously crossed you?'

'Nay.... Aye. I don't know. I'm not in anger. I just... you don't know what you've done. That coin was needed. I shall endure much trouble over this.'

The boards of the bed creaked as Alice moved across it. Her feet padded the few steps across the floor to where Robert sat. She embraced him from behind with an arm around his chest and another around his waist. Golden hair fell across Robert's shoulder and her breath was hot on his neck.

'Think not on this, Husband. Come abed.'

He sat for a few seconds longer, enjoying the uncommon embrace and the scent of the rosewater Alice used for perfume. He allowed her tender pull to encourage him to his feet.

Alice took his arm and guided him to the bed. She untied his hose and pulled them off his legs: such a rare act would usually have him excited beyond measure, but the mixture of melancholy over his lack of funds and overconsumption of ale had left him feeling empty and drained of will. Alice seemed to sense his deflated mood; she looked down on him with a pained expression. She put the candle back in its place and blew it out, then lay beside him, pulling the sheet over their shoulders and tugging her husband close.

The couple lay together in embrace. Alice's cheek rested on his. Her breath was soft on his ear. She rubbed his back as tenderly as one might a sleeping child's, and whispered hushes.

Robert closed his eyes against the warm wetness he felt in the corners of his eyes, daring not to move or make a sound in case his wife detect his weakness. He felt her fingertip softly trail across his eyelid, wiping away the salty moisture. Her lips touched his eyebrow. They said nothing.

XXIII

Robert fastened his doublet. He glanced across at Alice who was tying her hair into a crispinette. She wore her white dress, which like the crispinette, was adorned with beads intended to resemble pearls.

'You look as an angel, dearest.'

Alice turned and smiled faintly before returning to her rusty looking glass. Robert smoothed down the front of his doublet and watched his wife brush and tie her hair until it was neatly bundled into intricate nets at either side of her head. She admired herself in her reflection before picking up a piece of hazel twig from her small chest of accessories and implements. She used the frayed green end of the twig to scrub her teeth, picking out any small pieces of bark which came loose in her mouth. Once finished, she examined her teeth closely in the mirror. She frowned, turning to face Robert.

'Why do you observe me, Husband?'

'Why? Would be remiss not to - believe me well. Your visage maketh me feel greatly blessed.'

'Oh, Husband. You are always full of passions of one style or another.' Alice smiled at Robert's compliment, but her expression became downcast when she noticed him flinch at her words. 'Husband, I did not mean to rebuke you for this past night… I meant only that your heart is-'

Robert silenced her with an upheld hand but kept his gaze low. 'It matters not. I was betwixt rancour at my brother's indulgences and mine own indulgence in strong ale. We need not speak of it.'

Alice nodded solemnly. She closed the few steps between them and kissed him on the cheek. She held out the twig between forefinger and thumb. 'Here. Make use of this. Then we shall go to church.'

Robert took the twig and chewed the end to reveal more of the green. He peeled back the bark.

Alice watched him scrub his teeth. She chewed on her lower lip and released a heavy sigh. 'Husband, I will ask you not to make strong oaths against your kin- today of all days. Likewise, at church, if any should chastise you or look disagreeably upon you.'

Robert grimaced. 'I will not allow what has passed to go unspoken between Eustace and I, but I shall refrain from violent oaths. As for the congregation - those of Woodtown would dare not risk my ire. Those of Sampford I care not for their disdain, spoken or otherwise.'

Alice pinched his chin and held his gaze for some moments before nodding. She turned away, lifting the hem of her dress, she walked down the steps with a fashionable train of material dragging along behind her.

Robert found Eustace and Edmund sat at the table in the solar. Eustace was dressed in a fine coat and peacock feathered cap. He ate bread while wearing a disinterested scowl at whatever Edmund was talking about. They both looked up at Robert as he navigated around the privacy screen with a tut as his elbow nudged the gaudy wooden board.

'Morning, elder brother. How be thy head this holy morn?'

Robert walked over to the table and waved Edmund away. The clerk rose and left without a word. Robert took his seat.

Eustace's chewing slowed. His eyes narrowed. He leaned back to put a few inches further distance between them. 'Is all well, brother?'

Robert wiped some sleep from his eye and rested his forearms on the table. 'I'll make no bones, Eustace, but what has become of the coin you… lent off my wife?'

'Ah.,' Eustace paused with a piece of bread just short of his waiting mouth. He cautiously lowered the crust and swallowed a mouthful of saliva. 'Well, verily you are much gentler in the learning than I expected.'

'What has become of the coin?'

Eustace popped the piece of bread into his mouth and rolled his eyes around as if thinking as he chewed.

Robert put his left hand under the table and squeezed his own knee to steady his temper, while the fingertips of his right hand pressed onto the rough tabletop where splinters stabbed into his digits.

'Well…' Eustace said, pausing to swallow his food. 'Export taxes are much increased this last batch, to which I owed… the family owed that is, the balance. It's all in the account books. I know you will say I've spun your coin into cloth, and yes, I did purchase a new riding cloak and gloves, yet as the family representative to merchants buying our produce, I must maintain a visage of success. You see that, of course.'

Robert grunted. 'You've dispensed with it all already then?'

'It is all accounted for, Brother. I fully intend to repay you for the cloak and gloves, of course.'

Robert sniffed and stood, leaving the solar. There was no point in stressing how urgently the absent monies were needed. Such a discourse would only lead to the strong words he'd sworn to refrain from.

They left the house together: Robert walked arm in arm with Alice. Eustace, Edmund, and Guy followed a few step behind. Robert left his sword at home but wore a dagger on his belt; to draw any blade on consecrated ground was a sacrilege few would commit. Robert didn't expect violence but prepared for the possibility. He knew it was probable that most of the villagers attending mass would carry practical knives, as is normal, but his long-bladed dagger rather than a simple knife for everyday use might attract a few frowns.

The grass was fringed with the overnight droplets of rain and the path was puddled in places, but the sun rose warm, promising another hot day. Others from the hamlet made their way to the church, clustered together in their household groups. The men doffed their hats to Robert and Alice, Robert nodded in return. One man ahead on the path looked over his shoulder and quickened his pace: John Sherman.

Robert winced at John as the shearer's legs worked faster to put distance between himself and his landlord. Robert felt his arm squeezed by Alice, which came accompanied with a narrow, warning glance. He smiled, he hoped, disarmingly. He watched the hurrying figure of the shearer and allowed himself a small smile at the man's obvious alarm and savoured the thought that

John would have a difficult life in Woodtown: never sure when the master's ire might smite him.

They arrived at the church as the bells were ringing for Sunday mass. The population of Sampford Spiney, Woodtown, and the outlaying farms all filed into the church. Some attended mass daily, others less often, but all attended on the holy day: it was a mortal sin not to.

Robert removed his hat as he crossed the threshold. He glanced toward the altar where William's coffin had been the day before and then cast his gaze around the congregation, looking for Henry and prominent members of his household. He quickly spotted Henry and Mathilde sat on one of the front pews, their heads already bowed in solemn subjugation to the Lord. Other members of the seated lay community looked around at those shuffling in. Robert noted whispers behind hands and dark looks in his direction. He sucked his teeth and pretended not to notice; supposing that perhaps he was only imagining their scorn despite that it was the very reaction he anticipated. The expression on the Pastor's face indicated that he had probably not imagined it.

Randalf Hoccleave stood on the dais behind the altar, dressed in his colourless priest robes. His vision was firmly locked on Robert. His mouth hung slightly open, his nose wrinkled in disbelief or disgust.

Robert took his seat, feeling his skin warm at the mutterings and looks. What choice did he have? It wasn't optional to attend church. What right did the priest even have to look offended at Robert's arrival? He quietly fumed, staring between his knees while he waited for the service to begin.

Mass was given, as always, in Latin. Usually, some parishioners would fall asleep at various points only to be nudged awake by their neighbour, but Robert didn't notice any snoozing: many blatantly stared at him even during the recitals. The ill looks Robert received from all quarters distracted him from the unintelligible Latin Mass and English sermon alike, yet his ears and cheeks burned, smarting from the teachings of the service as he became increasingly aware that the Pastor was directing much of the English preaching at Robert.

'Whoever taketh man's life, shall be surely put to death!' The Pastor boomed, holding his hand high as if to invoke God's judgement. He flipped through more pages while continuing a diatribe about justice before finding a passage which he translated while looking directly at Robert. 'If anyone kills a man, the murderer shalt be put to death on evidence of witnesses! Thou shalt accept no ransom for the murderer's life. He who is guilty of death shall be put to death. So sayeth the Lord! We should not be pained by murderers in our midst. If thou should see evil among your neighbours, they must be brought to justice - as is the law of God!'

Robert grimaced and folded his arms. He noticed Guy further along the pew, shifting uncomfortably in his seat, his head turning this way and that to confront and deflect the stares of the congregation. Guy unblinkingly bore an irritated glance from the pastor, then stabbed his finger at a muttering farmer, widening his eyes in warning at the man. Alice sobbed quietly.

Robert gave thought to marching out of the service. Would Alice accompany him? They surely couldn't return to this church while he was under suspicion. They would likely have to travel into Tavistock to attend service. He was at the least glad he had convinced Alice not to attend William's funeral to endure a hostile reception alone.

Throughout the service Henry Spiney kept his attention on the priest. He stood when the pastor asked the congregation to rise, knelt when commanded, took the communion, but not once looked around at Robert. Mathilde however, looked about often with tear-streaked cheeks. Unlike the rest of the congregation, her expression didn't convey malice or hatred, but simple grief. Robert decided that the pure sorrow of her sad face with its red eyes and nose and blubbering lips were impossible to feign: she had nothing to do with her husband's demise. His list of possible murderers was becoming smaller, but it didn't feel like progress.

The service seemed to drag on much longer than usual. As the congregation finally filed out of the church they were careful to maintain a few paces gap before and after Robert. He ignored the offence and was glad to be outside in the sunshine. He took Alice's arm in his. Her lip trembled but she kept her composure.

'Murderer!' Someone called out.

Robert looked about for the source. Some of the Sampford Spiney residents stood glowering at him. Others walked hurriedly away with their families. The Woodtown spinners and fullers rushed past with their heads down.

'Why's he not hanging?' a black-toothed farmer sneered.

'Aye!' a female voice agreed.

'You'll stand well back if'n ye knows what's best for ye!' Guy snarled, standing protectively in front of Robert and Alice with his arms stretched out to form a barrier.

'Best we not remain but make haste,' Eustace whispered in Robert's ear.

It was not in Robert's creed to turn in the face of an enemy and walk away. He recalled that on campaign in France, bold English Knights would parade in front of the walls of a French castle, daring the French to come out and fight. He remembered John Sage's words; perhaps it was true that he held himself as greater than those villeins from who he ascended. He could rush among the churchgoers, striking and scolding them, but a few obstinates might become mob and turn on his family, and they might not be wrong to do so.

Henry Spiney exited the church. Dressed in his finest clothes of velvet and adorned with such cheap jewels and furs as a merchant of his standing could afford. The small crowd hushed. Henry cast a disdainful look at the group from Woodtown and extended his hand toward his mother whom he guided back toward the manor. He walked at a slow pace, as if parading through a cobbled city street, his nose pointed toward the horizon.

'Let us leave this wretched hamlet,' Robert said, turning away. He put his arm around Alice's shoulder.

The group walked back toward Woodtown with Guy and Edmund at the rear. A half dozen of the Sampford Spiney villeins followed them, shouting crude insults. One of them threw something: either mud or manure, striking Eustace in the back of the leg. Eustace cried out and paused to examine the cloth of his hose.

'Walk on!' Robert hissed.

Edmund reasoned with the farmers to stay their hand, insisting that Robert hadn't yet stood trial and was on the way to proving his innocence. The villeins paid the clerk no notice other than to insult his heritage and theorise on his sexual preferences. They were however wary of Guy's sharp tongue and snarled threats which kept them at a safe distance.

The nerve of the pursuing villeins ended at the boundary of Sampford Spiney, where the farmers had halted their pursuit and limited themselves to jeering. As Robert's group continued, the increased distance gave the villeins bravery enough to remark on Guy's scarred face and the rumours that he was cast out of Lord Courtenay's service either for theft or for sodomy. Guy didn't react to the insults and the villeins soon turned about and headed back to their furlongs.

'Oh! How can we ever return to church!' Alice sobbed, leaning heavily into Robert for support as she struggled to put one foot in front of the other.

'We'll attend Sunday mass at Tavistock,' Robert said, 'until this evil mess has been put to peace.'

'Tavistock?' Alice said, her face contorted and wet. 'What about daily service?'

'You've your own chapel. Use that!' Robert immediately regretted the harshness of his tone. It had always been his own reluctance to regularly attend mass that stopped Alice from going as often as she'd like.

Alice's head sunk low. Robert caught Eustace's reproachful look. A hard stare from Robert averted his brother's frown.

The group bundled into the longhouse like refugees from a severe storm. Robert helped his wife up the steps to the loft space and onto the bed. She lay face down, hugging the pillow and making a quiet sobbing sound. Robert sat beside her on the edge of the bed. Only a little natural light filtered through the interior window, so he lit a tallow candle at the bedside then stroked his wife's hair and back.

'Hush, my dearest. On the morrow I shall journey to Sutton and we shall, by God's will, find the name of the true murderer. We must endure but a few days and all will be well once more.'

Alice turned onto her side. She looked at him with one eye, the other remained pressed into the pillow. 'And what if you find not whatever it is you seek in Sutton?'

'Have faith, wife.' Robert smiled.

Alice put her hand on his forearm and squeezed. 'Run, Robert. They will hang you I am sure. If you find not what you seek in Sutton, you must flee. Go into Cornwall or Wessex with enough coin to start anew.'

'Without you?'

'You would have me outlawed and destitute, Husband? You are much hardier than I. You will thrive in any storm.'

Robert nodded and smiled weakly. He rested his hand on her shoulder. Alice soon fell asleep. Robert stifled the impulse to brush stray strands of her from her forehead and wipe the sticky, moistened area between her cheek and nose where the tears had run. He puffed out the candle to conserve it and sat in near darkness, accompanied only by the sounds of muffled voices and occasional footsteps from the solar and the bleating of goats and sheep from beyond the thatch.

***

'Master Wood!' Guy shouted from below. 'Master Wood!'

Alice stirred, putting her hand to her cheek, she groaned softly and turned on the bed then her eyes blinked open. 'Oh, how long did I sleep? Is it night?'

'Nay, wife. It is still morn. You slumbered but a short while in your grief.'

'Master Robert!'

'What is it, by God's cap!' Robert roared at the direction of the voice.

'You should come down with haste. There is ill news.'

'Stay. Rest.' Robert run his hand along Alice's sleeve and stood up from the bed and trudged down the steps into the larder.

Edmund stood in the larder doorway and indicated for Robert to walk into the central chamber where Guy stood, cap in hand.

'What be it?' Robert demanded.

'I be most sorry, Robert.' Guy crushed the hat in his hands and kept his eyes down.

'Well, what? Speak damn thee!'

'The bullock dagger. It be lost.'

'Lost?' Robert shook his head, bewildered. 'How be it lost? I gave it thee for the hiding - be you so addlepated as to forget where it be secreted?'

'It is stolen,' Edmund said, his expression as solemn as if he'd announced the death of a relative.

'Aye.' Guy nodded and gulped, he sucked in his lips and looked near to tears.

Robert snatched Guy's arm and shook it. 'Tell.'

Guy took a deep breath and nodded. 'I did as you bade. I stowed the dagger in the barn loft. Nery a soul ever went up there, so I put little thought to the hiding. I wrapped it inside me riding cloak. Now I find my cloak unravelled! I knew verily what had passed. Someone took it while we were at church!'

Robert released Guy's arm and groaned. He stumbled to the opposite wall and rested his forehead against it.

'Perhaps this is not ill news but fortuitous,' Edmund said, leaning against the wall beside Robert. He gave a thin smile as the three men eagerly awaited his explanation.

'Well? Damnit!' Robert seethed.

Edmund blinked and raised a palm for peace, realising his error in savouring his host's suspense for too long. 'The dagger is stolen. The murderer moves from shadow to reveal himself.'

Robert glanced at Guy who gave a confused shrug. Robert glared at Edmund.

'You see, Master Robert, few knew of the dagger. The one who took it must have been one of those few of us who knew of it and where it might be.'

Robert thought for a moment then shook his head. 'Nay. Any rogue can steal a dagger. Some lad snuck up there looking for a coin or piece of bread whilst everyone was at church.'

Edmund nodded almost imperceptibly and touched his lip with his forefinger. 'Verily, such a thing is possible. But would this young thief you speak of not take the riding cloak? And whatever else Master Guy may have to tempt such a thief.'

'No…' Robert wagged his finger in Edmund's face. 'This time, Scribe, you be wrong. Any hereabout would recognise it as Guy's cloak. The thief would be a fool to remove it.'

Edmund inclined his head in thought for a moment. 'Is the dagger not similarly noteworthy in the wrong hands?'

'Aye, the dagger is uncommon enough, but such a thing is easily hid then later sold away from here.'

'It seems not easily hid,' Eustace said with a smirk, emerging from the solar, carrying a clay goblet. 'What's of such import about a dagger? Is it some prize from glorious days in France or a gilded heirloom I've known naught about?'

Robert frowned and stared purposefully at the drink his brother cradled.

Eustace shrugged when it became clear that his questions were going to be left unanswered. 'Anyways, I agree with Robert. The whole hamlet was at mass. A wayward lad wouldn't be missed from church and can have snuck anywhere he pleased. Such things are known to happen.'

'Ah, Master Eustace.' Edmund nodded and stepped forward, interlacing his fingers before him. 'I grant that such things are not uncommon, but our thief has stolen one item only. Is it not so, Master Guy?'

Guy nodded.

'You are sure, Master Guy, that nothing else was taken from you? Not a fibre of cloth, a rusty spoon, nor a halved coin?'

'I keeps me spoon about my person. Same for such coin as I have. Not got much else. Wasn't no cloth taken. Nothing else neither. Just the bullock dagger.'

'You see,' said Eustace, 'the dagger was the only thing of value: any common thief will have taken it.'

'Aye. Twas ill hidden and taken by a common scoundrel,' Robert grumbled.

Edmund walked toward Guy and pushed him aside from the longhouse door.

Guy looked from Edmund to Robert with alarm, sputtering and unsure whether to be angry at being manhandled.

Edmund pulled open the door and gestured outside.

'As you say, Master Eustace, everyone was at mass. This door stood unbarred. As, I dare say, did every other cottage, hut, barn and longhouse in the hamlet and that of Sampford Spiney.

Yet I hear no hue and cry. No. Our thief went to one place only: the stable, where he stole only one possession.'

The four men looked at one another in silence.

'It can't be,' Robert said flatly.

'Let us recount who knew of the bullock dagger,' Edmund said, licking his lips excitedly. 'All of us here in this chamber save Eustace... the good lady Alice. Any other?'

'It wasn't any of us,' Robert scowled at the scribe. 'I will not hear of it. Anyway, we were all at mass. Your theorising is foolish.'

'Could not someone have paid this young thief your theorising has conjured up to steal the dagger in our absence?' Edmund said.

'Enough! Twas not I, nor my brother, nor Guy... and my wife? Impossible! I would sooner believe you as a thief than any those you named.'

Edmund held up a staying hand. 'Apologies, sir. I ask only if any others may know of the dagger.'

Robert jolted with sudden realisation. 'John Sage! Yes... I showed him the dagger yesterday and told him twas the murderer's tool.'

Eustace touched his temple and winced. 'Hold, Brother. Is this dagger thought to be the one which murdered William Spiney? And you spoke of your possession of it with the head man of the household that wishes you hanged for the very same offence?'

Robert paced, ignoring his brother. 'It must have been Sage! Ah, there is something bastardly about those named John, is there not?'

'Quite,' Eustace said without conviction.

'To arms!' Robert said, 'we shall arrest him and drag him to Lyford to answer.'

'Peace, Master Robert.' Edmund grabbed hold of Robert's shoulder. 'There is not proof. Not yet. Now, think... was this John Sage at mass today?'

Robert thought hard. He wasn't focused on who had been present other than those who had openly stared at him. He spent much of the service trying to ignore the other parishioners.

'I can't say.'

'Nor I,' said Guy.

'I think he was not,' offered Eustace with a shrug. 'But I wouldn't swear to it.'

'I saw him,' Edmund said, 'outside after the service. He walked with Master Spiney and his mother. I don't recollect him inside the church, but he was certainly outside.'

'So, he was there?' Guy said, wrinkling one side of his face.

'After Mass at least,' Edmund said thoughtfully. 'It might be that he only appeared once mass was done to give the impression of attendance. That is why I ask if any saw him inside the church.'

The three men shook their heads.

'We will need to ask the Lady Alice,' Edmund said, 'when she is fit to speak. We should also ask everyone in Woodtown if they saw Robert Sage or if anyone else was missing from mass. I would like to ask the same at Sampford Spiney, but I'd not feel safe to do so. We should also ask all the hamlet residents if any possession has gone missing since mass to confirm if there was a thief loose in the hamlet.'

Robert clapped Edmund's arm. 'Aye. Well reasoned. Then we shall journey to Sutton. I can describe the dagger to the smithy.'

Edmund nodded. 'It seems likely that this course will give us the name we seek. The killer will have only hidden the dagger if they feared the weapon might identify them.'

XXIV

Robert and Edmund exhaustively searched Guy's loft space, then examined the rest of stable and the surrounding area for footprints or any other indication of who may have taken the dagger. Despite the ground being softened from overnight rain the only discernible marks were the many horseshoe prints in the mud. Robert had been doubtful the exercise would produce result but deferred to Edmund's desire for thoroughness.

Guy and Robert readied a horse and donkey while Edmund visited nearby cottages, establishing that none in Woodtown had lost any property, nor found any evidence of intrusion during the church service.

They ate a meal of root vegetables in vinaigrette with cabbage and mustard. The Wood family, Guy, and Edmund sat shoulder to shoulder around the table in the solar. Each complimented Alice on the meal, then with the sun just past noon, Edmund and Robert set out for Plymouth.

It took Edmund a little while to regain his composure and confidence for riding the donkey. The beast circled as Edmund tried to mount it, and once they'd set off it stopped at will, but with firm commands and a nudge of the heel in the right place, Edmund was soon able to keep up with Robert.

Plymouth was about the same distance from Woodtown as Lydford, but in the opposite direction, and for much of the way the tracks were less well defined. Robert navigated from one stone cross marker to the next. At times Sutton harbour was in sight from certain promontories, even early in the journey. They skirted around bogs, over hillsides covered in granite lumps, and through hidden game trails among heather and bracken which brushed against the riders' boots. The route didn't meet a roadway until they were within a few miles of their destination - it was only then that they first encountered other travellers along the route: A few farmers transporting carts of produce between Plymouth and the communities and farms to the north, and a group of labourers from the tin mining industry who whipped a lame hose as it limped along under the burden of its load.

Smallholdings covered the landscape for a mile outside of Plymouth. Rows of long, narrow strips of farmland blanketed hillsides, giving the terrain the appearance of having been combed. Farmers and their beasts moved over the lynchets with bent-backed resilience. Occasional thatched buildings protruded between fields. The northern end of Plymouth was surrounded by a wooden palisade atop a continuous earthwork mound where labourers were busy building or rebuilding a long section of the wooden rampart. Hovels, houses, workshops, and huts had already overspilled beyond the perimeter wall, cramming the void between the farmland and the town. Thatch and slate roofs along with a few church steeples poked over the top of the palisade, promising a density of humanity within the walls. A wooden gatehouse arched over the path into the town, manned by a single guard in a worn and stained padded jacket who leaned against the jagged crenelations of the gatehouse with a bored expression - likely calculating the loss of a days' work he owed to his turn in sentry duty.

The stink of bodily waste mixed with decay and smoke permeated the town boundary by some distance. Edmund covered his mouth and nose with his hand. Robert merely grimaced at the stench. The road under the gatehouse had degraded into freshly churned muck, sucking and squelching at the hoofs of the mounts.

Within the town walls the buildings were mostly two levels tall: often with a granite ground floor and wooden or wattle and daub second floor. Black slate roofs dominated, while only a few of the poorer looking residences bore thatch. Faded and dirty business signs jutted into the narrow streets. The interior road was little better than under the gatehouse: stones had been thrown down in many places to make it more easily traversable but stagnant pools and filth, both human and animal, were visible in quantity.

The populace went about their business seemingly unperturbed by their neighbours' odours. They walked the streets with a collective ease, avoiding murky pools and more sodden spots while continuing conversation with their companions. Gulls flitted from one rooftop to the next, their cawing as ever-present as the sounds of hammering, coughing and the shouts of those hawking their wares.

Uneven and twisting streets diverged at each compass point. Robert continued straight ahead, ignoring various angled offshoots until they came onto a wider main street. The road ran East toward a large granite church. The Westerly path led deeper into the knotted chaos of the town. Robert called to a begging boy, asking if the Easterly route might lead them to the town's East gate, which the boy confirmed it did. Robert tossed him a coin and urged his horse into motion, following a slow-moving cart transporting two pigs.

'Guy tells that the smithy was on the harbour side of the East gate,' Robert said, 'can't be far.'

They harbour became apparent by the ship's rigging stretching above rooftops. Limp pennants hung from the summits of masts atop tied up, weather-stained canvas sails. The street soon opened into the cobbled seafront of Sutton Harbour. Dozens of merchant cogs were moored in the harbour and at the quayside. The harbourside was crammed with market stalls and beggars. Ships were being loaded or unloaded with workers pushing, pulling and rolling goods to and from the vessels. Conversations and shouting continued unabated in a variety of languages: Robert caught snatches of French and Welsh along with tongues he didn't recognise. A dark-skinned merchant in brightly striped attire argued in what Robert thought might've been Italian with a man whose clothes and long flowing hair boasted of some continental fashion.

'I feel as far from home as a man may ever be,' Edmund said slowly as his wide eyes darted from one sight to the next.

'Ha! When I fought the Bretons, we saw many a place much grander than this. They all stink the same. I expect that be why they build such mighty towers: so those better than us can dwell above the stench.' Robert pointed across the harbour where a stone castle was in the final stages of construction. The last of its four corner turrets was surrounded in scaffold and the walls topped by winches.

'I've been to Exeter,' Edmund said, 'the walls are grand and the cathedral mighty, but nothing so crowded as this.'

'Trade from here goes as far as Constantinople and beyond. It's as important a port as any, yet I have little use for this place. Wool goes up the coast from Plympton so it may be properly taxed. I shall need ask direction to our smith.'

Robert stopped three people before one of them could offer directions. A warty faced villein informed them that the smith was the third or fourth building up one of the side streets.

'We should find stabling firstly,' Robert said.

An inn was found near the harbour where stabling was available. Robert interred the mounts before continuing by foot to the blacksmith.

Edmund walked daintily with his eyes scanning the ground to avoid the worst he might have the misfortune to step in. A round-faced woman carrying a bundle of woollen cloth over her shoulder collided with him. He made a surprised sound and began to apologise but was cut-off by the woman's sneering curse before she continued on her way.

'Follow me. You may clean your befouled shoes later.' Robert grumbled, pushing on ahead.

The blacksmith forge was found easily enough: a sign depicted a hammer and anvil in flaking paint, and the sounds of iron on iron rang out with rapidity from the open-fronted forge. The street immediately outside was cleaner than most, having been strewn with a scattering of sawdust and ground up stones.

A furnace glowed red in the workshop while one man, naked except for his apron, hose, and gloves, gripped a pair of tongs which he used to hold an iron rod into the fire. A bald man hammered a glowing horseshoe with a black hammer. Behind him an assortment of tools, barrel rings and wheel arches in various stages of preparation hung from racks or from nails and hooks on the wall.

Robert waited for the bald man to pause his hammering before he ventured to enquire about purchasing a bullock dagger. The man directed him to the adjacent shop where the forge produce was sold.

Scents of leather, grease, and iron from within the shop struggled for dominance against the more repugnant exterior smells. A man with white hair and beard stood up from a stool in the corner. He gestured to his wares: an assortment of eating implements, farming tools, lanterns and a few weapons.

'I wish to purchase a bullock dagger,' Robert said, gazing over a small collection of sheathed daggers adorning a wooden pallet.

'Bullock ye say? Archer, be ye?' the man said in shrill voice as he scratched his temple. 'Not the manner o' thing we keeping about. Not much call for 'em these last years. I can make one for ye. It'll be three days. Perchance four. Or you can take a different manner o' dagger now from among such wares as I got.'

Robert glanced over the few daggers on display and selected one. The hilt showed the same mark as the missing bullock dagger. He slid the blade from its scabbard. It was clean and sharp, and the steel well oiled. The weapon felt firm in his hand and both grip and blade were unblemished. He put the dagger back and looked over to the shopkeeper.

'I was recommended to you, by a friend. Says he bought a bullock dagger hereabouts, but he couldn't remember which smith he bought from. It's a fine blade: I will buy only from the same smith and have travelled from Sampford Spiney to do so.'

The shopkeeper made a surprised but pleased sound. His smile created a knot of wrinkles around his eyes. 'There be three smiths in Sutton: of which I assure thee we are finest. As you see yourself.' The shopkeeper gestured grandly over the array of metalware lined up on benches, hanging from hooks and propped against walls.

'Indeed. Yet, good man, I must be sure I am speaking to the correct blacksmith. Do you recall crafting a bullock dagger in recent months for a man living south of Lydford?'

The shopkeeper scratched his stubble and wiggled his nose. 'We did make one fine dagger. Early in May methinks. Or April. I recall not where the customer be from, but surely he was an archer such as yourself.'

'Yes!' Robert clapped his hands. 'Do you remember the fellow? His name? His visage?'

The shopkeeper chuckled. 'Some days we've half dozen buying customers. I remember 'em not beyond a few days. The foreign ones are more easily marked. Last week, or twas it week before? Anyway, there was a Saracen dressed in the finest yellow cloth. Another fellow some months along, he had come from the borders of-'

'I care not for Saracens and borders, Shopkeeper,' Robert said quickly, forcing a smile. 'Please, it is past Sext and we've not supped. We are tired from our journey and eager for rest. Is there nothing you can tell us of the man who bade you craft the bullock dagger?'

'Well…' the shopkeeper looked off into the rafters, tapping his chin with his forefinger. 'perhaps you can describe your friend, then I will maybe remember him.'

Robert cast an irritated look toward Edmund who stepped forward with his hands clasped subserviently in front of him.

'Please, good sir. Perhaps your smiths… your sons, are they? Perchance their recollection is clearer?'

'That they be,' the shopkeeper's eyes disappeared into slits with his wrinkled smile. 'Me good, fine, strong sons. They are busy at work. I've nary a wish to disturb 'em.'

Robert took a deep breath. Edmund put a hand on his arm.

'Perhaps, Master Robert, we might leave the good smith to speak with his sons over their supper while we take ours. We can return in the morn after all are rested and with minds afresh. Perhaps a few coins for his trouble?'

Robert released his breath in a long slow deflation and opened his purse, removing two misshapen silver coins. He pressed them into the smith's waiting hand.

'I shall speak with my boys at length, good sirs. Be assured that if ye return in the morn, I will have such answer as best we might make.'

'Be sure you do,' Robert mumbled.

***

The harbourside Inn was grew boisterous with the dusk. Revellers engaged in dice games, singing, arguments and fights.

The fireplace remained unlit due to the evening warmth, yet the inn's occupants still congregated around it as the focal point.

Robert and Edmund sat eating a meal of hard bread and soft vegetables which they washed down with weak ale. Merchants, sailors, pilgrims, and labourers sat shoulder to shoulder along the benches. Any large arm movements risked spilling a neighbour's drink or nudging his eating arm, which carried the danger of harsh words or even violence.

Edmund ate carefully with his elbows tucked into his ribs, chewing his food carefully, cautiously watching the others around the table and looking down on his food when anyone made eye contact.

Robert ate with his face close to his wooden plate, using his stubby eating knife to carve up the food and shovel it into his mouth. When the man to his left knocked his arm, Robert shoved his shoulder and glared at the man until the fellow looked away. Once he was finished eating he pushed the plate from in front of him.

'You eat ravenously when away from home,' Edmund observed.

'Away from home I've no wife to comment on manners. I see you eat like a rabbit at all times, although lately as if a frightened one surrounded by foxes.'

Edmund frowned down at his plate, pushing the week-old vegetables about with the tip of his knife. 'Do you think the smith will remember the owner of the dagger?'

'Aye. Certain of such.'

'Truly?' Edmund said, raising his eyebrows expectantly.

'Nay. My meaning is that he will describe a fellow to us. Conjured from imagination if not memory.'

Edmund's shoulders dropped. 'Indeed. So, we are stuck with the same suspects.'

Robert looked sideways at Edmund while glugging from his tankard, then slammed it down and wiped his mouth with the back of his hand. 'What suspects?'

'Well… all those who knew of the dagger.'

'Nay. It'll be John Sage or someone we've not thought of. Not my wife, brother or Guy. I'll not hear otherwise.'

The attention of the two men was momentarily drawn to a crash from the table opposite, where someone had stood up with too much force and unbalanced the rickety bench, sending the two other patrons sitting on it sprawling onto their backs. The other customers laughed. Someone threw a handful of sloppy vegetables at the fallen men as they picked themselves up, cursing under their breath and glaring at the guffawing man who had tumbled the bench.

'Let me say, Master Robert: you may consider or disregard such suspects as you wish, but I hope you will not take offence if I keep open consideration.'

Robert curled his lip. 'I care not who you suspect while you keep such thoughts to yourself. Whoever the killer might be, it isn't my wife in any case.'

'Of course,' Edmund said, 'your wife will not have travelled to Sutton without your knowledge to buy a dagger. We may assume that much at least.'

'Nor done the killing,' Robert said, feeling his cheeks and neck warm.

'Of course, Sir. Yet, I have heard of instances of a woman killing a man. Usually the victim is her husband. Such things happen.'

'Verily,' Robert agreed, 'but not my wife. Our killer favours the left hand, does he not?'

'Yes. So we reasoned.'

'Alice favours the right.'

'Oh yes, I know.' Edmund smiled. 'I recall her using the right when stirring the pot.'

Robert's eyelids narrowed. 'Are you closely observing all in my household?'

'Oh yes,' Edmund enthused, then marking Robert's demeanour he returned his attention to his plate. 'I must consider all possibilities.'

***

Robert awoke early in a foul mood: he had been made to share a bed with Edmund while a pair of snoring men slept on the other bed in the room, but it was the coughing from the neighbouring room, chatter from the nearby ships, and the nocturnal cries of gulls which so thoroughly disturbed his sleep. Even at night when all should be abed, the night-time sounds were much more vibrant to that of the moorland hamlet.

Upon coming downstairs Robert was mildly disgusted to find the inn offered food and drink as early as the ringing of prime: an ungodly hour to break fast and before even the first task of a days' work could be glanced at.

The room was promptly paid for and Robert and Edmund were soon returned to the smith. The old shopkeeper was still sweeping the floor when they came in. He gave a friendly smile, creasing his entire weathered face in the process.

'What news have you?' Robert said, not wishing to waste a moment.

'Ah, yes. I spoke with both my sons and we spent much thought on the matter. Firstly, we couldn't agree who made an order for the bullock dagger, but me youngest... he got the keenest mind you see; he remembered well, and after much talk he-'

'Please old man, just speak what you know. We are in haste.'

The shopkeeper's eyebrows hopped. He grunted a single laugh. 'Always hurried with you it seems. Very well. I shall tell all I know.'

'With haste,' Robert said, forcing his lips into a thin smile.

'Of course. Now, my son, the youngest that is... he remembered your man. It was in early May he thinks. Mayhap you're not concerned with the timing, yes? Anyhow, your man, he come down by way of Lord Pomeroy's company. One of his archers, is it so?'

Robert sighed. The old man knew nothing. 'No, he wouldn't have been a Pomeroy.'

Edmund held up his hand. 'Let him finish. Please, Master Smithy. Tell us all you know of this man.'

'Well, the man I talk of, he was a Pomeroy man. Or was it a Courtney man? Didn't wear his livery, mind. Wore all black. Or mostly black. A blonde fellow. Maybe thirty years or just less than. A scar on his cheek just here, or perhaps the other side.'

Robert stood dumbfounded. The shopkeeper's words become drowned out by his own directionless thoughts and bewilderment. He became aware of the shopkeeper regarding him with a concerned frown. He felt Edmund's hand on his elbow which she shook off.

'Guy? It can't be Guy!' Robert said, pleading with the shopkeeper.

'I know not his name, only his appearance. Now I trust I have satisfied your condition. Do you want to buy a dagger or nay?'

'Guy?' Robert looked at Edmund for confirmation.

Edmund nodded. 'Guy.

XXV

Robert stormed to the stable, barking at the lad there to ready his horse. He paced the whole while, snapping that the boy was idle. He glared at Edmund's efforts to placate him and shook off the hand Edmund placed on his shoulder.

Once the mounts were ready Robert opened his purse and without looking at the contents, he plucked out a few coins and tossed them in the direction of the stable lad who darted about picking up the discarded handsome fee. A small boy in dirty clothes ran in from the street, snatching a silver coin before the stablehand could get to it. The stable boy ran after him, shouting and throwing his cap at the faster youth.

Robert swung his leg over his saddle as Edmund was still leading his donkey from the stable.

'Please, Master Robert, refrain from haste. I cannot keep up and know not the way back.'

Robert turned in his saddle, fuming quietly as the clerk mounted. He led his horse down the street, keeping the mount to a walk, growling at any who wandered into his path to move aside. Once they passed under the northern gatehouse, Robert put his heels to the flank of his mount and continued at a trot. Edmund tried to do likewise, but the donkey's pace quickly proved insufficient to keep up.

Robert waited near the first stone cross until Edmund caught up. The wait gave him time to clear the fog of anger from his mind, but he still struggled to focus his thoughts. Feelings of betrayal, bewilderment and sorrow overwhelmed him. He studied his shaking hands and wondered how other men controlled with their emotions. He stared at Edmund as the clerk approached, noting the clerk's firmly pressed together lips and wide-eyed countenance.

'You must help me, Scribe. My mind is bewitched by this betrayal. Is it truly Guy who has done all this to me?'

Edmund took a deep breath which he released as a low whistle. 'It would seem so. Although I confess, I am confused by much.'

'Aye? What confuses?' Robert spoke quickly.

Edmund scratched his nose as he thought for a moment before answering. 'It was Guy who directed us to the blacksmith. He has made himself his own hangman.'

'Aye. The fool. Mayhap he thought the blacksmith wouldn't recall him and I would waste a day or two of my time afore I must attend Lyford.'

Edmund hummed in such a way to suggest he was considering Robert's reasoning.

Robert arched an eyebrow. Sweat trickled down his temple as he waited for the clerk's reply. He clamped his jaw tight as he scrutinised Edmund, grinding his teeth to withhold an outburst as his impatience gave way to irritation and threatened to boil over into rage.

'I think it unlikely, Master Robert,' Edmund said thoughtfully, seemingly ignorant that every pause risked an explosive rage from his companion. 'Guy was under little suspicion. If we had been measuring him as the culprit perchance he'd make such a desperate diversion, but not as it is.'

'So ye think him innocent?' Robert winced at how gaspingly desperate he sounded to his own ears.

'We know only that he bought the dagger. We shall speak to him and find the truth of the matter.'

'He was one o' Lord Courtenay's men. It was well known that he was dismissed in disgrace. There were tales that it involved a theft or worse. None would give him work. I never asked the truth of the matter. I took the measure of him and balanced that whatever the crime were it can't have been so grievous since Lord Courtenay didn't hang him.'

Edmund nodded. They rode in silence for a time. Robert eyed the clerk, eager for his speculation but not wanting to disturb his thought.

The morning sun warmed and hardened the ground. The stench of the port town gave way to clean air through which birds of various sizes flittered and sang. Even at a walk they would be back at Woodtown by mid-afternoon. Robert was desperately eager to return and yet in equal measure, fearful of what he would face when he did.

'The morning of the slaying,' Edmund said, 'your brother and Guy went off to Plympton, is it not so?'

'Aye. Yet they had not long departed.'

'Indeed. Neither claimed knowledge of the murder.'

'That be so.'

'Which leaves in my mind only two possibilities.'

Robert felt his cheeks warm. He clenched his teeth at the clerk's pause and was about to snarl that the clerk had a dreadful habit and should say what he had to quickly, when Edmund continued.

'Firstly, that they together were responsible.' Edmund, glanced sideways at Robert, gauging his reaction.

Robert sniffed at the remark, but his rebuttal caught in his throat. Was it possible? Did his brother have some misplaced notion that if rid the Hundred of William Spiney that it would leave Robert free to ascend to Bailiff? Did his brother foolishly order Guy to do the deed out of misplaced loyalty? Perhaps expecting that it would better his own lifestyle.

'Or secondly,' Edmund continued, 'that Guy gifted, sold, or bet away the bullock dagger to the someone who used the weapon to kill William Spiney. Either way, Guy is the key. Have you seen such a dagger on his person?'

Robert shook his head. 'I know not. I 've been thinking... he always has a dagger, as do most, but I give little notice for such things. I think I've not seen him with it, but I wouldn't swear an oath to as much.'

Edmund hummed.

'There be a third chance,' Robert said slowly, trailing the same pause Edmund made him endure. 'Might be someone had a similar dagger and Guy asked the name of the maker.'

Edmund wiggled his eyebrows and puffed out his cheeks as he considered the theory. 'It could be, but then Guy could have led us to the murderer the moment he laid eyes on the weapon you discovered. Again, we shan't know until we speak with him. What will you do?'

'Speak to Guy, then Eustace, then act accordingly.'

Edmund cocked his head. 'Accordingly? You mean to say, if Guy is the one who did the killing, you will have him handed over the constable... or?'

Robert sniffed. 'I know not. He has been my closest friend. There be no constable in Spiney nor Woodtown neither, only Tavistock. If he has betrayed me...' Robert chewed his lip. He closed his eyes and shook his head as if to dislodge the notion that his confidant may well have plotted against him.

***

Robert increased his mount's gait as the first buildings of Woodtown came into view. Edmund tried to urge the donkey to keep up. He called out after Robert, asking him to wait but Robert paid no heed.

Robert cantered past John Sherman's hovel. The shearer dropped the bundle of logs he was carrying as he stood dumbly shaking, his head twitching from left to right as if desperately looking for a haven to flee to: perhaps thinking Robert intended to ride him down, but Robert passed by with barely a glance in his direction.

Robert reined the horse in right outside the longhouse. He slipped from the saddle as the door opened. Eustace and Alice emerged together.

'Where is he?' Robert barked. He handed the reins over to Eustace, who balked at taking it, but after a moment's hesitation he took the horse with a reproachful glance at his older brother.

'Where is whom?' Alice said, blinking. At either side of her face a dangling golden lock curled and delicately bounced under her veiled circlet.

'Guy!' Robert seethed, exasperated. He turned to the sound of footsteps.

Guy approached from the stable. His feint smile froze when he saw Robert's expression. He paused in mid stride. His face dropped and shoulders sank: the visage of a man who knew he was caught.

'Get in,' Robert said through his teeth. He glared at Eustace who still stood nearby holding the horse.

Guy walked past Robert into the cottage with his head bowed. Robert could only sigh in response to his wife's questioning expression as he followed behind Guy.

Alice followed behind her husband in and closed the door. Robert pointed at one of two knee-high stools on the far side of the firepit. Guy dutifully sat, staring into the pit's ashes. Robert studied him, the silence and lack of eye contact all but confirmed his guilt. Robert felt a strange sensation in his stomach; like it was empty but at the same time he couldn't bear the thought of food.

'Why?' It was all Robert could manage to ask: his mouth was dry, the word came out raspy.

Guy looked up and made eye contact at last. He blinked several times as if not understanding the question.

Robert turned away and paced to the wall, resting his forearm on a beam and his head upon the arm. 'I know it was your dagger. It weren't stolen from the stable, you hid it, did thou not?'
The silence was only interrupted by the sounds of breathing. Robert waited until his nerves could stand no more; he turned, facing his former confidant, anger rising in him.

'Speak, damn ye!'

Guy nodded slowly but kept his eyes down. 'Aye. Twas mine own dagger.'

Alice gasped and covered her mouth with both hands. Her eyes were wide as her gaze switched between the accused and her husband.

'Perhaps wife, you best be waiting outside with Eustace. Have someone send for the constable at Tavistock.'

Guy looked up. His features creased as if wounded. He shook his head and kneaded his temple with his palm.

The door swung open. Edmund stepped in, panting. His eyes darted, but then satisfied that nothing was amiss he calmed himself with a long exhalation. He quickly composed himself and folded his arms across his chest.

Alice hooked her arm around Edmund's elbow, clinging onto him for support. Edmund's eyes bulged. He looked sideways at

Alice and then apologetically at Robert. He stood firmly rooted on the spot like a dutiful guard or petrified rabbit.

'Let's hear it all,' Robert said, 'with witnesses beholding. It was your dagger that slew William Spiney, say it.'

'Twas,' Guy said, his attention firmly set in the ashes of the firepit.

'Did Eustace put you up to it?'

Guy closed his eyes. 'No. Wasn't that way.'

'You hid the truth of it from me: even when there was a likelihood I'd hang. You held your tongue, waiting for your master and benefactor to hang for your own crime.'

'No!' Guy shouted. He made as if to rise from the stool, anger flashing across his face. 'I'd not see you 'ang. I were ready to confess me hand in it if need be, but then you had a week to prove innocence and so I stayed my voice, but always inside I was burnin' to tell you truly.'

Robert's lip curled involuntarily. How could he have trusted this scoundrel? After saving him from a beggar's existence and taking him into his confidence his repayment was the most bitter betrayal.

The door opened again and Eustace walked in. He stood beside Alice and with a sideways glance at Edmund. He adjusted his chaperon and then took Alice's other arm in his.

'What's going on, Brother? What's your manservant done?' Eustace scoffed, looking down his nose at Guy.

'This I am trying to discover,' Robert snapped, 'and perchance something about your part in it. Guy, tell me truly... did Eustace put you up to this evil or was it your own doing?'

'Not either!' flecks of spittle landed on Robert's boot from the violence of Guy's denial. 'It were my blade but not by hand. I'll not take another's blame again!'

'His blade?' Eustace said, his voice reaching a whining pitch. 'The bullock dagger that did for Spiney... this... servant caused all this?'

'Be quiet, Eustace!' Robert snarled.

'Gut him, immediately!' Eustace said, drawing his dagger and pointing it at Guy.

Alice let go of Eustace's arm and clung onto Edmund with a small cry of alarm.

'Put your blunted child's knife away,' Robert grunted, 'before you lose it.'

Guy narrowed his eyes at the weapon and scowled at Eustace with undisguised disgust. His hand moved toward the sheathed dagger in his own belt, then paused. He glanced at Robert and let his hand drop.

'Master Guy,' Edmund said, clearing his throat. 'Why did you tell us where the dagger was made? You must have known it would lead back to you.'

Guy tutted and rubbed his palm over his face. 'A fool, I am. I suppose… I couldn't bear it. I wanted to confess, but I couldn't. I… I wanted the truth to be known but I'd not the courage to say it.'

Robert grimaced and balled his hands into fists. 'I tire of half answers. I will hear the whole truth of it. If I misbelieve a word you say, I shall gut you as you deserve.'

Edmund stepped forward and placed his arm on Robert's elbow but kept his sight fixed on Guy, who he scrutinized with a furrowed brow. 'Tell me, Master Guy, and be clear. Are you saying you didn't kill William Spiney?'

'Oh, of course he shall say such!' Eustace said, rolling his eyes up to the roofbeams. 'He's facing the hangman; he will say any such thing will put a slip between him and the noose.'

Guy wrinkled his nose at Eustace and sunk his face into his palms with a heavy sigh.

'Best you say quickly,' Robert said, his voice a low rumble.

'I did not slay William Spiney. Not he, nor anyone else neither.'

Robert exchanged a glance with Edmund. 'If you didn't kill Spiney, who did for him? Tell me now, Guy.'

Guy shook his head. 'I may not. I am bound by an oath hastily given in fear.'

Guy slumped over with his head between his knees. He clawed at his ears and scalp while making a low, anguished sound.

'Perhaps we should leave this for the bailiff,' Alice said.

'Nay,' Robert sniffed, 'I'll hear the truth of it now, or by God's own eyes I'll do for Guy as he or whomever did for Spiney.'

'Pray, please stay your hand,' Edmund said, 'it will do naught to aid you and may well see you yet in the noose. Others will think you slew him to stay his tongue. Certainly, killing him will do nothing to loosen it.'

'Did Henry Spiney put you up to this?' Robert snapped, 'Or the sheriff? Who? tell me!'

Guy rose only so far as to rest his elbows on his knees. He cupped his hands over his ears. His body trembled as he released an almost inaudible whimper through clenched teeth.

Robert spat into the firepit in disgust.

Alice put her hands on Robert's shoulders and tried to gently pull him away.

'Please husband, let's just leave this matter to the justices of the realm.'

Robert tried to stifle a grim laugh that became a snort. He shrugged off his wife's hands and turned to face her; incredulous at her urging of justice for the man he'd suffered in a dungeon pit for the sake of.

Alice slunk back, stopping with her back at the door. Edmund stepped in front of her, placing himself, awkwardly rigid, between man and wife.

Robert's eyes burned at the clerk. 'Forsooth! Do you think I shall lay a rough hand on mine own good wife? Many a husband may do such, but they'd not a wife as beautiful or pure.'

Robert looked at Alice: her trembling lip, ragged breathing, and pleading eyes betrayed her fear. Robert forced his mouth into the semblance of a smile and tried to relax his posture but found himself to be stiff in muscle and limb. He forced his fingers to unfurl from fists only to ball them up again to stop them trembling. He turned slowly to Eustace.

'You were with Guy on the morning of the slaying. Did you ride direct to Plympton? Tell me quickly, Brother, for my wrath will not be stayed long even for you.'

Eustace shrugged. 'We went straight... no wait - we'd just cleared the woods and he said he'd left behind his purse and was afraid it would be stolen in his absence. He rode hard back to fetch it but, I think he was gone just some moments.'

'You never thought to say this before?' Edmund said sourly before Robert could ask the same.

Eustace shook his head and shrugged one shoulder. 'It was such a little thing. Nothing really. It left my mind until Robert put the memory back with his question.'

Rain pattered on the thatch. Light through the windows dimmed. Everyone glanced up at the rafters at the sound of the rain; the downfall always sounded heavier against the compacted straw.

Robert looked sideways at Guy, not wanting to face the wretch directly. 'Does he speak truly?'

'Verily, you ask a killer and thief if I speak truly?' Eustace squealed.

'Silence!' Robert sneered.

Guy slowly raised his head. His eyes were ringed with red which made the rest of his face look pale and sickly. 'I am sworn to say naught,' he said in a quavering voice, 'but I'll not be named killer, thief, or liar, for I am none.'

'You're already proven liar,' Robert said, turning away from him. 'I care not what you swore. You will say who put you up to it.'

The downpour soaked into the thatch, releasing scents of earth, mildew and various muck mixed in with the straw and wheat.

'You swore an oath? On religious artefacts?' Edmund demanded.

Guy nodded. 'A prayer book 'n a cross. Had I known what I swore to I would not have said it.'

Edmund sighed and entwined his fingers in front of him at his navel. 'It is a grave matter, Master Robert, as fellow Christians we cannot compel him to forsake his vow.'

Robert regarded the clerk for a moment, unsure if he was being taken for a fool. Seeing that Edmund spoke in all seriousness, he stammered and sputtered as he struggled to formulate his outraged response.

Edmund held up his palms, splaying his fingers. 'Peace, Master Robert. Please.'

'Peace?' Robert demanded. 'Peace say ye? I stand forsaken. Without this wretch's full confession, I am condemned - all he will speak of is what we know; that it be his dagger! Swore an oath? Bah! Tis a cruel lie to befuddle us. I will not hang alongside him, that much I swear!'

Robert lunged across the firepit, his hands outstretched toward Guy, who in his haste to scramble away from his assailant, fell backwards off the stool and slumped against the wall.

Shouts of protest followed Robert's sudden attack. Alice and Edmund's cries combined in shock and alarm.

Robert gripped Guy's shirt and pulled him close, so the tips of their noses almost touched. He could smell Guy's hot breath and see every detail of his wide, panicked eyes in which the blue-grey irises were devoured by expanding black pupils.

'Tell me now, who put you up to this evil?'

Guy shook his head. His mouth downturned, his lower lip protruded, his usually handsome face creased. Tears rolled from the corners of his eyes. His lips blubbered wetly.

Robert shook him. He lowered him to the floor and raked his fingers across Guy's face.

Guy released a grieving sob compressed through gritted teeth.

'Release him, this doesn't serve you, m'Lord!' Edmund shouted.

Guy gasped. His eyes and mouth opened wide. His piteous sobbing caught in his throat. For several seconds he remained petrified, frozen in the moment.

Robert released his grip on Guy's shirt and pulled his dagger blade from Guy's gut with a sudden jerking motion which made Guy gasp again.

Dark blood dripped from the long-bladed bullock dagger on the floor where it soaked into the dirt and reeds. Guy looked down at his torso; his fingers tearing at his clothes trying to find the source of the injury. A dark stain spread across his black hose.

The white undershirt when revealed was wet with red. He looked up at Robert with a pleading expression and whimpered.

XXVI

Robert studied the dagger, fixating on the wet, red blade. Behind him Alice screamed; her high-pitched cry jerked him from his grim trance. He turned to face her, opening his mouth to speak but the words caught in his throat.

Alice clung onto Edmund's sleeve with one hand. The clerk stared, dumbfounded. Eustace regarded Robert with a confused expression, as if he couldn't fathom why Robert had done what he had, despite Eustace's urging in the matter.

Robert lowered the dagger and took a cautious step toward his wife with an open palm outstretched to her. He blinked, failing to comprehend why she was suddenly so terrified of him: surely she didn't believe he'd hurt her?

Alice picked up the front of her dress and ran into the larder. Edmund glanced from the husband to wife and then dashed after her. Footfalls slammed the steps up to the sleeping space in the loft. Robert looked at his brother who still wore a confused expression. Eustace swallowed and smoothed down the front of his tunic in an apparent effort to compose himself.

A groan brought Robert's attention back to Guy, writhing on the ground. Rushes from the floor stuck to the sleeves of his tunic. His heels scraped on the floor, knocking against the rim of the firepit. He clasped his wound with both hands. Dark blood seeped through his trembling fingers.

'M-my apologies, Master,' Guy coughed.

'Put him through again!' Eustace snarled, 'you did well, Brother. Now, do the wretch to death.'

Robert tossed his weapon into the firepit where it landed with a dull thump, creating small cloud of ash. He knelt beside Guy and held the dying man's shoulder.

'I forgive thee.' It was all Robert could think to say. It didn't feel enough. He knew he had killed his friend: the dark blood was a sign of a mortal belly wound. An apology was absurd. Guy would not outlive the next hour. His strained attempt to maintain composure despite his obvious pain betrayed that he knew his fate.

Guy gripped Robert's forearm and winced, twisting on the ground, baring his teeth against the pain. 'I... I couldn't say. I was sworn. I wish it were otherwise.'

'Hush. Take your rest. Do you wish water? Ale?'

Guy shook his head.

'Have you any request?' Robert said gently.

Guy's peered over Robert's shoulder. He nodded in the direction of his gaze and winced.

'Don't trust he.'

Robert turned and made eye contact with Eustace, who shook his head, sniffed loudly and idly tugged on the hem of his tunic. Robert narrowed his eyes at his brother.

'Oh, for the Lord's sake, Robert! He'll speak any such words as may stop you putting the dagger to him again, which you should do with haste.' Eustace said, stabbing an accusing finger at the fallen man.

Robert looked back at Guy. His eyes were clamped shut and teeth gritted in pain. His grip tightened on Robert's arm.

'Peace, Guy. Rest.'

Footsteps slowly descended from the loft: Edmund's, Robert knew before the clerk appeared; Alice's footfalls were tender and more deliberately placed than the haphazard, clumsy, almost tumbling descent of the clerk.

Robert turned back to Eustace. 'Verily, you art keen for me to slay my friend. Why be that so, Brother?'

Eustace shrugged nonchalantly, wrinkled his nose and toyed with the dangling velvet tails of his chaperon. 'Do as you will with the traitor.'

Robert turned his attention back to his friend. There would be time to deal with his brother; he wasn't going to leave Guy alone in his last moments.

Guy's muscles were tensed, braced against the pain, at times he jerked and twisted, and with a stifled cry his fingers dug more firmly into Robert's arm.

'I shall not stand and watch you gloom over a dying rouge,' Eustace said, 'I will take a horse and ensure the constable is called out.'

'That would be to err on your part, Master Eustace,' Edmund said.

Robert turned to look at the clerk who stood holding a riding boot, frowning in scrutiny at the sole.

'You hold no dominion over me, Clerk,' Eustace snapped. He made for the door, but Edmund took a long sidestep to block his exit.

'A moment, please, Master Eustace,' Edmund said. His pose was casual, but his expression was firm.

'Brother...' Eustace said, 'with which hand did you slay poor Guy?'

'What?' Robert looked down at his hands, only then realising the significance.

''Twas the left, was it not? The killer you seek is a left-handed devil, is he not, Clerk?' Eustace's lip curled in a cruel smile.

'What are you saying, Brother?' Robert snarled. He realised that because he had held Guy with his right hand it was his left that had gone to the dagger - if he'd had both hands free it would've naturally been his right which drew the dagger.

Edmund allowed a thin smile. 'A timely observation, Master Eustace.' His eyes flicked to Robert, the smile still on his lips, his attention then turned back to Eustace. He held forth the boot like he was presenting a gift. 'This is a fine riding boot. Best leather. Well sewn. You should take better care with it.'

'I care not for the damned boot, you fool!' Eustace said, he made to snatch the boot, but Edmund turned away, shielding the item with his body.

'Bah! I've not time for this,' Robert growled.

'Just a moment, if you please,' Edmund said, 'but first, I must be sure: there is to be no more slaying. May we swear to it?'

Robert waved dismissively. 'Say what you will, quickly.'

'Firstly, your oath,' Edmund insisted.

'Aye. No slaying. Would you have me swear it on articles?'

222

Edmund shook his head. 'That will not be in the needing. Now, this boot. This very fine boot, it belongs to you Eustace, is that so?'

'Verily you know it,' Eustace snapped, 'now return it or I'll have you named thief.'

Edmund's eyebrows quirked and his cheeks puffed in a short expulsion of laughter. 'We are beyond a matter of thievery I think thou well know.' Edmund turned the boot over his in his hands so that the sole was upturned. 'It was a funny matter; I hurried after Lady Alice, being as worried for her health as my own. She took to the bed in tears and I sat in comfort of her when I saw this boot on the floor and it worried me. I didn't know why at first: it was just a boot, I'd seen it before. Merely a muddy boot.

'You really should have better care for such a fine boot, Master Eustace. I suppose it is rare you clean your own boots, but on examining it I realised that although it is just a little dirty, not all is dirt. Unless, that is, hereabout there is soil the colour of dried blood?'

'Is not blood, you fool.' Eustace reached for the boot, but Edmund again turned aside and held it out of reach.

Eustace grabbed Edmund's shoulder, trying to turn him about while his grasping hand reached over his shoulder him. They scuffled for a few seconds before Robert rose and lurched forward, clamping his hands on his brother's shoulders and pulling him back. Eustace clung to Edmund and the two of them stumbled together. Robert pushed Edmund one way and pulled Eustace the other, prising the two apart. He held his brother by a fistful of his doublet, shaking him until he ceased his struggle.

Robert pointed at the far wall near the solar. 'Stand there, Brother. Move not a single pace.' He glanced down at Guy who convulsed in a spasm of pain.

Edmund held out the boot for inspection. It was flecked with light brown mud, but there was dark matter not dissimilar to blood around some of the shoe nails. Edmund turned the boot over, showing staining on the toe of the boot that could have been blood, but might as easily have been red wine. Robert looked in askance at the clerk, who in response only gave one of his thin, apologetic smiles.

Robert turned back to Guy and knelt beside him again. 'We'll make you as comfortable as we can. Clerk, bring a woollen blanket and sheepskin from the bed.'

'Of course…' Edmund's footfalls moved into the pantry and up the steps.

'It… it's not Spiney's blood,' Eustace said. 'It was from a chicken I killed while at Plympton. The clerk is a fool.'

Guy shook his head and winced. Robert was unsure if it was to dispute Eustace's words or from the pain.

Robert smiled at his friend, turning his head only fractionally toward Eustace. 'You could've said the stain were wine. I might believe wine sooner than I'd believe you'd bother to kill your own chicken. Even so, it's not so much blood as to lead to the hangman, even though there were a shoe print in Spiney's blood.'

'So, you don't believe the clerk?'

Robert grunted a solitary laugh. 'I see now his purpose.'

'Purpose? What purpose?'

'The stain might be from the slaying or might be not. The truth of it is in your fear and desperation when the clerk confronted you with it.'

'What?'

'Your ashen face when the clerk brought the boot was enough, but then you named me killer and fought with the clerk for possession of the boot. I am thankful that our mother is not present to see you betray your own kin so.'

'I see.'

Robert heard Eustace step forward and the unmistakable sound of a blade sliding against the brass ring around the leather sheath.

XXVII

Four paces separated the brothers. Eustace rushed the distance.

Robert spun. A sliver of steel arced down on him; his right-hand clamped around Eustace's wrist, stopping the dagger short of its mark. Robert's left hand instinctively gripped his brother's throat. He dug his fingertips into skin.

Eustace's eyes bulged either from fright, surprise, or both. He bared his teeth, spraying spittle. The folds of his chaperon fell over his eyes, forcing him to swipe the hat from his head before he could grip Robert's wrist and try to prise the choking hold from his throat. Eustace attempted to twist his arm free of his Robert's grip, but the wrist was held fast, denying the movement required to even bury the prick of the blade into his brother's arm. He made a strangled, panicked sound. His usually handsome face contorted into creases and his lips peeled back over the gums as he blubbered. His tall, thin frame and unworked muscles wilted under the toil hardened grip of his brother.

Robert kept a tight hold on Eustace's throat, ignorant of the scrabbling fingers futilely tugging on his forearm. He didn't close his grasp enough to completely shut off the airway: only enough to hold him subdued. He studied his brother's face with a mixture of disappointment and disgust while simultaneously twisting Eustace's arm until the blade clattered to the floor.

There were no words which could vocalise Robert's feeling of betrayal; he could only shake his head as he lifted his brother off his feet, slamming him into the wall. Iron pots rattled and fell. He pressed Eustace's head into the thatch where old hard straw scratched his scalp.

'Unhand him!' The shriek belonged to Alice.

Robert hadn't heard her descend from the loft. He held his brother firm. Unsure what he would do next. Eustace kicked uselessly at his shins.

'Robert! Husband! Unhand him!'

Eustace's pleading eyes frantically searched as if looking for escape. Robert held his brother in place, transfixed by his desperate, piteous expression. He searched Eustace's features for understanding of what might turn one brother against the other.

'Wait!' Edmund cried, 'Lady Alice, no-'

Thonk!

A pain split across the back of Robert's head. The force of the blow sent him falling against his brother whom he involuntarily released. Jagged ends of thatch scratched Robert's face. He slumped against Eustace, blinked, and pushed himself off his brother and stumbled back a step. Remembering Guy on the floor, he turned and reeled as his foot caught the edge of the firepit but steadied himself against the wall. He gingerly touched the back of his throbbing head - the light pressure caused the dull pain to throb. Robert looked at his fingers, expecting blood, finding them unstained.

A flurry of motion in his peripheral vision caught his attention. Edmund was trying to wrestle a black pot from Alice. They both pulled on the black iron implement: Alice squealing and panting, Edmund stuttering placating words pleading with Alice to desist her struggles. He might have torn the implement from her hands, but he seemed reluctant to make any overt action to secure it.

Eustace lunged, reaching for the dropped dagger. Robert slammed his boot on the weapon, causing Eustace to slink backwards against the wall.

'Both of you, stop with that damned pot!' Robert roared.

Edmund relinquished his grip as suddenly as if the iron were red hot - his open hands springing up to his shoulders. The abrupt release caused Alice to stumble back, she righted her balance, glaring at Edmund before turning to Robert, holding the pot ready to strike.

Robert gently touched the back of his head again, wincing and giving Alice a reproachful look. 'You hit me. I'm hamsoken by mine own wife and brother.'

'Don't you lay your foul hand on poor Eustace!' Alice said, her features hardened by her deep frown.

Eustace cowered against the wall, crouched as if he might crawl away unnoticed. He froze like a startled rabbit when Robert turned his gaze upon him.

'Wife, perhaps you heard not what was said. Twas mine own brother who did for William Spiney. I'm yet to hear the how and why. Let us hear it now.' Robert grabbed Eustace by a tuft of his long dark hair and pulled before Alice.

'Now... brother, tell me... twas you who swore Guy to secrecy, yes? You best tell all. With haste.' Robert's every muscle tingled with outrage, his voice wavered with adrenaline and suppressed fury. Had it not been his own kin, he would have crushed Eustace's skull: his mind having already played out the very scenario.

Eustace opened his mouth to speak. His jaw stammered uselessly until he gulped, licked his lips and blinked, composing himself. 'I did. I swore him to secrecy. I had to slay Spiney... had to! He made our family appear foolish. I did it for you. I am your brother, have mercy.'

Robert twisted the handful of hair, making Eustace wince.

'For me, eh? Then tell me. The morning of the slaying what happened?'

'We... we, uh... rode a little way out and I asked to see Guy's dagger... the one he bought on our prior trip to Sutton. I told Guy I must ride back as I'd forgotten something or other. I told him ride on slowly.'

'And you rode back to lay in wait for Spiney?'

Eustace looked down, hesitating to speak until Robert twisted his hair again.

'Yes. I... I knew he was taking his morning ride. It is known he takes a ride at dawn. I... I thought I might catch him out alone, but he'd not yet departed so I tied up at the gate and hid in the stable. He soon came and I... did such as needed doing but there was a sound from the manor, a door or window shutter... In my fright I dropped the dagger into the trough, jumped the wall and rode back to Guy.'

Edmund listened attentively with his chin held between forefinger and thumb. Alice still held the pot as ready to defend herself, her eyes darting from Robert to Eustace, her jaw set firm.

'How'd you fool Guy into swearing for you?'

'Ah, well... I told him I'd been set upon by a vagabond and forced to defend myself with the dagger, slaying the rogue. I bade

Guy promise not to breathe that I'd parted his company, or it would be his dagger that would be found, thusly we'd be in the same trouble. I'd taken Alice's bible with me and I had my cross, so I bade him swear upon them, which he did.'

Robert released Eustace and staggered away, rubbing his eyes and brow as he tried to accept what he'd heard.

'So,' Edmund said, 'Master Guy thought he was protecting you, and you used the good man's faith to secure his silence. What of the lost weapon? You took it from Guy's loft?'

'I knew he'd hid it and I knew it to be in the barn. While you all slept off your fill of strong ale and wine, I crept out. It took but a short time to find the weapon, bury it, and return. I couldn't risk that the finding of the dagger would loosen his tongue.'

'Although, it seems it had not, for he'd spoken nothing of the crime, nor even his innocence when presented with his own dagger as the device of the slaying.' Edmund spoke in a point-of-fact tone, as if he were assimilating information from a book or scroll.

Robert dropped to his knees beside Guy's prone form. Guy no longer cradled his wound, his hands merely rested upon the dark mess. Robert took a limp, pale, bloodied hand in his.

'Never has there been a better friend or retainer,' Robert said, 'but twas foolishness to keep your silence. You should've spoken to me.'

Guy's eyelids slowly parted, the effort seeming almost too much. 'I couldn't break my oath. Tis all I have.' His voice was hoarse and feint, barely above a whisper.

'I can only wish I were a better master... and friend,' Robert said.

Guy gave a short weak smile. 'I must tell you... I never told anyone. I was cast from Courtenay's service on a lie. Twas a theft, blamed on me by the culprits. Two oaths against one. I never did steal a thing, but who would believe me?'

'Peace, Guy. I am certain Lord Courtenay doubted their lie or he'd have you brought afore the justices. A banishment is as near to a pardon as can be without showing weakness.'

Guy closed his eyes. His breathing came slow and shallow.

'Forgive me Guy, for slaying you.' The words sounded pathetic, but Robert knew if he didn't ask, he'd have to live with the regret.

'Aye,' Guy said between breaths, his lips moved slightly as if he tried to say more but no sound came.

'We should summon witnesses,' Edmund said, 'there are two more things which trouble me greatly. Firstly, Eustace, who told thee of the dagger? And why were your riding boots in the bedchamber?'

Robert brushed Guy's hair and turned to Edmund to speak - just in time to see the black pot swing toward the clerk, slamming into his forehead.

XXVIII

The pot clunked off the side of Edmund's head, sending him sprawling to the floor, crashing face first into the ashes of the firepit.

The wild swing unbalanced Alice: she staggered a step before righting herself. Her nostrils flared and she bared her teeth, snarling, glaring at her husband.

'Alice, what the hells are you doing?' Robert roared.

Alice shrieked in pure fury. She rushed at Robert hefting the pot overhead, her wild eyes fixed on him as she bore down.

There was no room to manoeuvre out of her way without scrambling over Guy's prone body and so Robert raised his hands to catch the pot as it arced down: swung with as much force as Alice could muster, aiming directly at Robert's head. He absorbed the force of the attack with his open palms, the shock knocking him back against the wall with hands numbed but tingling.

Alice lifted her makeshift weapon up over her head again. Her eyes were as wild as those of a warrior lost in frenzied bloodlust. Spittle sprayed from her lips. She screamed and swung the black utensil down again.

'Wife, no!'

Robert sunk down into a ball against the wall and protected his head with his arms. The pot pounded his forearms, striking flesh and muscle rather than bone. In a moment the weight was lifted. The sharp inhalation that punctuated Alice's shrieking signified that she was summoning the strength for the next assault. Robert parted his shielding arms to see Alice raising the pot. He had to act, or she'd brain him before coming to her senses. His first reaction was to pull at one of her ankles to fell her, but even as he moved his aching and prickling fingers to the task he hesitated: he couldn't risk injuring her if she fell badly. Then it was too late.

The black iron utensil descended. Robert could only put out a protective hand and wince awaiting the inevitable impact. It didn't arrive.

Alice overswung her attack: standing too near to the wall, the pot struck the inward slope of the thatch, sending her stumbling off-balance. She dropped the pot as she put out a hand to steady herself against the wall.

Eustace stood near the screen to the solar. He looked from Alice to Robert then turned, darting into the solar, sending the privacy screen crashing to the dirt.

Edmund stirred from the firepit, his arms, head and sleeves covered in ash. He groaned and touched his head, wincing.

Every digit of Robert's hands was numbed, he could bend the fingers, but only just. He pushed himself off the ground and stood, advancing on his wife as she was reaching for the pot.

Alice gasped and pressed her back against the wall. The pot lay on the floor just beyond her reach. Her tense, snarling features relaxed in an instant, then collapsed into creases as she began to sob. Her trembling fingers covered her blubbering mouth.

'Oh, husband what came over me? I... I was possessed!' Alice made the sign of the cross and sank to the floor, weeping into her hands.

'Possessed indeed,' Robert said, standing over her. He resisted the urge to offer his hand. 'You always stood for my brother when I'm against him, but never with such violence. What was it possessed you, woman? The Devil, or your passion for my softer, more educated and courtly kin?'

Alice wailed. She tore the circlet and veil from her head and threw them to the floor. She tore at her thick blonde curls until Robert snatched her wrist to prevent her from pulling her hair out.

'Peace, wife.'

Robert knelt beside her. She threw her arms around his neck and blubbered against his chest. Robert heard Edmund tutting and dusting himself off behind him, and then a rush off footfalls from the solar. Robert turned his head to glimpse Eustace holding the longsword. Alice's arms tightened around Robert's neck. He tried to push her aside so he might move her from danger and disarm his brother, but she remained fastened to him.

'Run him through, now! Now!' Alice screamed.

Guy stood in an awkward stance, holding the sword at waist level, his tongue protruded from the corner of his mouth like he was attending a delicate task. He aimed the blade point at Robert's midsection and drew the weapon back ready to strike.

Robert seized his wife's shoulders and shoved her aside with all the force he could muster, sending her sprawling. He turned back to his brother as the sword blade stabbed toward him.

Edmund threw himself at Eustace. He slammed into Eustace's side, sending both men tumbling together to the floor. The sword skidded across the rushes and compacted dirt until it clattered against the wall. Two men struggled on the floor, each trying to pin the other down. They rolled, pushing, pulling, and tearing at each other.

Robert sighed, drew his bullock dagger and grabbed a handful of Eustace's hair, dragging him from his struggle with the clerk. Eustace's legs flailed and fingers scratched at Robert's arms. Once he was apart from the clerk, Robert put the dagger to Eustace's throat. All violence drained out of his brother; he remained motionless, not even daring to breathe.

In the corner Alice stirred, brushing her dishevelled hair from her face. She gasped at the sight of her husband holding Eustace by the hair with the blade pressed tight under his chin.

'Don't kill him, Master Robert!' Edmund implored. He stood, brushing his hose and tunic down. An acorn sized lump adorned his head where he had been struck by the pot.

'I intend no such thing. Yet.'

'Don't you harm him,' Alice said, her face was stern, her tone demanding rather than pleading.

'Indeed,' Edmund said bitterly. 'Perhaps we might all cease efforts at bloodshed. This is the most violent family it has ever been my misfortune to encounter. I should never have doubted that William Spiney's killer slept within these walls.'

Robert ignored the clerk, his attention remaining fixed on Alice. 'Tell me… *wife*. Are you in love with mine own brother?'

Alice's lips spread into a wide smile. She chuckled a mirthless and mocking laugh. 'It is not a matter of love, Husband. It is a matter of necessity.'

'Say your meaning or I'll open his throat.'

Robert pressed the flat of the blade harder under Guy's jaw, making his prisoner whimper until a sharp twist of his hair quieted him.

'You are a terrible, vile husband,' Alice said, almost spitting the words. 'You always were. Oh, it took me some years to realise such. Truly, I loved you once, but you are more beast than man. Your violence, uncouth habits, uncourtly ways... I might have bore it, but you are uneducated and seedless to match. Oh, how you have poisoned my virtues and patience. I have grown to hate thee.'

Robert blinked. 'Lies. Why do you say such evil? You art truly possessed!'

She laughed, showing her straight, white teeth. Her whole body shook, causing her tangled hair to gently wave.

'Stop!' Robert growled.

'You fool. I might have told you that I am possessed by witchcraft and you would readily believe as much, yet the clerk, even though cloistered near his whole life, would see the lie of it where you couldn't.

'More than a dozen childless years we are wed, Husband. Never did you think yourself seedless. I always knew your brother loved me and I came to see that by him I've a chance at a true family and position.'

'That is why the boots bothered me,' Edmund said, 'they were heaped on the floor along with your simple dress and a shirt I recognised as belonging to Eustace. It indicated to me you had undressed together. Then I recalled the other day when you barred your husband and I from entering - you had descended from the loft saying you had slept during the day. In truth, you barred us from entry because Eustace was abed with you, is it not so?'

The dagger almost fell from Robert's shaking fingers. He struggled to keep his hand steady. Eustace gulped.

'How long?' Robert said, his voice come as a dry rasp.

Alice glanced at Eustace. Robert felt Eustace's head shake no.

'Near on four years,' Alice said with a faint smile.

The walls seemed to bend and arc inward. Robert pressed his eyes shut. His stomach churned. He held onto Eustace as much for support as restraint.

'Four years?' Edmund said. 'Lady Alice, if you've been trying to beget a child with Master Eustace for four years, I think perhaps tis yourself barren rather than Robert seedless.'

'Fool,' Alice snapped, 'I would not allow Eustace to put me with a child which all would believe is Robert's. Oh, what I endured by my husband! I made every excuse and reason to keep him from my bed for I cannot bear his grunting and vile... uh!' She wrinkled her nose and regarded her husband through narrowed eyes.

'Did you know Eustace killed William?' Edmund said with a deep frown.

'Not until he confessed with his own words,' Alice said, meeting Edmund's gaze with a haughty defiance.

Edmund walked a few steps tapping his lips with his forefinger. 'Love Eustace or nay, why did you defend him once he was uncovered as the killer? I don't fathom the logic, Lady Alice.'

'I will not go back to having that beast beside me while a suitable husband is cold in the ground. I... saw a chance.'

Edmund nodded and regarded the floor as he inclined his head in thought.

'Betrayed,' Robert muttered, 'by wife and brother.' He pushed his brother's head away, sheathed the knife and walked over to his sword, retrieving the blade, he moved to Guy's side. His friend remained in the same unmoving and prone. Robert knelt and touched his neck: the skin was warm but clammy, yet there was no heartbeat or sign of breathing. Robert made the sign of the cross and sat down beside him.

Eustace scuttled across the floor to sit beside Alice who embraced him, gently patting his head as she glared defiantly at Robert.

'I don't believe you, Lady Alice,' Eustace said.

All eyes looked at the clerk. He turned to address Robert.

'Lady Alice did not just discover Eustace's guilt and decide so suddenly to cast her lot with him, now of all times. They plotted this together. By what I know of Eustace, he is not bold enough to kill on his own... for what reason did he say, the family honour?'

Robert scowled. 'Honour? I believe that not either. Nor will the jury.'

'Indeed. If Lady Alice wanted to raise a child, she might've begot one with Eustace and claimed it yours, but that wasn't enough: she wanted rid of you. What was it she said? That you were uneducated? Yes. Unlearned enough to bar the way to bailiff. Eustace, of course, is educated. He couldn't simply kill you and marry Alice or he'd surely fall under suspicion and likely hang for it.'

'He could not kill me,' Robert grunted, 'not unless it were in my sleep or some other cowardly method.'

'Verily. Whichever way they might slay you, suspicion would hang around their necks like the heaviest chain. Yet slay William Spiney right after you'd sworn to do that very thing: your guilt would be beyond doubt. Once you're hung, there's nothing to stop Eustace succeeding you as husband of Alice and succeeding William Spiney as bailiff. Their comfort and position advanced, they might have as many children as they please.'

Eustace watched from the protection of Alice's arms with eyes wide and frightened, he looked every bit a child hiding behind his mother's skirts. Alice's chin was raised in defiance. She held her husband's stare and returned it with cold hatred. Robert shook his head. He didn't even need to hear her admit the truth of the clerk's words to see the legitimacy of it in his wife's countenance.

'These last four years... all a mummery,' Robert said, 'every day you played a loving and good wife. You prayed at every holy hour, chastised me for my manners and curses, and yet you plotted such a sin as murder. Did I ever know thee... wife?'

'I told you, I loved you once. I was sixteen when we married. You were a hero fresh from war in France: as near to a Knight as I, a merchant's daughter, might hope to have. By the time I was twenty I came to realise I could never have true courtly love with you... such are your oaths and habits. The day came when I ceased praying for your salvation and began praying to be saved from you, somehow, but I had to be a dutiful wife. Now I am almost an old woman: twenty-nine! I knew if I was ever to have the chance of respectable position and a full family, I had to act myself.'

'And damn yourself in the process?'

Alice shrugged. 'One can pray for forgiveness. I prayed for my other sins each day in my chapel. The sins of my heart and my mind. One day, when I am deathly frail, I shall confess them to a priest. I never intend to pass from this world unconfessed. You spoiled my life Robert Wood, but you'll not spoil my soul.'

Edmund's eyebrow's twitched. 'You've spoiled your own life, Lady Alice. As for your soul - I am sure you will have the chance for confession prior to your hanging.'

'No!' Robert thundered. 'I'll not allow it!'

XXIX

'There shall be no trial. No jury. No hanging.' Robert sighed, closed his eyes and ran his fingers through his hair. He felt drained. He walked to the longhouse doorway and opened the door, leaning against the fame he sucked in fresh moorland air.

Muriel and her husband were standing on the dirt road, looking at the house, clearly having heard some commotion. They startled at the sight of Robert and scurried back toward their own abode. One of the fullers' young boys peaked out from behind the broken old cart beside the barn and grinned, displaying vast gaps between his teeth.

Robert thought it unlikely that any of the nearby residents who had heard the ruckus knew the extent of the confrontation or the cause, although Muriel's flight upon seeing him betrayed that they thought it likely that he was the source and cause of any violence.

'Master Robert,' Edmund said, his words slow and cautious. 'I must record the tidings of what has come to pass here. You must see that if the true murderers are not brought to justice the sheriff, coroner, and bailiff will have you hanged in their stead.'

Robert looked about the hamlet: Chickens pecked at tufts of grass for hidden morsels. One of the dyers' husbands carried a bushel of wheat from his June harvest; the small stretch of land he farmed produced little coin for his family and barely enough to sustain them when combined with his wife's earnings. The Easterly wind carried some of the stench from the latrine pit Robert had dug too close to the cottages. A carrion bird circled some distance above, biding its time.

'Write your findings, Clerk,' Robert said, still surveying his hamlet. 'You will write that you detected the killer of William Spiney by way of the shoe and the dagger. The murderer became enraged and tried to slay the household, killing Guy who had gallantly defended them. It was as all had thought: Robert Wood was guilty of murder.'

Nobody spoke for long moments. The heavily freckled boy behind the cart grew tired of his spying game and ran off, looking over his shoulder at the longhouse until a chicken ran across his path and the boy gave chase to it.

'Master Robert... I will record no such untruth.'

Robert pushed himself off the doorframe and trudged toward Edmund who startled and backed up at a step at Robert's approach. Robert snatched his arm and dragged him outside. Robert felt the clerk's racing pulse through his doublet sleeve. When they were far enough from the longhouse Robert released him.

'You're a good man, Clerk. Foolish in many ways and bothersome in many more ways, but you'll do as I beseech.'

Edmund stood tall and straight, raising his chin. 'I shall not. I will not see an innocent man hang while to evil doers go unpunished. You are bewitched by your wife's charms. She has done much evil-'

Robert held up his palm for silence and clamped his teeth on his lower lip to prevent oaths from tumbling out. 'None shall go free, nor shall I hang. Truly, I should for the slaying of dear Guy...'

'A jury will decide if that was murder.'

'Twas murder in the truest sense, now hold your tongue! Much of this evil is the produce of my own behaviours. I've driven both wife and brother to desperate acts to rid themselves of the tyrant I never saw myself to be. I shall suffer all blame for the killing: that will satisfy the Spineys' and account for my wrongs to me own kin. I deserve no less for slaying poor Guy.

'Furthermore, I will not submit to having mine enemies see me hang. I shall flee this land. There be nought here for me. I will go, perhaps, to France. To pilgrimage somewhere. I will be declared outlaw and Alice shall become owner of all my possessions, yet her and Eustace shall not escape all justice: the family will suffer fines and they will fall foul of Sir John's ploy to confiscate my lands and trade. They will even need make sale of the Plympton house to meet the debt.'

Edmund's frown deepened as Robert spoke. He pursed his lips but remained silent. Robert clapped his hand on the clerk's shoulder.

'You will be thought a man of great mind for your successful inquisition. I'm sure the Sheriff will award you well. My punishment will be life as a humble man with no domain. Alice and Eustace will be together, as perchance they should have always been, but they will lose all wealth. Mayhap she will spin wool or sew while he scrapes such means as he can by way of being a market trader or perchance even a clerk.'

Edmund regarded Robert with his head inclined and a quizzical expression. He walked a few paces then stopped and nodded. 'I consider that there is little enough true justice in the land. Perhaps moral justice can be served. I see the wisdom of your words. I do not know if you get away lightly, but it is perhaps just that you bear the burden of blame for the slaying of William Spiney: In such short time I have known thee, you have slain twice as many men as the very murderer we sought.'

Robert glowered, unsure if he was being mocked, but Edmund's smooth, place face remained expressionless.

'You should leave quickly, Master Robert. The hamlet is not ignorant to the sounds of violence from your home. We should not be seen talking out here.'

'Aye. I will gather my belongings, ready my horse and begone. Allow me some short time before raising the hue and cry. Say I took the road to Sutton.'

'So, you will go by Exeter?'

Robert ground his teeth. 'I said no such thing.'

'Well, I am sure you will not go by Tavistock or Lyford for fear of capture. That leaves only Exeter.'

'You are an annoying fellow, yet you are a good friend.'

Edmund shook his head. 'I do not act as a friend. I do not believe I've ever known a friend. I merely serve my idea of what is right and just.'

Robert nodded and walked back into the longhouse with Edmund following. Inside, he found Eustace and Alice whispering. They huddled together as Robert crossed the threshold.

'Bah! Restrain yourselves. And if either of you have a notion to rush me with anything you should stand ready to ingest the implement of your assault. Now listen: I am to take the blame for your killing. You two will be together. Take the land, the trade, and such wealth as there is to be had. I shall take only such coin as is in my purse. That's all I will say on it.'

Robert strode past them, they still clutched to each other, recoiling as if he might strike them as he walked by. He went into the solar took up the glaive. The wood was rough, chipped, worn and flaking off in places. The curved blade was sharp but bore a few small patches of rust. He set the weapon back by the fireplace.

There were a dozen coins in his purse: pennies, groats, and farthings. Robert pushed the coins around his palm and satisfied himself that there was enough for two weeks necessities and for transportation abroad. He tipped the coins back into his purse, picked up his arming jacket and pushed his arms into the sleeves. He removed the empty sword sheath from his belt and dropped it onto the floor but kept his bullock dagger. From the larder he fetched enough scraps to make a meal and wrapped them into a bundle.

Alice, Eustace, and Edmund waited for him by the firepit. Robert glanced at Guy's body and then to Edmund. 'See he is buried well.'

Edmund nodded.

'There be a man held in Lyford gaol. A miller named Cedric. He is much abused by our good sheriff and in need of justice. Do what you can for him.'

Edmund nodded again and allowed a thin smile.

'We thank you, Husb... Robert, for what you sacrifice for us,' Alice said with her head bowed and hands clasped penitently in front of her.

'Bah! Tis as much for I as thee. The clerk will support the claim of my guilt so don't think to slay him when I'm beyond sight.'

Edmund's eyes widened. He gulped and choked on his own saliva, doubling over and coughing into his fist.

Neither Alice nor Eustace would meet Robert's gaze, both keeping their eyes low. Robert opened his mouth to say something more to his wife but found he had no parting words that felt sufficient to the occasion. He pushed through the door and headed to the stable.

The horse was quickly saddled. Robert led it south of the hamlet; it would be best to be seen taking the path toward Sutton before heading across the moors to Exeter.

A door slammed on his right as he was passing the last cottage. Robert turned to see John Sherman leaving his abode.

The Sherman stopped midstride. He dropped the jug he was carrying. Milk spilled into the mud and grass. He snatched the linen coif off his head and mashed it up in his hands as he sank to his knees, clutching his hands to his chest as if in prayer. 'M'Lord!'

'Bah! Stand,' Robert growled. 'You're not a sot more of a bastard than any other in this accursed place.'

Robert opened his purse. The first coin he pulled out was a farthing. He tossed it toward John, who remained petrified in a pose of contrite devotion. The coin rolled into the grass just beyond John's reach. The glint of silver broke the spell and the young man lunged forward, his hands combing the green blades.

Robert patted his horse's neck, made a clicking sound and dug his heels into the flanks to encourage the beast into a canter. Perhaps he would find absolution for his sins on the continent - maybe in Nantes, or if not, elsewhere. Or perhaps his punishment was to interminably seek it.

Historical notes

Sampford Spiney is a real place on the edge of Dartmoor, although I have taken some liberties with the details. There is a small, privately owned late medieval manor which has been extensively renovated over the years and most of the medieval parts no longer exist. There is a stone cross, but it post-dates the events in the novel.

I based the church on St. Mary's church in Sampford Spiney, although as the dedication was post-medieval, the novel refers to it merely as 'the church'. Churches of this period didn't tend to have pews, making the church in this story unusual. After the sermon the parishioners leave the church – this is also unusual as the church was the focal point of a medieval community and a social event, but it suited the story to have them leave promptly.

Woodtown exists pretty much in the location described in the novel, however it is not medieval: the earliest records date back to the mid 1700's. I've taken the liberty of predating it and adopting its name for Robert's surname. None of the features in the fictional Woodtown relate to those which may be found there.

Lydford Castle stands as described in the novel, albeit in a ruined state. It is open to the public and free to visit, but a castle in name only: it bears the resemblance of a square stone keep but it was never intended as a defensive structure. It served as the stannary court from the Middle Ages onward and has a terrible reputation for 'Lyford law'. William Browne's famous poem describes how the magistrate would hang the guilty and then sit in judgement after: if death sentence was passed by a county court, it had to be confirmed by the royal court, which could take many months. To expediate things, those found guilty of a capital offence might be executed promptly and then the sentence confirmed by the Royal Court after the fact. The real Sampford Spiney wasn't under the administration of the Lydford Hundred, but I took the liberty of changing it for the purpose of the enabling the use of the notorious Lydford gaol.

The wool trade was very important in medieval England and was prominent in Devon, as in the novel. Sheep from the lowlands were grazed on the moor during the summer months - an activity known as transhumance. Much of the wool was transported via a port from Plympton until the river silted up due to residue from tin mining: it was that very occurrence in 1510 which caused member of parliament Robert Strode to complain about the activities of Devon tin miners, who then angrily threw him into Lyford gaol. Strode protested that Lydford was one of the 'most detestable places within this realm'.

All locations mentioned in passing existed. Brentor is the site of a church built upon the remains of an Iron Age hillfort and is visible for many miles. Tavistock was (and is) a major market town.

Sir John Herle was the Sheriff of Devon in 1402. He served two non-consecutive, year-long terms as Sheriff: November 1401-1402 and November 1406-1407. As in popular culture, many sheriffs were known to be corrupt. There is some evidence of Herle's shenanigans: he was fined for obtaining land and property dishonestly, and even linked to the attempted assassination of Henry IV in 1400, although he managed to distance himself from the plot and escaped punishment. He died in 1418. The Courtenay family, who are mentioned in passing within these pages, were the most powerful family in Devon in the fifteenth century, owning large amounts of land and many estates.

None of the other characters in *The Sampford Slaying* existed. The Spiney family initially owned the estate, although to my knowledge, none of them were murdered. By 1400 the hamlet was owned by William Dymmok, who owned other estates and may not have resided at Sampford Spiney. I decided to keep my fictional owners as the Spiney family.

Robert Wood isn't based on a historical character but represents that small number of men who went to war in France and returned with booty enough to increase their station in society. The Breton campaign Robert refers to was led by Thomas of Woodstock in 1380-1. The siege of Nantes took place during the campaign, and it is likely (as was common) that prisoners, such as the unnamed Breton noble, were ransomed for huge sums of money. Only a knight or greater could ransom a noble prisoner; a surrendering noble would tend to yield to another noble and not a commoner, however if a commoner was able to capture a knight then the lord he served would collect the ransom and the commoner could expect a small share of the money. As a commoner, Robert would have likely been recruited as an archer. It didn't suit his character to be a veteran archer as he thinks he's superior to the average person, so I've given him the hand injury which disabled him from using a bow which could have a draw weight of up to a massive 150lbs. The injury enables Robert to have fought instead with a glaive in the ranks with the men-at-arms: that is to say, knights, their squires and retainers. In reality, being unable to shot a bow would have more likely resulted in Robert being directed to guard the baggage train or some non-combat role.

Some of the things that occur in the book may seem a bit strange to the modern reader - Robert and Alice sharing a bed with Eustace probably stands out. Medieval longhouses didn't have private bedrooms - many may not have even have a bed as such. For bed owners it was considered good manners to share your bed with guests of an equal social standing: not to do so would be perceived as an arrogant insult. Similarly, strangers at a tavern might be expected to share a bed: a common practice until well after the medieval period.

Releasing a prisoner on parole wouldn't likely have occurred unless that prisoner was a noble. A prisoner might bribe their way out of gaol, but to then be tasked with detecting the culprit of the crime they've been accused of is not likely to have occurred and is a liberty I've taken on the basis of the John Herle's corruption: In 15th century medieval judicial law, almost anything goes provided it suits those presiding over affairs.

Thank you

I hope you have enjoyed reading *The Sampford Slaying*. If you can spare a minute, please leave a review on Amazon or Goodreads. I do read reviews and they are greatly appreciated as they increase the visibility of my books and let me know how you've enjoyed it.

If you wish to be kept up to date on future releases, please sign up to my mailing list at andrewmcauleyauthor.com I am also on Twitter under the name AndrewM1428 which is my first point for announcing any news and where I also post about Dartmoor, local history and other such other subjects that may fit into a tweet.

Also by Andrew McAuley:

The March of the Dragons
The Circle in the Woods

Battles of Devon (coming soon)

Andrew McAuley lives in Devon with his daughter and her budgerigar. Andrew can often be found somewhere on Dartmoor, regardless of the weather, where he spends a disproportionate amount of time photographing historic and prehistoric monuments and will navigate a great deal of blanket bog in order to photograph vague bumps which were once Bronze Age hut circles. Andrew is currently working on a history of the battles of Devon which should be released in 2022/3. Future projects include a set of Wargaming miniature rules which have been in a drawer for a couple of years and then a follow-up to *The Sampford Slaying* which will take place in 1403 and feature Edmund as the central character.

Printed in Great Britain
by Amazon